I0524283

Shall I loathe you now

When it stirs my sin?

I will never be saved.

I am clothed in agony.

There is no escaping it.

And thee shall suffer.

PROLOGUE

S.T.R.G

SPECIAL TACTICAL RESPONSE GROUP

Commonly nicknamed in the police force as T.A.C.

They were ready, positioned outside the house, watching and waiting. The T.A.C. team leader, Gary Richardson, could feel the tension all around him. He stood at six-ten and bulged in his uniform. He was stuck waiting for some lame-ass superintendent sitting in his comfy office to give him the word to move. *Ha! Isn't that how it always goes?* The law regarding forced entry had recently changed, a call had to be received for permission to break the door down, and Gary wondered who the hell came up with that stupid idea.

The A.F.P.'s T.A.C department, specializes in major criminal acts. Serial sex offenders, terrorism, international child sex traffickers, child pornography, serial killers, and hostage rescue. They had been staking out the area near the house for the past three hours. It was a modern, two-story house—nothing unusual except for the bars covering the windows and the purposely blacked-out glass.

It was a stinking hot day. All of them were wearing Kevlar, helmets, gas canisters, and half a dozen other gadgets on their utility belts. They were also heavily armed, and Gary could feel his hands sweating through his gloves as he kept shifting his grip on his firearm. When his team had arrived, it had taken a frustrating ten minutes for Gary to get everyone else out of the way and his team into position. He thought whoever was inside would have plenty of time to be ready for them. They were dealing with an extremely dangerous target; someone wanted for the torture and murder of six people, including the kidnapping and rape of a young woman. The media named the suspect the east coast slasher. They had been hunting for this killer for over five years now. The case had gone cold after just one year, then, just a few days ago, they got a tip from an informant, the first real break in the case. Now they were at the slasher's house, Gary and his team were ready. *This ends today,* Gary assured himself.

The public demanded results, and this slasher's head had to roll. Gary finally got the ok, and they moved in. They went in formations of three, flanked left and right. A small team moved around the side of the house, down a small path to the rear. Gary and three others silently approached the house. Gary scoped the door. He judged that it could be broken down with the right amount of force. He listened closely for any sounds; sweat was trickling down the back of his neck, he heard none. He raised his hand and made the signal for his next man to break the door down with the ram, nicknamed Batty. They entered through the door like a rugby scrum, shouting, screaming, and threatening. Their guns pointing at everything and anything and fanned out to search the house.

The upstairs area, living room, bedrooms, and the garage

with a white van and sliding door were clear. There was a large door near the kitchen, and they forced the lock. They moved like cats down the stairs and came to another door; they waited until enough officers were with them, then threw the bolt across and pushed through the open door. What they saw shocked them. The team rushed in and took up their firing positions in every direction. The room was filled with a dull red glow, blood-covered chains connected to pulleys in various fixed positions hanging from the ceiling. The walls were covered with saws and cutting tools, all polished and set in their places. A naked young girl was chained to a bed inside another room. Her body was emancipated; it was too late; she was dead. The look in her eyes was of desperation and anguish. No one spoke. A large table with assortments of knives, sharp objects, and tools was in the middle of the room. They checked the entire basement and searched all the boxes and crates methodically. A few of the team called Gary over to another door next to the opposite side of the basement. There was a large mirror on the wall, and his eyes went back again to the door on the side. His team had already broken through, and Gary walked into an array of video equipment pointing at the see-through mirror overlooking the basement.

What the fuck is this? The three video cameras on tripods had a substance all over them that was eating the metal. Gary ordered his men to get a team in there with protective suits and get the equipment cleared for inspection. He hoped there might be something salvageable. The coroner was called and was waiting outside to come in and inspect the dead girl. Gary gave the all-clear. He looked at the main wall of the basement again and noticed the blood on the floor and on the manacles that were chained to the wall. "Fuck me!" he said out loud to no one. *This psycho is still out there!*

The aftermath of the raid had yielded few clues since the killer had rented the house under a false name, and an unknown proxy had paid a full year's rent. The owners of the house who lived overseas had no idea the horrors that had been happening on their property. The renter had provided false information, and the background checks were of no use. There were very few neighbors near the house, and none knew who lived there. Although the killings had stopped after the raid, it was by no means over, and with a few million dollars more, the police were no closer to catching the slasher. Gary was sure the killer had gone underground and would most likely stay that way until he got hungry for death and couldn't suppress himself. It was a bad ending for them. The major investigative task team dropped the case. They sent it to the cold case team. There, it would continue to be investigated. Gary was also sure the killer had been tipped off. Someone out there didn't want the police to solve this case. Someone very high up, and all he could do now was wait for that dreaded phone call. Then all of it would begin again.

Chapter One

Herman Kapper, a patient, sat on his bed in his room of the psychiatric ward of the Aradale Asylum Clinic for the Criminally Insane. He mindlessly shuffled a deck of cards, gazing through the wire-meshed window at the white clouds jostling for position, dreaming of a faraway place. It was a sharp contrast to the gray-walled building, sitting among the freshly mowed green grass.

Herman was a good-looking young man, so he thought, with dark green eyes and short thick black hair and a slim build. He looked around the ten by twelve room, only slightly larger than the prison cell he'd come from. The walls were a dull white covered in stains that told the stories of the inmates who'd been caged there before him. The chessboard floor, tiled in black and white, was big enough to hold the bed he sat on, steel sink in the corner, table for the occasional game of cards, and not much more. He'd been at the clinic now for five years. Initially, a guest at the state prison–the crimes being especially brutal, they'd determined Aradale more suitable for such a violent person and the crimes that he had committed.

Reduced to a lab rat, the doctors salivated like thirsty dogs at the chance to poke and prod and study the brain of this anomaly, this mistake of nature. Surely there must be *something* dysfunctional, something broken. Normal young men don't do these sorts of things. Despite their best efforts, intensive psychoanalysis treatments and constantly changing drug therapies still left them scratching their heads. But Herman knew. He held all the answers they desperately sought. They were simply not asking the right questions. He had no desire to tell them.

Chapter Two

Five Years Earlier

Herman was seventeen years old—so close to freedom—in the state-run home for boys when he stole a piece of wood about eight inches long from the woodwork shop. It was wide at one end and came to a blunt point. He took some sandpaper and quickly sanded the blunt point until it was sharpened, then kept it near at all times. He didn't know when to use it, but he was too afraid to continue without it.

Everyday Herman tried to mind his own business, but it didn't take long on his way to take his daily shower for those boys to come at him again. He pretended to be submissive, complying as they forced him to his knees. One boy walked up to him, unzipped his fly, and lowered his pants, standing in front of him, smiling. The second he forced himself inside Herman's mouth, Herman bit down as hard as he could. The metallic taste of blood filled his mouth, and the boy released a subhuman howl.

Rage took over, and the room turned as red as the blood filling Herman's mouth. His teeth continued to tear the boy's flesh like a starving wild animal feeding on its prey. The boy keeled over and fell to the floor, writhing and screaming in a fetal position, holding his crotch.

The other two boys froze, stiff and still as the concrete walls surrounding them, their eyes wide in disbelief. Herman stood and removed the carefully crafted piece of wood from the waistline of his pants, then slammed it into one of the boy's eyes. For a second, the boy just stood there. His mouth fell open, and blood spurted from his eye socket, splashing Herman's face. The boy screamed in agony and brought one of his hands up to his destroyed eye. Numb, as if someone or something else was controlling his body, Herman's manner controlled and calm, observing the chaos surrounding him.

The boy, despite his injury, managed to sputter two last words, "No, please—"

Before he could finish, Herman drove the stake further into the injured boy's skull. A popping sounded, more blood spurted from the destroyed socket. The boy fell to the floor, and Herman quickly pulled the piece of wood out of the boys skull and stabbed the boy with the mangled penis, in his throat.

The remaining boy turned to run. Herman lunged at him, grabbed his head, and bit deep into his soft cheek with all his strength. Herman shook his head, growling like a rabid dog, holding the boy's head, determined to bite deeper. The boy struggled but lost his strength quickly as Herman's teeth buried further into the boy's flesh.

The correctional officers arrived soon after, the first one slipping on the blood-covered floor. Herman stood in the center of the bloody mess, the three boys sprawled on the floor around him, covered in blood and gore.

Once the shock wore off, they grabbed Herman and marched him straight to the restraining room, still covered in the three boys' blood, who were rushed to the hospital. One boy with a stabbed eye socket; died on the way to the hospital. The other boy's penis had been so badly mangled it had to be amputated. An emergency blood transfusion saved his life from his punctured throat. The last boy had also survived. Surgeons attempted to restore the mangled half of his face. The boy went on to spend the rest of his life disfigured.

Herman was charged with and quickly convicted of murder, attempted murder, and assault with a deadly weapon causing grievous bodily harm. The court on appeal—because of the almost daily sexual abuse he'd endured as a child compounded by the continued sexual abuse at the state-run boy's home—reduced the charges down to diminished responsibility and sentenced him instead to ten years at the Aradale Asylum Clinic for the

Criminally Insane; with a provision of early release after a full mental assessment.

Herman wasn't born a killer. He was an ordinary boy, shy, introverted, innocent, and kind. But even the most moral and normal of us—can reach their limits. Herman had reached his that day.

****

Herman stopped shuffling the cards and closed his eyes. His younger sister Beth's smiling face materialized behind his darkened lids, golden-haired, blue-eyed, with a smile as bright as the sun. The two would play card games to escape their miserable lives as children. Each card had represented a faraway make-believe place. Then they would ask each other which of those places they would like to run away to. Then they would deal the cards to each other, and whoever got their favorite place card got to keep the card and go to that place. To feel free, happy, and safe.

He pulled out a card, turning it over. The last words he'd

said to his dying sister echoed in his mind, "Why couldn't you wait for me, Beth? Why didn't you wait? We could go together!" The deck slipped from his hands, and cards scattered onto the worn floor. His right finger lightly traced the fading scar on his left wrist. After releasing a long sigh, he told the empty room, hoping his sister, or perhaps her spirit may hear him, "I tried to come. I failed you in death too."

What Herman didn't know, as he sat in that room thinking of his long-dead sister, was a major scandal involving the Aradale Clinic was being exposed. It turns out Herman wasn't the only one with buried secrets.

Herman looked up at the sound of the door's metal hinges creaking. A doctor slid into the room and quickly closed the door behind him. "I'm sure you've heard," he said, face impassive, leaving Herman unsure of what he was about to relinquish on him. A new treatment plan, yet a different drug regiment, or maybe they'd finally decided to kill him, put him out of his misery for good. "Heard what?" Herman asked. The doctor's face hardened. "You're being transferred, effective immediately. Have your belongings packed and ready to go by tomorrow morning."

Herman laughed at the thought of needing a night to pack. With his meager belongings, he could have stood, thrown a few items in a bag, and been ready in five minutes. The doctor left as quickly as he came, and Herman's mood plummeted. *Where are they taking me?*

He later learned one of the major television stations ran a story on the hospital. Over 13,000 patients had died there since its opening almost 126 years ago. Most unexplained. The outcry from the public and several politicians was successful; the hospital closed less than four months later. The patient's records received new assessments and revisions, including Herman's, and some were lost. The next day he was transferred to a low-security halfway ward for out-patients.

Chapter Three

The next day, Herman was loaded onto the bus to take him to his new home. Excitement buzzed in the air. The patients had to be told several times to settle down. Herman leaned his head on the dusty window, drinking in the outside world, imagining what it would be like to one day be part of it again.

The young nurse in charge of his intake enthusiastically explained his new living conditions. After an evaluation period, he'd be permitted supervised visits to the local parks and lakes with good behavior.

"We find these outings beneficial to our patients' mental well-being and recovery," she said, nodding her head as if she were the one just granted freedom. "Calm and peaceful locations, so as not to cause stress, agitation or anxiety."

He forced his face into what he hoped was a convincing smile. He was determined to prove he wasn't a threat. He would always appear quiet, passive, and soft-spoken on the outside, but on the inside, no one had to know that he was a ticking time bomb.

"Our doctors are just the best. You'll see. We have a very high rate of success. With the right attitude and some hard work, you'll be ready to re-join society live a normal life. Doesn't that sound lovely, Herman?"

"Yes, it certainly does," he replied. Meaning every single word.

***

As time passed Herman kept his head down, followed the rules, and participated in his therapy sessions with the vigor of a man determined to heal; or escape, but they didn't need to know that.

Herman was lying on his bed, feet crossed, hands beneath his head, when a friendly knock tapped on his open door.

"Down for a game of cards?" Robert Jeffries stood in the door frame with a broad smile, holding up a deck of cards. Herman never interacted with the other patients; most were much farther gone than he was, although their crimes were less brutal. Instead, he befriended Robert, a middle-aged orderly. Robert was taller than his other colleagues, athletically fit with short dark hair and a strong jaw.

"Sure, sounds great," Herman said. He pulled himself off the bed and met Robert at the small table. Robert shuffled the cards and began dealing.

Robert was the one spot of color in Herman's dulled, gray existence. He showed him a kindness that he hadn't felt since his sister died. When others looked at Herman, he could see it in their eyes, the fear swirling, as if at any moment Herman would lunge at them like a wild animal. Not Robert. Robert looked at Herman like he was human, with thoughts, feelings, hopes, and dreams.

"I dreamed about a girl like Beth last night," Herman said.

Robert cleared his throat and finished dealing. "I know you miss your sister, Herman. But what about those girls we saw last weekend? I mean that one blonde with the legs. I think she had eyes for you, my friend." Robert winked. "That's who you should be dreaming about. She's your age too. Maybe we'll see her out later today. It's Saturday, you know, big day out."

Herman nodded and focused his attention on his hand. He was going to win again. Robert once told Herman he found it difficult to connect this young man with the horrific crimes he had committed. Robert squirmed in his seat. It always made him uncomfortable when Herman talked about Beth, especially the time he shared that he wished to marry a girl just like Beth one day. He was empathetic and kind and appreciated that Herman still grieved Beth's death. However, he mentioned that he wished Herman would focus on girls his own age on more than one occasion.

They finished their game in comfortable silence. Robert tossed his cards on the table. "You did it again. You win." He went to reach into his pocket.

"No. Keep your money. You know I won't take it."

Robert shook his head and laughed. "You won. Fair and square. But alright."

He pushed his chair back from the table and walked to the door. He told Herman to get ready with two taps on the door jamb. The patients were allowed out on the weekends, and the bus was leaving in an hour.

Herman sat in his chair, staring at the empty spot left by Robert. He'd had fantasies for quite some time. Girls with Beth's face or Beth's body or Beth's laugh floated in and out of his dreams. They were becoming more intense. He trusted Robert, but not enough to open up completely and tell him what happened in the dreams. Herman knew that Robert, while a friend, still had a job to do. If he shared his dark secrets, they would just keep him in longer than he wanted to be. He still appreciated his friendship. After what happened to him in that boy's home, he disappeared further into himself. He was depressed and possibly suicidal. Robert helped Herman get through the worst of it; he's not sure what would have become of him if he hadn't had Robert in his life.

****

The internet was restricted for most patients, but Robert managed permission to use it with Herman under his supervision. Herman was hungry to learn, and when they weren't playing cards, Robert and Herman would be online, Robert helping him gobble up information as fast as the computer could deliver it. Computers fascinated Herman. He remembered the laptop he had as a young teen. It was the first time he had seen one. He had not understood it but always loved learning how they worked.

It was a Monday; Robert and Herman sat in front of the monitor, the light from the computer making their faces glow.

"Robert, have I ever told you about my inheritance trust?"

Robert's eyes widened slightly. "No, Herman, I don't believe you have."

"Yes. I have a trust fund. My father owned a good bit of land. When he died in prison, the courts sold the house and the land it was on, with no other living relatives that money goes to me once I turn 21. When I get out of here, I'll get my inheritance. That will be nice, don't you think?"

Robert rubbed his chin, deep in thought. "You know you should invest some of that money in crypto currencies. Crypto is huge now, lots of people making lots of money without really doing anything."

"That sounds like it might be a scam. Nothing's ever free." Herman's eyes narrowed.

"Yeah, it's a bit risky, but I'm telling you, Herman, most

people are making good money. Here, let me show you."

Robert leaned across and pulled up a website where he stored his investment sheets. He walked Herman through the data, showing him the tidy profit he had made the last couple of years.

"My little nest egg," Robert said, sitting back smiling proudly.

Robert's eyes flitted across the screen, absorbing all the numbers, taking it all in. "Yes." He nodded. "Yes, I'd like to learn about this cryptocurrency. I want to do this when I get out."

Robert taught him how to invest using online currency platforms. He told Herman that now was the time he should invest because Bitcoin was taking off and soon would be worth a lot of money.

They started spending much less time playing cards and more time in front of the computer. Robert showed him which investment platforms to use, how to use them, and avoid getting scammed. Herman became obsessed. Whatever time the clinic allocated to him, although restricted, he would spend on a computer learning the intricacies of this new world with Robert by his side. There to encourage him and answer any questions. He was ready to get out, put this new knowledge into action, and start his new life.

Chapter Four

Six years in the hospital, exactly thirty-two days after Herman's twenty-eighth birthday, Herman was released. He stepped outside on that first day with a small bag and his freedom; the air smelled different, fresher. The first thing he did was grab a cab with a few borrowed dollars from Robert and immediately headed to the bank.

$800,000, more money than he'd ever dreamed of. He had the cab take him to the electronics store, purchased a new computer, then, last stop, his new home—at least for the next thirty days. A small apartment Robert had helped him find the week before his release. Fully furnished, clean, and nice, according to the photos online. It was the first day of his new life. And it scared him.

He collapsed on his new couch and pulled out the phone Robert bought him. There was only one number programmed in so far.

"Hey! Herman, how's it feel to be out in the real world?" Robert said when he answered.

"A bit strange, if I'm being honest." Herman's gaze swept the room. The apartment was modest, but it felt enormous after spending the last decade in concrete rooms locked from the outside.

"I was able to get access to my trust. I plan on investing $100,000 in Bitcoin."

A long, drawn-out whistle sounded through the phone's receiver.

"A hundred K. Whew, that's a good chunk of change. I'm sure it will work out great for you."

"I think so. Yes. I believe it will."

"Just—are you sure you don't want to ease into it? Start

with maybe a few grand?"

Herman gripped the phone tighter. Robert had been a great help, but he was confident he knew what he was doing and didn't need anyone telling him what to do with his money. He'd spent too many years bending to the will of everyone around him.

"No, I'm sure. I'm going to look for houses soon. Can you send me that real estate agent's number?"

"Sure, of course. Anything I can do to help you out, you know where to find me." The phone vibrated when they hung up, and a text came through with what seemed to be a contact. Smartphones had only been available when Herman first got sent away, and he'd never used one and was still getting used to the thing. But after a few clicks, he figured out how to add the agent to his phone contacts. And now he had two.

The real estate agent got back to him right away. They made plans to get together and tour some properties. He wanted to find a place as far as possible from his abusive father's house, but his parole regulations required him to remain within the state; he didn't tell the agent that and simply gave her the areas he was hoping to find a place in. After three houses, he found one.

Herman bought himself a nice two-bedroom brick house on the outskirts of the nearest town. It had a lock-up garage, a large basement, and sat on a few acres of land. He modestly furnished it and bought himself a new van after getting a driver's license. He paid cash for everything. Not having to worry about money was great, but he didn't want to sit around like a bum, so he got a job through a friend of Robert's working at a local packing company. Herman spent his days working and his evenings frequenting the underground card games around town. From the outside, life was normal. He was great, but thoughts of his sister, the inner torment of what had happened to her, continued to haunt him. Especially when he was alone, the pain bubbled to the surface. He would get the cards out and play their special game, pretending she was there with him. He'd dream of wonderful faraway places, being there together with her, free and safe again.

***

The first few months after his release from the clinic were intense. He read newspapers and watched as much as he could, all day, every day. He was immersing himself in the completely changed world around him. So many things were the same, but a lot had changed, or maybe he was the changed one. He tried to learn to acclimate to this new world as much as possible. Being removed from society for over a decade takes its toll on you. He felt completely out of place, like he didn't quite belong anymore.

He soon realized the doctors never wanted him to understand the harsh reality of life and what it was truly like. All the dark people, all the horrid things people did to each other. Things he was sure existed but had never seen before. When he was in the clinic, some of his deepest fantasies were now easy to access, a click of a remote or tap of a few keys, and they'd play out right in front of him, right there on his new T.V. and computer.

The internet was a chasm of filth and unknown depravity, and Herman got quickly sucked in. It was so easy. The deeper he went, the more he clicked, the greater his insatiable appetite for porn and violence grew. *The internet has changed so much since my school days before.* He thought about what he used to watch as a boy, on that first laptop Lilly Steen bought him, and how those videos back then were very real to him.

His worthless father drove their mother to suicide. And being an iron ore worker meant he'd be away in the mines for weeks. With no mother, their father hired an old ex-prostitute friend. That's how Lilly Steen came to be. She was a middle-aged alcoholic meth user. She'd worn too much makeup, smoked heavily, and hardly ate. Since Herman and Beth were only allowed to eat when she did, that meant they hardly ate either. She hated kids, and never wanted any of her own, so she certainly hadn't wanted Herman or Beth.

The laptop had been a bribe. Herman knew all about Lilly's occupation and clients. Things she had made them do. But gifting him with a laptop, she got both his silence and peace. Enthralled, Herman would sit on that laptop day and night, not understanding how it really works.

Now, in his new house, in his re-started life, it was like someone had pulled back the curtain and exposed the man working the strings. He expanded and searched any subject that came to mind, natural disasters, drug cartels, terrorism, and crime. Robert had warned him about certain sites on the internet and to, 'Not go crazy.'

"There are things on the internet you need to stay away from, Herman. Those things are evil and will corrupt your mind. Certain places on the internet can be dangerous. You don't need that shit in your life!" Robert's warning only increased his desire to know. *Dangerous? Intriguing.* He wanted to know more.

He *was* on the dark side when he murdered and maimed those boys. Herman needed to know more about his sickness and searched the internet for the root causes of why his mind was different, broken, dark.

One evening, he discovered some dark chat rooms. He

wasn't alone. There were others out there who had the same dark fantasies. These secret fantasies, the ones that hid in the depths of his mind, the ones he had never shared with anyone, there were other people with the same devious thoughts- fantasies of kidnapping a young girl, helpless, vulnerable, and submissive. And they were talking about these things he'd never thought he'd be able to talk about. *Maybe I'm not so different after all.*

Kidnappers, murderers, rapists. They were everywhere online and on T.V. He noticed these other kidnappers, serial killers, and serial rapists followed specific protocols and patterns. The ones who didn't, the ones who made mistakes, got caught. He spent hours watching and studying documentaries; Ted Bundy, The Night Stalker, The Toolbox killers, The Ariel Castro kidnappings, The Leonard Lake and Charles Ng kidnappings, and the Marc Dutroux kidnappings.

He discovered David Parker Ray, also known as the Toy Box Killer. He didn't know why they called him a serial killer. Herman found out that he had released most of his victims after he finished with them, and Herman liked that idea very much. He admired the tenacity of the man. Ray had built a complete self-storage sex trailer, then kidnapped young girls holding them captive for one to three months, sexually abusing them. Keeping them healthy and well, while he and his wife lived out their fantasies with them. Before letting them go, he would drug them for days to erase their memories, then leave them somewhere far away.

These evil men and women, these dredges of society, were hated but also famously admired. They captivated many during their reigns of terror, imprinting their names into history. They were envied by thousands of potential rapists, killers, and pedophiles worldwide. Loved by women who wanted to marry them, even bear their children. Herman couldn't understand the women who fell so deeply for these notorious criminals, but he wanted to know why they did. *Understanding this would be the key, the door would unlock, and he'd finally access everything he wanted. The love he wanted.*

It became clear to Herman the common factor in each of these criminals' demise. The authorities learned their patterns; they studied them. There are experts in the field of criminal minds. A ghost haunting a city can be brought to life by these profilers. Their age, sex, race, upbringing, and fears. These profilers create a human from nothing. It was captivating.

It became pretty evident to Herman if he were to turn his fantasies into reality, his moves had to be unique and different from theirs. He would be more random without a predictable pattern. He would carefully think through his intentions. It was at this point there was no turning back. He would be moving forward with his plans. He would be kidnapping a girl. Then he would be admired. *People liked when someone unique came along,* he thought. *Someone who was much more clever than the last, no matter what type of crime, it was how they did it that mattered.* The public was fascinated by criminals. The more sinister the crime, the more fascinated they became, especially if the police couldn't catch the perpetrator. Especially the ones who the longer they remained free, the more daring they became, purposely leaving clues and taunting the police. The public ate it up. Through these news programs and documentaries, Herman soon realized there was always someone who wanted to do much better than the last person. This kept the media constantly flushed with content, the police frustrated, and the public well-fed.

Do I want fame? I know it would create news if I snatch a beautiful young girl. I would achieve fame whether I liked it or not. How much fame depends on several factors. How young she is. What I do to her when I have her. How long I keep her for. What I do with her after I grow tired of her. The more shocking and horrific the crime, the more twisted and demented the person, the longer you stay on the news. If you can be unique enough, depraved enough, your name will be permanently written into the history books. Herman knew he needed to be admired, envied, and even loved. His whole life had been so mundane, so dull and lifeless. It had to change.

There had recently been a serial rapist-murderer caught.

The media followed him, trying to film him when they could, plastering his photo across the T.V. screens in everyone's homes. Every newspaper and online news site featured articles on his life, dissecting every second he'd walked this earth. The story had chat forums and social platforms buzzing. Constant repetitive videos of him being led to and from the courthouse. The public strained their eyes to get a glimpse of what kind of person could do those things to another human being, how he could remain so calm about his crimes. Everyone was in awe, and all wanted to see this freak of nature up close. Herman was just as obsessed. He was impressed by the attention this person received. Envious of the sexual shock gratification that the rapist-killer must have gotten when he inflicted his desires on his victims. The fact that Herman's fascination with kidnappers, serial killers, and serial rapists had grown didn't bother him.

These thoughts of these killers consumed him every waking hour. He wondered about their childhoods. *Were they similar to mine and Beth's? Maybe they can help me understand why my family did all those terrible things to Beth and me! They were not born like that! Just like Beth and I were not born that way. Why did they do this to me? They made me like this! They turned me into a monster. A perverted, sexually sadistic loner!*

Deep down, he knew he needed help, but he also knew no one cared enough to give him what he needed. This was a deep, burning rage in his mind and through his body. *No one will ever answer those questions for me!* He thought with a deep sense of hatred. *They could never answer them!* Suddenly he felt rage ignite within him. He screamed out as loud and hard as he could. He wanted to lash out, stab, kill, mutilate. He wanted to hurt someone. Make everyone feel the pain and hurt he'd endured. *Fucking bitches and bastards, all of you!* His head throbbed, and his throat hurt. The lack of awareness he was forced to have during those times at the clinic and hospital. They had cocooned him in that place for so long, denying him normalcy.

Murders, rapes, torture, suicides, armed robbery, stalking

for kidnapping, and other serious crimes were never exposed to him. Of course not. That would be too upsetting for someone like him. When he had asked Robert about how violent the outside world was, Robert had replied. "Better you don't know," he had said. "Herman, you're not the only sick person out there. They can't lock a lot of them up as they did with you."

He thought about his time at the hospital. *They could never get inside my head. They tried many times, but I only gave them the thoughts I wanted them to have. To satisfy them, to appease their sense of duty of care, to give them enough so they could feel like they were doing their jobs.* The patient fooling the doctor syndrome was famous. He had read about this. *Convince them you're much better. Get released. Commit your crimes all over again. That's why most serial rapists and killers don't kill themselves. Why should they? Why should they die? Why do most of them want to get caught instead? Because they want to be famous. They think they are smarter than everyone else! They are more powerful and superior! More clever in eluding capture, with their higher I.Q.s. Some take their own lives. But no matter whether they're caught or not, or die by their hand, they are famous. When they're shot to death by police, or put to death by a justice system, do they finally lose their notoriety? Even then, they live on in the nightmares of those who are either enthralled or traumatized by them.*

The serial killers and rapists he read about were not rich. They just had the right homes, locations. The right van to take girls. And they looked just like everyone else. Some of them had very high I.Q.'S, which he found strange. *If you're so smart, how come you can claim insanity when you're captured? You can't figure out what is right and wrong? How come you get caught?* Herman knew the difference between right and wrong. *I may not know everything now or how perfectly my sexual desires work. But my lust for control is absolute.* It had become too strong for him to ignore any longer. But he knew not to get caught. He'd lost his freedom once, never again.

He jumped out of the desk chair he'd been sitting in scrolling the chat rooms and paced the room. Herman wanted to go straight

to his van. *I want to find one now! No more waiting! This could*

be my only relief, my only salvation! He began to plan.

Chapter Five

Herman's Bitcoin investment was shooting through the roof in the nearly eight months since he had been released. Thousands of dollars were pouring into his account. When he wasn't exploring the devious side of the web, he was continuing his Bitcoin education.

Robert specifically warned him against the dark web and the deep dark web.

"Everything in there is illegal, Herman," he said. "You could be sent back to prison if you get involved with that!"

But Herman had to know why it was so dangerous and forbidden. He learned he needed a Tor browser to continue. This would make his I.P. address untraceable. Herman was scared more than excited. He downloaded the T.O.R. and waited. He knew nothing about the deep dark web, but he was sure he would like it there.

During Herman's online chats, he met someone with the username 'Swift!' Swift guided him through the maze and brought him to the dark web. There it was. Herman gazed in wonderment and scrolled. His nervousness increased the deeper he went. You could buy anything. Fake passports, driver's licenses, birth certificates, college degrees, any type of drug. Killing knives, guns, and of course, more graphic and real-looking bondage-rape videos. Only a few were free to watch, and Swift warned him that many of these sites had viruses and spam, and he had to be careful of what he watched. He didn't listen at first and had to factory reset his computer two times before buying expensive ant-virus software.

The chat forums he found especially useful. Most users helped each other to enjoy these forbidden sites safely. Herman and Swift chatted daily, and through him, Herman found much better sites and went much deeper into the dark web until he found the deep dark web where he discovered the Red Rooms. Here you could watch anything like real rapes and murders—no actors and actresses. Herman delved deeper and was surprised to learn they required large Bitcoin memberships; some cost as much as $40,000. He wasn't ready to join yet. They were costly, and he had no desire to spend that much money on something he didn't fully understand. He needed more experience and advice from Swift first. He was also a little scared of what he would find and thought it would be better to ease in via less expensive sites. Still interesting, but a lot less dangerous. Although his I.P. address was now encrypted, Swift warned him that people on the deep dark web were very good at tracing and finding people, which frightened Herman.

On the deep and deep dark web, he wasn't known as Herman, he was the Card Collector, and he used his Bitcoin to join some of the more easily accessible sites. These cost hundreds of dollars to join instead of thousands. Not that money was an issue. He was making good money with his online trading, and it wasn't like he had anything better to spend it on.

He spent hours watching videos, imagining what it would be like to be one of those guys doing those things to a young girl with people paying money to watch. But it still wasn't enough. On the dark web, the girls looked much younger than eighteen, but the message said they were eighteen before each video played. He still hadn't fully satisfied his desires. He wasn't even completely sure what those desires were, but he was sure he'd know when he found them.

There was never a doubt in his mind that sooner or later, he would come across child porn. *When I do, will it shock me? Will I be sick? Will it fascinate me? Is that what's in the Red Rooms?* Swift had told him that there were videos of children being killed in some of the Red Rooms. That idea made bile burn his throat. It disturbed him to think there were people out there who enjoyed watching something like that. The worst were the videos of the rapes, killings, or maiming of children. He didn't understand that at all. The thought of killing a pure, innocent child made his stomach churn.

Jeff Kapper—Herman's father—had always been an alcoholic abuser. His beatings drove his mother to suicide. After her death, and then after losing his job, things only got worse. One night one of Lilly's clients sodomized Beth. When their father had come home later that night, drunk, Lilly quickly lied and said Herman and Beth had had an inappropriate sexual relationship. Jeff lost his mind. He beat both Herman and Beth nearly to death and forced them to perform sexual acts on each other.

He remembered Beth's blue eyes filling with tears. "It's all wrong, Herman, it's all wrong. Everything we've been made to do, it's all bad." Herman felt completely helpless, with no idea how to react or what to say to her. He hugged her for a very long time, her head on his shoulders, listening to her cry until she could cry no more.

The next day, Beth killed herself. The second person Herman loved was gone because of Jeff Kapper.

The videos made him remember, the anger as fresh as it had

happened yesterday. He suddenly imagined torturing and killing Lilly and his father. *I should have killed them both before Beth died. But I never would have gotten away with it. You killed that boy, stabbed him in the eye and his throat. Did it make me feel good?* It was the same question he always came back to. The abject of cruelty. *No! I'm not like that; I want to be normal. I had to kill them for protection. I could never kill for fun. No! I couldn't! Never!* The more gruesome he imagined the crimes committed against children, the sicker he became. When Swift told him all about those Red Rooms, he had cried for the children he never knew but were now dead. If he saw something like that on the deep dark web, he would want to know who the killer was. *I would kill him myself! Yes! Myself! What sort of maniac could do that to a child and feel no remorse?* Herman liked to see young girls tied up and submissive, but he didn't enjoy watching a beautiful young girl being tortured. And that, in Herman's mind, made him much different from those men who create those Red Room videos.

The idea of torture was a curious one. He rolled the word around in his mouth. He was trying to distinguish his version of torture, the kind that excited him, and the type of videos that disgusted him. He decided to look up the definition. 'The action or practice to inflict severe pain or suffering on someone as a punishment to force them to do something or say something.' In his version of torture, he'd inflict an uncontrollable desire or ecstasy, driving a young girl to the point of an orgasm, even when she didn't want to have one. He couldn't watch a beautiful young girl being physically tortured, which led to marking her, bleeding, or bruising her perfect skin. This, for him, would make her undesirable, dirty, disgusting. *She is not supposed to suffer pain. Why kill someone so young and beautiful when you can drug her, kidnap her, have her many times over? Then release her somewhere, drugged again.* These thoughts only made things worse for Herman. He blamed those maniacs for his frustrations. He knew his fantasies were different, and until he acted and kidnapped a girl, his agitation would only grow.

I know I have to take one. Why should I miss out and be denied the same experience? Why should all these other people get to enjoy themselves and not me? The reason was simple. It was because he didn't think he was clever enough yet. He would be captured and sent back to life in captivity if he tried. And not the low-security clinic he was use to. It would be a high-security prison, where he would most likely be tortured and raped daily.

Herman was sure it would be better to stay in the corners of the deep dark web until he was ready. *Yes! This will be my salvation.* It would protect him, nurture him, hide him from prying eyes. And when he was ready, he had the money now and a large basement that he could convert, where he could safely take his captives without the worry of any neighbors or anyone knowing what was going on.

He used the deep web and Swift to continue planning. He knew he needed drugs for the entire thing to work. Certain drugs can render their memory useless for some time. He asked Swift what drugs could wipe memories and make a person incapacitated. He told him about a drug called the 'Devil's Breath.' Swift explained this drug renders the victim completely complacent.

Herman obsessed over this idea and reveled in its perfection. *All my fantasies will come true with a beautiful girl of my choice. Willing to do anything I say. Without screaming or crying. Only her moans of pleasure.* It was perfect. There were other things to think about, like the location of his house was quite remote. There were no girls that he knew of nearby. This was probably for the best. The further the girl lived, the less likely they would connect him to her disappearance. He thought about the beach and the young girls sunbathing and dancing in the waves. He would need to spend hours there. He had many ideas on how to expose himself to young girls through trickery. A large beach towel hides his nakedness, then waits for young girls to walk by, opening his legs if they glance at him. He would find places that were located far away enough away from the crowds that would notice him. Then a great idea crossed his mind. He could rent an apartment under a false name close to the beach. *I could stay there as long as it took. Follow them. Then when the time is right, drug them and bring them to my house at night.*

The next morning, he drove to the beach. His plan had to work out perfectly; his imagination ran wild, identifying strategic spots from which he could watch young girls. He finally arrived and parked at a good middle part of the coast and explored. That day he saw many young girls he liked and fantasized about all of them, bringing them to his basement and doing whatever he wanted with them. He searched around for an apartment or condo to rent and found a two-bedroom apartment right across the road from the beach. It was a small block with a swimming pool. Herman took it and paid cash for three months' rent.

Chapter Six

Herman spent nearly the whole summer at the beach stalking and exposing himself to young girls. The opportunity still hadn't presented itself where it would be safe to take one, though. He was getting restless, his frustration and anger growing.

By the end of summer, he had raped a young girl in a secluded rocky area of the beach coastline. He had tricked her into looking inside a small rock cave on her hands and knees for an octopus, and had forced her to stay still, pulled down her bikini bottom, and raped her from behind. He had escaped, leaving her there, threatening her not to move until he was gone. A few days later, he read about himself in the newspaper, or at least what he'd done. The victim didn't want to be identified, and the police hoped they would catch the rapist soon. Since the attack, another woman had come forward and also complained of being sexually harassed in the same location. His hands shook as he read the words. He knew they were talking about him. He tried relaxing his mind. Convincing himself, it was fine that he looked like any other guy with a hat and sunglasses. He got rid of everything, his towel, swimsuit, cap, and glasses as a precaution. The paper explained the undercover police and beach guards would be patrolling the headland. The community demanded more be done to make them feel safe. *That's it then,* he thought. *What do I do now?* Herman stopped going to the beach completely and gave notice that he'd be ending his apartment lease. He returned to his house, and it was just as well. It became apparent to Herman he wasn't capable of living anywhere near the beach. He couldn't control himself, not after all the things he had done with young girls over the summer.

***

Herman was mindlessly scrolling the internet when he received an email invitation to his high school reunion. He had no idea how they got his email address; Robert was the one who had set it up for him, but after all he'd learned on the internet, he knew you could find anything and anyone if you looked hard enough.

The details in the email said that it would be at some dance hall in a few weeks, and below the invitation was his old class photo. Herman didn't want to go- even looking at himself in that photo dredged up horrible memories.

He scanned the photo, and his gaze landed on John Gooding's face. Sudden rage filled his stomach. He fisted his hands until his knuckles turned white. John was the first boy Herman met at school. He lived close to Herman, and they became close friends. As he got to know John, he remembered that they began to share their deep emotional problems. Herman would become John's trusted companion. Herman and John would go everywhere together. One boy they met was a guy named Roscoe Mcfee. As with Herman and John, Roscoe also had no real friends. Roscoe was a heavy pot-smoking, long-haired, short, ugly boy with pasty skin from lack of sunlight and rotten teeth.

Roscoe hardly attended school. He was an avid book reader and had an artistic ability that impressed John and Herman. He lived with his aging mother in a two-story house near a lake in Herman's neighborhood. Roscoe's father had left his mother when he was very young, and she never remarried. She was also a bordering alcoholic; she didn't work and lived off government welfare. There was a little flat out the back of the house where his brother Peter sometimes lived. Peter Mcfee was a dope dealer, and like his brother, had long hair, pasty skin, and was skinny. It eventually became an ideal place for everyone to hang out. There was a mix in the group at the house, and the girls would hang around because Roscoe's brother was cool, good-looking, and had lots of dope. John and Herman became part of the group and would spend every day at Roscoe's after school. Herman closed his eyes and traveled back to that day when everything changed.

Herman went along with whatever John said. Maybe if his home life hadn't been so miserable, if he hadn't been so lonely, he wouldn't have needed John. But in Herman's young mind, he did. They needed each other.

Herman remembered one day John suddenly came out and told him something that made Herman very uncomfortable. John said that he would often have thoughts about kissing young, good-looking boys when he was very young. He would fantasize about having sex with some of them. He explained to Herman he had tried putting it out of his mind, but he would become aroused every time he thought about it. Herman was silent and a little shocked. He felt John wanted to tell him much more, but Herman didn't want to hear this talk, but he was afraid to say anything. He hoped it was only because of their close friendship. There was something about John that started to scare Herman. One day John molested Herman in John's parents' swimming pool. Herman had trusted John, and it changed everything.

Herman went home that day, his mind spinning from

humiliation and betrayal, his body shaking from the shock of his only friend touching him. After that, he didn't trust anyone in school and spent the rest of his days except for Beth, alone.

There were a few girls Herman remembered, but the one he would never forget was Annie Leason. Herman stared at her in the photo, tracing her face with his finger. He had been in love with her since the first time he laid eyes on her. She was slim, tanned, fit, with long golden blonde hair down to her buttocks. A blemish-free small face with deep blue eyes and white teeth smile. He had been fixated on her and would stare at her during class, fantasizing about what it would be like to date her, to hold her hand, to tie her up and have her helpless at his mercy. He was too shy to talk to her, so he just admired her from afar.

John Gooding also desired her, the entire school did, but John's desires were much more disturbing than Herman's. Back before, when they were friends, the two discussed what they would love to do to Annie Leason, joking together about drugging her, kidnapping her, and raping her together. John told him he had fantasies before about killing young girls. He didn't know why; he would only watch porn every day. He did, however, get pleasure in thinking about defenseless young girls, watching them begging for their lives, he would touch himself, but he never saw himself kill them in his fantasies. When he did climax and opened his eyes, they were already dead. John would constantly go on about what he'd like to do to Annie. Herman wondered if John would treat Annie the same way he would treat his other fantasy girls. Herman had these fantasies, but he was sure nowhere near as violent as John's.

Herman could tell John was changing. His feelings got stranger and weirder. Herman slowly realized that John had gay tendencies, but Herman said nothing. Then the swimming pool incident happened, and Herman avoided John and the other boys as much as possible until John cornered him at school one day.

"I heard Annie likes you. She said she wants to talk to you, to know if you are ok," John said. Herman didn't respond; he wanted to forgive John for what had happened but couldn't. No matter what reasons he thought of to forget what he did to him in that pool, he couldn't.

Annie had gone to John's house to ask him to send a message to Herman to contact her. Instead, desperate to win back Herman's favour, John confessed to Herman that he had taken his dick out in front of her in his room. John had thought Annie was there for him, she wore her tight short school uniform, and he had cried to Herman he had lost control, but John never did give that message to him until that day, when it was too late.

Herman remembered the last ever words he had shouted to John, "You betrayed me, all this time she wanted me, and you kept it to yourself so that I couldn't have her, the one girl I wanted to have, the one girl that liked me. You fucked me up! I trusted you! I trusted you as my friend! And you fucked me up! I fucking hate you, John Gooding! I fucking hate you!" He would never speak to him again.

Looking at the old photo and seeing John's face brought back too many bad memories. The confusion, the hurt, the nights of gay dreams. He couldn't stand to look any more.

He finally spotted the boy much worse than John, Brady Wightly. Herman hated Wightly the most. Everyone was terrified of him. He was the school bully, a criminal, and a thug. He used to make fun of Herman in front of Annie, humiliating him. Herman would picture all the ways he would kill him in his head. If Wightly ever turned up dead, he wouldn't care, and neither would anyone else. Wightly was short, with long slicked back brown hair that he kept tied in a ponytail, his skin was scaled by the sun, and he was built like a little bulldog.

He looked at his smug smile in the faded scanned photo. *Maybe I should kidnap him and kill him!* Herman looked at Annie again; her beautiful smile shining in the photo took his breath away. It was almost as if she was smiling at him only. *I wonder what she looks like now after all this time? Would she even talk to me after all I've been through? Does everyone know about my crimes and time in jail and the hospitals?*

His thoughts shifted from the horrible things he could do to Wightly, and instead pictured Annie, bound and gagged in his carefully built basement. *She could be my prize!* He stared at the photo and felt his loins stir.

Chapter Seven

Brady Wightly was sitting on the porch of his little backyard flat as he took a mouthful of beer, swallowed it, and cursed out loud. It was late Friday afternoon. He had big plans for that evening and was supposed to be on his way out. Instead, he was sitting brooding and waiting for his brother Ian to come home and give him his weekly supply of meth to sell.

His older brother, Ian had been bossing him around and bullying Brady his whole life. Even as an adult, he was still afraid of him. When Ian left earlier, he told Brady to clean out his garage. Brady did it without question. As he finished, he had come across his old school yearbook and was now flicking through it. He remembered he'd received an email invitation for a school reunion party and would most likely go for some sort of revenge. He stopped short on a photo page. Herman Kapper stared back at him. If only he had taught Kapper a lesson back then, he and his bum buddy, psycho John Gooding. Brady still hated them both. For many reasons, but one particular moment stood out among the rest. After school one day, Brady had found out that Annie Leason, the hottest girl in school, was chasing Herman Kapper. Of all people to like, weirdo Herman. Brady had been giving Kapper a hard time all afternoon, and Gooding had stood up to him. There was something in Gooding's eyes that scared Brady. He didn't look right, crazy, unhinged. He'd been scared that day, and no one ever scared him.

His brother always warned him never to fuck with the crazy ones, and Gooding was exactly that. A madman. *That stupid, weird fucker!* It was why Brady didn't fight him, because he knew Gooding wouldn't stop until Gooding killed him. Brady had a pretty shit life, but that didn't mean he wanted to die.

Ian finally showed up and gave Brady enough meth to make a nice profit for the evening. Brady took the satchel and left. It would be the last time Ian would see his brother alive.

Chapter Eight

Annie Leason was beautiful. At twenty-six, she was studying at university for an arts degree. She was sitting out on her balcony sipping chardonnay with her longtime friend Sally Wui, who she'd known since high school. They were huddled over Annie's laptop, reading an email Annie received for their high school reunion. Neither of them was sure if they would go. High school was filled with bad memories; she had grown past all of that and was glad they were nothing but memories. She wanted a good life. She was happy, had big plans for her future, and had no desire to move backwards.

"Oh my God, do you remember that one kid Herman Kapper?" Sally asked, laughing. "Your old flame."

"He was *not* my old flame, ok? I had a crush on him, that's all." Annie smiled and wondered what had happened to him. She looked at his face in the photo and frowned. When she heard what happened to his sister, then his father being arrested and sent to prison, she felt so sad for him. She had cried for him. But after school, their paths never crossed again. He disappeared. No one had any idea where he went. She sometimes asked herself why they never stayed in touch. Then she remembered that creep John Gooding and she was done reminiscing for the night. She slammed the lid of the laptop closed and forced a smile on her face.

"Ready to get going? Let's start with drinks at D.D.'S Bar and go from there."

Chapter Nine

Brady lit a joint and leaned against a dumpster, taking a long, deep inhale, waiting for the pungent smoke to fill his lungs before exhaling. He had just been kicked out of Feisty's for slapping a black woman and pulling a knife on her friends who ran to her defense. "Fuck 'em," he said, coughing.

Two beams of light lit the dark alley as a car approached. He slunk back into the shadows, pushing his back against the wall. *Ah shit, someone called the cops.* As the lights grew brighter, he realized it wasn't the police but a van. The blinding lights made it impossible to see which type though. *Who the fuck is this?* As the van approached, he tried to make out the driver, but he couldn't tell if it was a man or a woman. The van stopped. No movement. Brady took a step forward to see who was inside, but he couldn't see through the tinted glass. His reflection stared back at him. He shivered, knowing they could see him, but he still had no idea who stared back from within. His first thought was the mafia, but they don't drive vans like this one. He then thought it might be someone in the club who followed him here seeking revenge.

It can't be them. No one saw him come down this alley, and he was sure of that. It must be some fucking drunk who pulled in here to sleep it off and hadn't seen him standing there. And the idiot was blocking him in.

He tapped on the glass and said, "Hey, asshole! Move your fucking van, will ya? You're blocking me in here!" There was no response. *Maybe this dickhead passed out.* He leaned against the door and knocked on the window again harder. "Hey, dickhead! What the fuck do you think you're doing? Move this fucking pile of shit!" He cupped his hands around his eyes and peered into the window. The window suddenly slid down, and a powerful arm reached out and grabbed the back of his neck, pulling his head inside the car. Before Brady could react, he felt a prick in his neck. He tried to struggle, but he felt his legs collapse underneath him within a few seconds. His vision blurred and clouded over. After a few more seconds, he slumped and collapsed onto the alley road. The driver's door opened, and a figure walked around to Brady's unconscious body. He slid the van's side door open and, with two powerful arms, reached down and pulled Brady inside before slamming the door shut. He then casually walked back around to the driver's side, got in, started the van, and drove off.

***

Hours passed, and Brady finally woke from his dream-like state. His body felt numb, and he couldn't move. The last thing he remembered was standing behind a dumpster smoking a joint. There was a hood over his head, making it impossible to see where he'd been taken, and when he moved, he felt something locked around his wrists. He tugged on it and felt the sudden jolt of a chain locked tight. *What the fuck?* He jerked his hands again, but the same thing happened. Then again, harder, until pain shot through his wrists. Panic took over. He struggled violently, but whatever chains held him down was too strong. His skin was rubbing against a bare mattress, and he realized he was naked except for his underwear. His heart started pounding. *Did the mafia kidnap me? Who have I pissed off this time?* His brain searched for a reason but came up with nothing.

Brady squinted his eyes to try and see through the thick canvas covering his head. He could just barely make out a small table beside him and strained to see what looked like a toilet and shower in the corner. He finally snapped and screamed. When he finally stopped, he was met with silence.

He heard a lock click, and a door opened. He yelled, "Hey, what the fuck is going on, man? Is this a joke or something? Let me the fuck up! Who the fuck are you?"

Heavy footsteps pounded towards him; they were getting closer, and he strained to see through the hood. He could barely make out a colossal figure coming towards him, blocking what little light penetrated his hood. Then he felt a stinging welt snap across his face as if someone had just whipped him. He fell back on the bed and writhed in pain. "What the fuck, man? What are you doing? Who the fuck are you?" He could sense whoever was there was standing very close to him. Brady lashed out with his leg, trying to kick the figure and another strong welt from the mysterious object connected with his head. He buckled in pain. "Hey, listen, man! My brother has a lot of money, ok? He can pay you whatever you want! Just let me go, and I will get it for you! Just let me go, please!"

The footsteps walked away, and the door slammed shut, the key turned, and the lock clicked. He was alone again. "What the fuck is going on?" he cursed. *Maybe one of my brother's customers kidnapped me and held me for ransom.* "Yes!" he said to the empty room. "That's it! Ok, my brother will get me out. Just need to hang in there." He breathed out a sigh of relief. "This will all be over soon."

Brady slowly felt the energy draining from his body; the booze and dope were taking over. Even the welt from whoever hit him couldn't stop the sleep that was about to consume him. He closed his eyes and fell asleep.

Chapter Ten

The days turned dark and cold for Herman. He wouldn't even go outside to buy food. Everything he needed he bought online and had it delivered. Herman was becoming very savvy with his hands and learned how to fix and repair things in his house by watching videos on the internet. He became a hermit, no one came inside, and all deliveries were left on the front porch. He felt safe and out of sight, hidden away in his house.

He no longer feared the deep dark web, and he became smarter and hardened. His daily doses of the deep dark web were so dramatically intense that there was nothing he couldn't handle. His lust for depraved and bizarre sexual deviance increased the more he spent online. He sat in front of his computer watching videos being live-streamed. People doing things to other people; he could never have imagined possible. Although he vowed never to watch certain things, there was no escaping what kept popping up on his browser—especially with his most bizarre searches.

Herman had asked Swift to help him find a Red Room that might be more suited to what Herman was looking for. Swift had suggested he join *The Hood's* Red Room. He said it was one of the best on the deep dark web. He sent him the link, and the front page was saturated in a foggy red mist. Among the mist were sex toys, whips, chains, bondage machines, cutting tools, and blood splatters. In the middle was an image of a large brown hood that looked to be made from a potato sack with jagged, rough stitches through it. An image of a young girl screaming was superimposed on the page. Below was a description of the room and instructions in blood dripping letters.

Welcome to the red room of

"THE HOOD!"

Your membership guarantees you the best.

To be present at our events will be an incredible experience,

like nothing you've ever seen.

Sit back and enjoy the spectacle.

Bloody torture, rape, and inexorable death of pretty girls.

You will have a front-row seat for the torture.

For the fee of 00.5 Bitcoin, you will receive a

lifetime membership and the ability to make requests and

personal bids! Please see your application code to complete your

payment. We will be in touch with confirmation and further

instructions.

Herman had done the calculation. It came to $27,000; it was a lot of money, but it gave him a lifetime membership. He liked the option of making personalized requests. So he joined. A few hours later, he received a confirmation message and his membership I.D.

Herman held his breath and pressed enter.

Chapter Eleven

The sound of the door unlocking and opening ripped Brady from his sleep. *Finally, my brother has got me out of this shit. I wonder how much it cost him? How much will I have to pay him back?* Brady didn't care. He was just glad it was over. The sooner he was out of wherever he was, the better. He sensed the figure coming close to him and felt his leg chain unlocked. His capture had come in and handcuffed his hands behind his back when he was asleep, and he waited with anticipation for him to unlock those too.

He felt the two powerful hands grab him, pulling him roughly off the bed, then he was pushed and shoved out of the room with the hood still over his head and his hands cuffed behind his back. He tried to focus his vision again, but he couldn't see where he was going. He didn't understand why they hadn't given him his clothes back.

Brady didn't make a noise. Knowing it was best not to aggravate these people. He was sure he was being released and didn't want to screw it up. Brady was waiting for the rush of fresh cool air to hit him any moment now. But instead, he was dragged into what seemed to be a large, empty room. He couldn't see much, but he could tell the room was lit with red lights. He was shoved against a wall, and his arms lifted and chained above his head. "Hey, what the fuck is going on, man? My brother has paid you, hasn't he? Why am I still here? Let me the fuck go! Didn't you get your money?" There was no reply. He sensed his captor walk away, then return a few minutes later, coming very close to him now. Brady waited.

The figure ripped the hood off Brady's head. His eyes struggled to adjust to the red glow playing tricks on his eyes. As his vision sharpened, he noticed he was standing on a large plastic sheet. He lifted his head to see the man standing a few feet in front of him. At first, Brady smirked, then he thought he was tripping. Brady's mouth tried to say something, but nothing came out. What stood before him was something out of a bizarre fairy tale. The man had a large potato sack on his head. It looked roughly stitched together with slots cut out for the eyes, nose, and mouth. The sack came to a point at the top, like a witch's hat. The man was shirtless, except for a black leather apron that went to his knees. The man wore khaki shorts and long black rubber boots adorned with shiny buckles.

Brady wanted to laugh, and at that very moment, he almost did. Being chained to a wall didn't seem to matter anymore compared to what stood before him. He was sure it was a joke. It had to be.

He burst out laughing. "What the fuck man, what is this? Are you some sort of medieval clown or something? I knew this was a joke." He was calmer now. "Someone is playing a fucking good joke on me, maybe my brother, eh? Is he trying to teach me some sort of lesson?" he asked, still grinning.

His eyes now fully adjusted, he looked around the room. It was completely lit in a dull, red glow. There was no furniture except for a large table and what looked like a dildo machine. Brady laughed again, but this time a nervous laugh. Doubt crept in. When he saw all the sex toys, leather restraints, sharp objects, and hooks hanging on the rough old brickwork walls, he was no longer grinning. A wave of panic shot through him.

His eyes went back to the hooded man, and he looked at the table with two sets of drawers draped in a black cloth. Beyond that was a long wall mirror. *I'm in the custody of some weird hospital ward!* He realized that was not possible. Cops and doctors don't kidnap people. Anxiety and panic coursed through his body.

"Ok!" he said with determination. "You've had your fun guys! Enough of the fucking jokes! Ok? You got me! You made me shit myself! Now let me the fuck out of here!" He looked around the room desperately for a way to escape. He struggled violently in vain, his arms tight and secured. The big hooded man stood silently, watching him. "Listen to me, you fucker! Stop with this shit now! If you don't let me loose, I'm gonna cut your fucking balls off!" There was no response. The large man just stood there in front of him, still watching.

The hooded man turned and walked to the large table. With one quick movement, he angrily pulled the black sheet off. Brady's confusion and panicked horror increased. The table was covered with sharp metal objects, curved knives, small steel hooks attached to long chains, pliers, knives of different sizes, and some sort of dentist tools. There was a roll of barbed wire, long sharp metal phallic-looking rods, and different-sized dildos.

Brady stuttered. "The fuck?..Hey! What the fuck is this?" Brady's mind screamed out in desperate shock. *What the fuck is happening? Who is this guy? Why am I here? Is this a mafia hit? Is this guy going to torture me? Please somebody help.* Brady watched in horror as the hooded man opened a laptop and began typing. He stopped, looked back at Brady, then continued typing. Brady yelled at him, "Look, man, I don't know what the fuck is happening. What did I do, man? Who the fuck are you?"

The man completely ignored him, and after a few minutes, Brady watched him pick up a pair of pliers and a small serrated knife. He came towards Brady, and that's when he realized it wasn't a prank or a joke. He started whimpering. "Listen, man, please don't! I did nothing wrong! Come on, man, please? What the fuck?" The large man walked up to him and stood there for a few seconds. He took the pliers and tightened them on one of Brady's nipples. Brady let out a scream, and with one quick motion of his other hand, the hood took a knife and sawed through the soft skin, severing the nipple at the base. Brady felt the tearing of the knife and howled. The man held up the pliers holding Brady's bloody nipple in front of him. Brady, in shock, looked down to see the bloody wound where his nipple had been.

Brady's usual tough facade completely drained away. He whimpered like a little boy. "Please! Man!" he pleaded. "Don't hurt me, please stop!" Brady watched as the large man opened the pliers and let the nipple fall onto the plastic sheet. He reached over to the other side of Brady's chest and, using the pliers, again grabbed the other nipple. Brady begged, "No! No! No! Don't!" The hood pulled hard on the nipple and, with the knife, sliced it off in a saw-like fashion. Brady screamed again and almost pissed himself.

The hood returned to his computer and started typing again. Brady's chest was thumping, and his breathing was erratic; blood gushed from his chest down his abdomen. Streaks of pain soared through the mangled area. He tried to cry out but was too weak.

The hooded man returned to the table of horrors and turned to show Brady what he had in his hand. It looked like a large oversize fishing hook, connected to a thin silver chain that ran down to the floor and out of sight. Brady pleaded with him. "Please help me! Please, man! Don't do this! What the fuck are you doing? Why are you doing this to me?" The Hood walked over to Brady and held his head with one hand; he brought the hook under Brady's chin with the other. His eyes bulged when the cold metal of the hook touched his skin. Before he could react,

The Hood rammed the hook upwards through his chin and up into his mouth with one strong hard motion. Brady's eyes bulged even wider, but he couldn't scream; his tongue involuntarily whipped the sharp tip of the hook. He choked on the blood filling his mouth. His body wiggled and shook like a fish. He tried to scream, but his lungs had drained of air. He thrashed about; tears poured from his eyes. Despite the pain, he felt warm liquid run down his leg. He'd finally pissed himself.

Brady could feel the blood mixing with his urine running down his thighs. He had suddenly been injected with something, and it gave him a weird burst of energy and lit up every nerve in his body; the pain intensified. The hooded man walked to Brady's side and started winding a winch connected to the chain. The chain screeched through a pulley; as it tightened, the hook pulled his head upwards. He tried screaming, but all that came out was a gurgled mess. His head was now completely facing the ceiling. The chain kept pulling him, and the pain burned across Brady's entire face. His jaw felt like it was being ripped out of its socket.

His heels slowly lifted off the ground, and his weight shifted to the balls of his feet. The hooded man stopped pulling on the chain and looked down to check how far Brady's feet had lifted from the ground. He grabbed the chain again and pulled some more until he heard a cracking sound from Brady's jaw breaking. He stopped pulling on the chain and walked back to the computer. Brady's eyes strained in their sockets to see what torture was next. The hooded man took a vice of some sort, and Brady's panic sent his heart racing. The hooded man slipped on a pair of rubber gloves, came back over, and pulled Brady's underwear down; he placed the small vise around Brady's testicles and slowly turned the handle. Brady felt the pain shoot through his abdomen into his brain and screamed a silent scream. The pressure increased until his testicles burst through his scrotum skin like two cracked eggs.

There was an indescribable searing pain in his groin. Bright flashes of light filled his vision before he passed out.

Chapter Twelve

The Hood stopped turning the vise and left it hanging on Brady's scrotum. He returned to the table and grabbed some gauze pads, tape, and a Bunsen burner. He opened a drawer from the table and took out an IV bag with tubing and catheter and a syringe filled with adrenaline. He walked back over to Brady and hooked the plastic bag with the saline solution to a stand, and inserted the IV into Brady's hand. Then injected the adrenaline into Brady's arm. The adrenaline hit Brady in an instant. His eyes flew open, bringing him out of his nightmarish dream and into a foul-tasting synthetic reality. He attempted to speak but only gurgled. Spit mixed with blood and snot from his nose dripped down his face.

Brady was still alive, dizzy, and fogged from the pain. The Hood knew his victim was beyond understanding what was happening to him. Tears poured from Brady's eyes. His body pulled up so high that he couldn't keep a regular balance on his toes. Every time he slightly moved off-balance, the hook would grind into his jaw; it almost supported his total weight. Every time he coughed or choked, he would fall off balance and cry out from the massive pain in his jaw. The room smelled of metal from the blood pouring from his wounds. The vise on his testicles was still left hanging there by its weight. Guttural moaning sounds came from his lips. He finally blacked out again. Then his eyes fluttered open again, and The Hood stood watching him, head cocked to one side. Then he retrieved another needle and the Bunsen burner to stop Brady's scrotum from bleeding out anymore. The Hood didn't want him dying just yet. He checked the adrenaline dosage once more and returned to Brady's mutilated body. He took Brady's arm and tapped it to bring up a vein. It would be a long time yet before Brady would die that night.

Chapter Thirteen

When the room opened, Herman wasn't completely certain of what he saw. No. He couldn't be completely sure, but if he was right, he was watching something that would stay with him for the rest of his life. The Hood was brutally torturing a man to death.

The man's face was covered in blood, so it was hard to make it out, but Herman was sure he knew him from somewhere; he just couldn't quite place it. He was new and not sure how it all worked, so he didn't make any personal requests, but whoever they were, was certainly getting their money's worth.

The Hood was not only mutilating the man but also sexually torturing him, so much that he almost found it hard to watch. Yet he couldn't force his eyes from the screen. The man was close to death, and despite his obsession, he would be glad when it was over.

He wasn't sure if he could watch something like this again and hoped not all The Hood's shows were like this. He was a lifetime member now, though, which frightened and excited him. Until now, he wanted to avoid watching murders in the Red Rooms. That was his plan anyway, but since the live stream had begun, he couldn't help himself; he couldn't stop watching. Herman continued to watch the brutal torture until The Hood cut the man's throat. It was flashing through Herman's mind. Then it came to him. He suddenly realized that although the man's face was bloody and his body bruised and mutilated, he was sure that the victim looked and sounded just like Brady Wightly. Herman hadn't seen him since school, but that familiar grating, bullying voice was unmistakable. *How did Brady Wightly end up in this room?* He couldn't believe he didn't pick up on it right away. He was suddenly scared, angry, and quite disappointed he hadn't put in a bid for a personalized request.

Chapter Fourteen

The air outside was brisk. The night was darker than usual, the perfect cover. He watched her walk quickly towards her garage, she stopped, looked around then wrapped her arms around herself. *Does she sense me watching her?* When she reached the garage entrance, she looked at the van. It must have stood out from the vehicles filling the parking area. She kept looking over her shoulder as if she knew she was being followed.

When she reached her car, a hand-pulled her shoulder, jerking her backwards, and a needle pierced her neck. She passed out straight away and was bundled quickly into the van. The Hood drove out of the garage quickly but not too quickly to attract unwanted attention. He drove her to his location, and when he arrived, he checked to make sure he had given her the correct dosage. He picked her up and carried her to what he likes to call his "waiting room." The special room where he would prepare his victims for whatever his customers ordered. Laying her down on the bed, he took off her clothes, leaving her underwear on. *Hmm, she is lovely, my customer has excellent taste.* He secured her wrist and ankles to the chains connected to the bed and left her to sleep for a few hours.

He was quite pleased with the special drug Swift had given him. *I wonder where he is now.*

"If you want to kidnap and release, The Devil's Breath is the way to go," Swift had told him years ago. "It leaves them helpless and willing, but after, the victim has no memory of what happened to them," Swift warned him to be careful with the doses, or it could kill them. The Hood figured this one would be out for at least two hours more. He was good at this; he'd perfected his craft. He also knew exactly how much adrenaline to give to a subject to bring them back to consciousness. His customers preferred them to be awake for the torture. He aimed to please.

She'd be lethargic and helpless when she woke, and that's how he needed her to be. He went out to his main room to set up for the show. He checked the various restraints he had placed on the two main pillars and around the room. The floor and walls still had blood splatter from the last show, and he'd need to clean that. His last one had been a brutal killing, but the customer had paid well. A $25,000 deposit along with the name of the victim. He was sure he'd pleased his customer; he'd done everything requested; the customer's requests were harsh even for him but explicit. The order included specific instructions on how the victim was tortured and killed. It was one of the most brutal killings he had done so far. For the right price, though, he could easily do another. To him, it was just another meaningless victim who most likely deserved what he got.

The man had kept shouting at him and treating him like he was some sort of mafia hoodlum. He was a professional, not some two-bit mafia soldier.

He checked his cameras to ensure they were in working order

and angled properly. He then logged onto his computer. *The show will start in two hours,* and he typed out. He posted a photo of her and described her innocence to them, a nice teaser to build the anticipation. After cleaning, he left the room and went to his private chambers. Although he had a fairly large house, he spent most of his time downstairs, in his chambers. He had a fridge, a minibar, TV, stereo, a bed, and a couch. It was also where he kept all his tools and accessories. He opened his fridge and made himself a sandwich. *This will be one of the more enjoyable shows,* he thought. She was beautiful, and the excitement of ravishing her thrilled him immensely. He hoped that's what his customers wanted. It was all up to them. It was always up to them. The Hood was loyal to his customers, and most were loyal to him. Sitting down on his couch to eat, he thought about his past girls. There were a few favorites he had on his wall, mementos. *Few of them, though, have been like this one,* he smiled to himself. *I'm going to enjoy her.*

****

When he was working, his mind was blank except for the show. He smiled to himself, feeling smug, *The Hood* they nicknamed him. He looked at the girls on the wall but felt nothing other than pride. Each of them represented a show, nothing more, nothing less. *Am I without empathy or emotion? Of course! How else could I have done all these things?* He remembered what his father had taught him, 'Never feel for others! No one would ever feel anything for you in the real world!' His father was right. His father never lied to him. He grew up with his father constantly reminding him that he was the only one who cared about him; he was the only one he could trust. His father was all he ever had or ever knew. He was a career criminal before The Hood was born and had done a stint in the army. He was dishonorably discharged for striking an officer; it didn't help that he was constantly drunk and disorderly. He met his mother on the streets soon after. She had been a drugged-out, underage prostitute. As soon as The Hood was born, she left. She had no desire to be a mother and wanted nothing to do with a baby.

His father wasn't too keen on raising a baby alone and tried to find someone to take The Hood off his hands. No one wanted him, but that was fine. He decided to raise him and show him what the world was really like, his world. His son would be his legacy, built to survive the cruel world he'd been born into. *"That's why everyone is so bad in this world,"* his father would tell him. The Hood grew into a very tough young man, and his father taught him how to fight, steal, cheat, and even kill when necessary to survive. The Hood spent most of his time traveling around the country with his father, sleeping in parks hotels when they had money, or in people's houses, they broke into when the owners were away on holiday. They eventually bought a van they could sleep in and started targeting houses to rob them. Sometimes they would run out the back just as the family was pulling up the drive. The Hood never had a girlfriend, and he never wanted one. It had been drilled into his head that women were bad, all of them.

"Worthless, except to be abused and thrown away," his

father would say.

His father had a bottle of chloroform he carried around with him and taught The Hood how to hunt and capture them. They always kept them drugged, then left somewhere far from where they took them.

He was only fifteen the first time he saw his father kill someone. They were in a home they had just broken into. A neighbor who had become suspicious came out of nowhere through the back door and caught them sitting in the kitchen. His father pounced on the man, hitting him over the head repeatedly with a metal pot. He then took a knife and stabbed the man to ensure he was good and dead. He felt nothing. His father showed him how to clean up and not leave any evidence.

"You gotta protect yourself in this shit life," he said. "People will always want you to do things for them. You gotta always get money for that, you understand? Nothings free!" The Hood understood, and he wanted to know what it felt like to kill someone, so his father helped him kill a young girl. He showed him what to do, then stood back while The Hood did his best to impress him. It was messy. They never used guns; his father would say, *"it's too easy to trace back to us, or someone you know, and they make too much noise."*

The Hood perfected his craft over time. He was much cleaner, more precise. One day, they kidnapped a girl and tied her to a chair in the living room of a house they had just broken into the day before. The automatic garage whirred to life; the owner had come home early. They couldn't run and leave the girl, and there was no time to kill her and clean up. His father motioned for him to hide while he waited with a knife. As the man walked through the door, his father had lunged at him but miscalculated and missed, only wounding him. The man turned out to be a special forces soldier. Within a minute, he'd overpowered his father and killed him with the same knife. The Hood fled and never turned back. He was grateful that the girl had been drugged since they took her, and she remained unconscious when he had fled. Just to be safe, he left the state and spent the rest of his teen years on the city's streets, working for criminal gangs.

He would sometimes kill for people or work as a debt collector. Eventually, he worked for an internet scammer and drug dealer who made his money using the deep dark web. The Hood became his bodyguard and enforcer. The man introduced him to his online criminal business and taught him how to use cryptocurrency. He showed him how much money there was to be made if he was willing to do certain things for rich people.

"They like to watch things being done to young girls or their enemies. They give you the names, and you do their dirty work. They sit and watch from the comfort of their homes. No blood on their hands, and they can feel good about themselves. Explain away any guilt. It's not them committing the crime, so nothing to weigh on their conscience." The Hood didn't have a conscience, and he liked money, so it sounded perfect for him. A crypto bank account was opened for him, and he set him up in a basement building with everything he needed. At first, they used young prostitutes who would do it for the money. Then teenage runaways, and eventually, he kidnapped young teen girls. The Hood learned quickly, and he made his boss very rich.

They were hanging out one night high on cocaine and drunk on booze. His boss accused him of stealing money and compromising his business. They argued fiercely, and The Hood ended up stabbing the man to death. He took his computer, his contacts, and his Bitcoin and became his own free agent. He found new clients on the deep dark web, and although he was selective about who they were, he would do almost whatever they wanted him to do. He got the requests and bids, took the money, and did his job. His reputation on the deep dark web grew, and now he had a decent list of rich clients. Some of them, he was sure, were politicians, lawyers, and industrialists, who would pay him thousands of dollars to fulfill their fantasies or special requests on a live stream. He did everything himself. It was the main reason he never got caught. He would kidnap the victims and do all the things asked of him, then dispose of them, alive or dead. He had his system worked out perfectly.

Despite his careful planning, one incident almost brought the entire operation crashing down. When he first heard the police were coming, he frantically searched his mind for how they'd found him. He'd always been so careful. His IP address was untraceable, and he registered the house and his car in a false name. Then he realized the tip-off came from an acquaintance of his, Swift. The Hood was sure Swift ratted him out, only he knew his address. Then he must have had a change of heart. He only had less than an hour before they would be there and had burned all his tapes and took his main laptop, and destroyed everything else with acid. He left the girl he had drugged up and chained to a bed because he had no time to deal with her. He had taken her almost three days before. He didn't know if she was still unconscious or dead when he left his house. He didn't care; There was no way she could recognize him, and he had no time; he was never to return.

Now here he was in his new place and set up. Things were good. He could retire soon. He had almost a million dollars stashed in cash and another cool million in Bitcoin. *Soon*, he thought, *just a few more shows, and then I'm out*. He finished his sandwich and took a long shot of whiskey to wash it down. *I love this lifestyle; what if I can't give it up?* He put on his outfit, went outside to his main room, and scanned that everything was ready. Ok, he smiled, *here we go again*.

Chapter Fifteen

Herman was now tuning into The Hood's room every day. He was a member of eight rooms, including The Hood's, which catered to everything he wanted and didn't want. He'd spent $150,000, but he didn't care. He loved it every day; there was something new and different to watch. Out of all this, there was still a nagging thought. His actual participation, his involvement. *Why am I always watching? Why is it I can never actually feel what it's like? I need to know. I'm so caught up in the deep dark web I'm missing out on what I want, my girl.*

He had slowly converted his basement into a Hood-style red room, and now it was getting closer to perfection. He had chains and pulleys in place and two state-of-the-art video cameras. He painted the walls a light shade of pink, choosing that color to put his girls more erotically at ease. The red lights he installed made the entire basement glow a beautiful reddish rose color. He built himself two special bondage benches with fur-covered leather straps and restraints. Like the Hood's room, he had chains with soft restraints connected to pulleys fixed to the ceiling and the walls. These chains could secure the wrists or ankles without hurting or bruising when the girls struggled. They were strong enough to hold them. The length could be adjusted with the pulleys. His favorite was the sex chair he built himself. His design was exceptional, original, and unique. His design was different from those he'd seen on the web, as well as adding all his own specifications. Made of wood and steel, with many movable parts, the work had taken him months to finish. This would be his key feature, and he designed it to be used safely and comfortably to secure a girl.

A notification popped up from The Hood. He was about to live stream a video with a beautiful girl. The posting said she was clueless about what would happen to her. *They always were.* Herman grinned. He studied the photo of the girl. *Hmm, she looks good.* He leaned in closer. *She looks familiar.* A weird feeling shot through his stomach; he thought of the Brady-looking man and his horrific death. Surely he must be imagining things. There couldn't be two people he knew on The Hood's show. He entered his login and opened The Hood's room. The screen glowed the usual eerie red. *Soon I won't have to watch any of these red rooms.* He smiled to himself. *Soon everyone will log into the CardCollectors' room. It will be the best show on earth.*

Chapter Sixteen

Annie opened her eyes to blurred vision. *What happened? Where the hell am I?* Some type of cloth hood covered her head. Her body felt heavy; she couldn't move it. She realized her clothes were gone, and she tried to cover herself, but her arms wouldn't cooperate, her muscles were too weak, then she realized she was chained to the bed. She jerked her arm. It rattled, and freezing fear shot down her spine. Her mind screamed. *What was happening? God, what is going on?* She could see a red light through the hood, what looked like a camera lens fixed high in the room's corner, like a large glass eye staring at her.

"Hello? Is there someone there? Help, please." She tugged hard on the chain again, and her heart raced. She struggled to push herself up. Something tugged at her leg, and she realized her ankle was also chained. She whimpered and tried to claw at the cloth covering her face. She tried to get off the bed but couldn't. The chain's deafening rattling in the empty room made her anxiety increase. She fell back down on the bed and raised her head to the ceiling. There was one dim light. She yelled out again, but her voice sounded muffled as if she was shouting into a pillow.

Where am I? Her head was spinning, and she laid down and tried to focus on what had happened to her. *What do I remember? I left my apartment walked to my car, someone came up to me, and it felt like I was stuck in the neck with a needle.* She still felt groggy, and there was little energy in her body. Before she knew it, she was passing out again. Her mind drifted in and out of a daze like she was half awake and half asleep. Annie slowly woke. She tried to lift her head, but it was too heavy. She moaned and tried to shift her body, but she was too weak. There was someone in the room with her. Her mind was spinning, she was being carried somewhere; her vision blurred. It was a giant shadow moving around. She felt a prick, her eyes popped open, and she let out a loud groan. Suddenly she could see, whatever was over her head was gone. Her body was on fire; she felt a sudden strength in her limbs. *This must be a dream, a nightmare. I'll wake up any minute in my bed and laugh at how strange it was.* It was not a dream, though, or a nightmare. Her vision acute, she quickly realized this, as she felt the chains and looked down and could see her half-naked body chained to two beams. A tall, muscular heavyset man, wearing some crazy type of get up, with a pointed hood, stood in front of her. She tried to make out the eyes, but he wasn't close enough. There was just blackness in the openings.

"What are you doing? Who are you? Let me out of this thing!" She struggled but couldn't move her arms more than a few inches. She looked down to see her legs chained apart. Sheer panic soared through her body.

Chapter Seventeen

The Hood injected the woman, and her head flew up, revealing her face; Herman gasped. *It was her. Fuck! I can't believe it, Annie Leason.* He stared at his monitor with his mouth open in shock. *No, not her, it can't be, goddammit!*

Herman found it hard to breathe. He always dreamed of having her this way but never imagined she would end up in someone else's grip. Now there she was, and he could do nothing about it. *Wait. I can bid. Yes, I can bid not to harm her, maybe even get him to let her go.* To take control, he had to be the highest bidder. Thoughts were drastically running through his mind. *Since she was already there, she was going to be raped. That was a certainty. I can determine how, though. I know that much to be true,* he told himself. *Then I can bid to see if The Hood could later release her. If not, he will kill her!* He knew that for sure, the highest bidder would kill her at the end of the show. He had to save her.

He watched the hood move around the room, preparing his various devices. Herman mentally calculated what he should bid. He needed to take control now and bid. He didn't know what the other people who were watching wanted, but he was sure that most of them were hoping she'd be tortured, raped, beaten, then murdered. The Hood was studying his large monitor screen near the girl and had it positioned so he could look at it closely. Herman hesitated. He wasn't sure what he should type in first. The Hood's Red Room was for many things, not just sexual abuse, so he wasn't sure what sort of things The Hood might inflict on her first. He had to think fast; the bids were already coming in. Herman checked the chat-feed, looking at what the others were bidding on. He looked back at the room, and his heart sank a little, but his loins stirred. The Hood looked at the monitor for a moment longer, then went and stood in front of the girl. With one aggressive swipe, he grabbed her panties and ripped them off her body. He brought a knife up to her neckline, grabbed her bra, and cut the center strap, exposing her breasts. He looked back to the screen, then turned and slapped her, then slapped her again. Herman panicked. He furiously started typing and made a bid of one thousand dollars not to have her slapped again. He watched as The Hood looked at the monitor and shrugged. He turned back to spread her legs apart one by one.

One of The Red Room bidding rules was to wait for your turn. You couldn't dominate the room unless you became the highest bidder, and then your bids had to stay that way. Each time Herman made a bid, he would have to wait until someone bid higher than him or wait for his turn to come around again. In the meantime, other higher bidders had their requests carried out. All Herman could do was watch and hope that someone wouldn't bid very high to hurt her.

When he and John were kids, they dreamed of this happening,

of sexually abusing Annie. Since he had first seen her in school, he wanted it. This was all different, though; it was not on his terms. Having her there now was torture for him, *but why did I want to get pleasure from it as well?* He just prayed some of the other bidders thought she was too beautiful to be beaten.

"Come on, Annie!" he said out loud. "You can get through this baby!" He passed on bidding to see what the others wanted to be done to her. He would throw in a very high bid to stop it if it got violent. He was thankful that The Hood hadn't slapped her too hard. If the hood bruised her body or marked her perfect face, he would double his bid and put a stop to it. Though Herman would get pleasure from watching Annie's body being ravished sexually, watching her bleed would not turn him on at all. If it were any other girl, he wouldn't even watch once she started to bleed. He'd leave the room if the girl suffered too much or was going to be murdered.

Herman watched as The Hood used various-sized toys on her. He checked the chat and watched the bidders selecting which ones for him to use. Herman stirred. They weren't large, and Herman couldn't help but enjoy watching Annie squirm as The Hood used them on her. Herman could hear her moaning and crying. *I love it. Oh Jesus!* She screamed in anguish. Her voice was weak; tears flowed from her eyes. Herman checked to see when it was his turn and saw one more bidder before him. And they increased the bid.

Herman watched The Hood take Annie from her chains and dragged her over to a thin, long wooden beam. He threw her over it so he could tie her wrists to her ankles. Herman was sure this was the previous bidder's request, so he had to wait. He wanted to see what the customer had in mind for her. The hood placed two metal clips on her nipples, and Herman heard her cry out. The clips were connected to wires that ran somewhere that Herman couldn't see. Annie was screaming in panic. She closed her eyes and winced in pain. Herman hadn't seen that before; it was something he wouldn't do with a girl. He watched The Hood hold a cat of nine tails in his hand, and his trepidation increased. The whip had leather tips instead of metal ones; Herman knew this would not make her bleed but would still leave welt marks on her. He wasn't sure he'd be able to tolerate it. The Hood changed his position to avoid blocking the cameras and brought the whip down on Annie's bare ass. She screamed. He brought the whip down again, and she cried out again. Herman felt powerless. He wished it would stop, but the bid was for ten whips. Herman wanted her pain to stop; he bid two thousand dollars and waited for The Hood to finish. Herman counted each whip. Finally, it was over, and The Hood returned the whip to the table. He went over and checked his monitor, then walked back to her and untied her from the bench. She collapsed to the floor. Herman had control for a brief time but then had to give someone else their turn to outbid him.

***

The Hood was keeping the orders fulfilled. The bids were hot and fast and increasing by the minute. He enjoyed this one and would get his pleasure himself with her before killing her.

Herman was reading the chats fly in and knew almost everything that would be done to her. He wondered how much longer she could take; it seemed she was losing the battle to stay alive. Every time Annie passed out, The Hood would revive her with a small injection. Herman was pretty sure it was adrenaline.

He watched The Hood put her in many secured positions in the chair. Another bid came in. She screamed and begged for it to end. Her eyes moved everywhere. Her body was convulsing with pain or panic; Herman didn't know. After a few minutes, The Hood walked back over to the table and took a serrated knife, placing it in his apron. Annie screamed and thrashed in the chair. Herman decided he had seen enough. He wasn't sure what would happen to Annie after the chair, but he was pretty sure The Hood would kill her. He usually did after the machine. The previous bidder finished, and the bidding flattened out. Herman knew now was the time.

The Hood checked his monitor. There were two more bids to

go. The next bid was for him to do whatever he wanted to her. The Hood was pulling her out of the chair when she tried to sideswipe him with a punch. She still had some energy from her last adrenaline shot. He laughed out loud and punched her in the face, almost knocking her out. Herman wanted to punch his monitor, he typed his bid, but The Hood had dragged her to the beam stand and bent her over the bench. Herman felt for her, she had come around from his punch, and he could hear her screaming and crying. *Enough! She has been through enough, don't worry, Annie, I will try to get you out of this.*

Chapter Eighteen

When The Hood had finished with her, he went back to his computer and checked for the last bid. *It was a good show tonight.* He informed his customers that there was one last bid, then the show would end, and the killing bid would start. Spit and blood were seeping from Annie's mouth. She vomited involuntarily. The Hood's eyebrows raised in surprise. One of his customers, The CardCollector, had just made a costly bid and an unusual request. This was unconventional for The Hood but not impossible to complete. He had done it before, but not this late in the show, and he still wasn't sure what his other special customer wanted.

The cardcollector would offer to bid $10,000 to release the girl without harm. *This was interesting*, so he wrote back he would offer other bidders their chance to decide. He typed in the information and waited. He turned to the girl and said under his breath, "This might be your lucky day" Herman made his bid and waited. Ten thousand dollars was a lot of money, but he didn't want Annie to die, and he could easily afford it. He only hoped that none of the other members would refuse and bid higher to watch her die. The Hood's special customer had allowed him to accept the outcome of her fate to the highest bidder. As Herman waited, he thought about the others he went to school with. So far, he had watched Brady Wightly die and now Annie being raped and abused, both in The Hood's room. He looked at the screen again and saw that the bidding had ended.

Congratulations CardCollector! You have won the highest bid. The girl will be released.

The Hood thanked his members for joining the show and promised them another soon. He made sure the CardCollector's payment went through, and when it did, he smiled, looking down at her. She seemed broken to him, slumped over on the floor. He picked her up and took her back to the room, and would release her in the early hours before anyone would normally be up in the morning. The hood would have liked to have kept her for another two days, then kill her, but business was business.

She was crying and pleading on the bed as he chained her back up and went to retrieve his needle and vial. As he came back into the room, she saw him with the needle in his hand. She watched him draw the liquid from the vial, and then he came towards her.

"No, please don't, don't kill me, please!" She tried to struggle.

He took her arm and injected her with the liquid. She held onto him, helplessly pleading with him, crying, her tears covering her cheeks.

The Hood unchained her again and brought her to the shower. He washed every inch of her body and hair to ensure none of his DNA was left on her, then dried her and put her clothes back on, minus her underwear. He chained her back to the bed, put her car keys in her handbag, and left it beside her on the bed. *It was best to keep her sedated until the right time tonight*. Then he would leave her in her car to wake up. No one would even know he was there.

"Honey, you did well today!" He said to her, even though she couldn't hear him. "Very well."

Chapter Nineteen

Herman had won the bid. He couldn't believe The Hood agreed to release her unharmed. Herman wasn't concerned about whether he'd keep his word. He was one of the best on the deep dark web. He breathed a heavy sigh of relief. He had just saved Annie's life, and she didn't even know it. Maybe he should find her one day and tell her everything. *No! That would be a mistake. I had bid on her abuse.* The question was, though, what was she doing in The Hood's room? He thought of his old school friends again.

Maybe someone was exacting some sort of revenge? He could understand why someone would want to watch Brady Wightly die, but who? He was glad he didn't go to that reunion party. *Maybe that's why these things were happening? No! That's not possible,* he assured himself. He felt safe in his house, and he had powerful contacts now on the deep dark web. He could have anyone killed who became a threat if he wanted to, for the right price. Then he realized he could have one of those asshole friends of Wightly's killed, like Caughly or Cullen. He thought of Annie's friends. Maybe he could get one of them to his basement, Diane and Jenny; he liked them very much as well but he would not want to harm them, just use them for gratification. There were many possibilities, but he knew what he had to do. Now that he had seen how The Hood operated. Tomorrow he would begin. Tomorrow would be the start of an alternative lifestyle that only he had control of.

Chapter Twenty

Sally Wui was from a mixed family. Her father was Australian, and her mother was Korean. Her mother had immigrated to Australia and had met her father on a dating site. They fell in love and were married within a year. Sally, their only child, was born the year after. The marriage didn't last though, and her father left her mother for another woman.

Her mother put her through school and university, where she met Annie, and the two became close friends. While in university, Sally enrolled in a modeling course. A well-known agency immediately hired her after she submitted her portfolio. The high-end modeling agency kept her very busy.

When Annie never showed up the night they were supposed to meet, she tried calling Annie's phone several times. It went straight to voicemail. It wasn't like Annie to not show up without a text or call. She paced her apartment, not sure what to do. She tried to come up with a reasonable explanation, but nothing made sense. It just wasn't like Annie. She knew Annie could take care of herself, but it didn't ease her worries. Sally spent the whole evening in the empty apartment calling Annie's phone. She went to bed feeling uneasy. It was a dangerous world out there, and a girl had to be careful in the city. When she checked her phone the next morning, there was still no word from Annie. She decided she would give Annie the benefit of the doubt and wait until the afternoon. If she didn't hear from her after that, she would start phoning their mutual friends.

When the day passed with still no word from Annie, she started to panic and started phoning people. The other girls told Sally they hadn't seen or heard from Annie either. She decided if she didn't hear from her by the next morning, she would call the police. Sally went to bed that night, hoping her friend was safe. She was sure her best friend was in trouble; she would never go that long without getting in touch. She fell into a restless sleep, imagining all the horrible things that could have happened to Annie.

Chapter Twenty-One

Bob Sharot was a tough, burly 25-year veteran of the Australian police force. He had been a homicide detective for 15 years, who had seen more than his fair share of serious crimes. Bob commanded respect at six foot six, tall, short dark hair, firm jaw, and a casual bodybuilder. A golden glove boxer, he was as unforgiving of an opponent as he was a cop. He was a detective that sometimes bent the rules to get what he needed, but he was damn good at his job. His superiors would usually look the other way if he brought those to justice.

He was a single man who lived alone. Bob had no kids and didn't want them because he had seen many failed families and what some people do to children. He couldn't go through that if something like that happened to one of his own. He was currently in a part-time relationship with a rape counselor named Sherry Miller. To him, she was the sweetest thing he had in his life. She could also be tough as nails. She had a daughter of her own, who she was extremely protective of. He knew Sherry had been through a traumatic experience when she was a young child, but she had never shared the details. Bob was sure it was the main reason she became a social worker and eventually a rape counselor. Sherry could be volatile sometimes; she didn't take shit from anyone, including him. He liked the way she handled her cases. They had worked on a few together that had brought about rightful justice for the victims. They had a healthy mutual respect and would see each other when they had the time, which was not often.

Bob was a detective who was quick to cut through the red tape when necessary and never laid down from any cases handed to him. People generally liked him, he thought, but he knew it couldn't be for his good looks, which he found didn't exist. He rarely looked at himself in the mirror and never wore aftershave.

His superiors had told him occasionally that they considered him one of the best homicide investigators in the department they ever had. Bob didn't care for the compliments and really couldn't handle them. He did, however, have no unsolved cases and had a 99% conviction rate.

The rookie cops looked up to him, and most of the older ones, those who had been around him almost as long as he had, respected him. He could get away with many things other cops couldn't, but he never abused that privilege. He had the respect of the streets, even among organized crime figures. Many feared him. No one wanted to be on the receiving end of Bob Sharot's rage. Even hardened criminals stayed away from his wrath. He knew all this but didn't care. His time was up soon. He could have retired five years ago but stayed on because he loved the job. Now they had him confined to a desk, or so they tried, for the rest of what little time he had left in the force. The reason was for an unjustifiable homicide—the L.E.C.C. The Law Enforcement Conduct Commission had given him a choice, stay at his desk, or lose his pension. In Bob's mind, he would have had no problem working until he dropped dead right there at his desk. He wasn't ready to retire or to go anywhere on holiday. He hated bureaucracy and resented some of the up-and-coming brass who had contributed to where he was sitting now.

Those in the brass cared less about catching criminals and more about promotions and sucking up to the ones that would get them cushy, high-paid desk jobs. Most of them were afraid to work on the streets. There were so many psychos out there these days; a person could get shot or maimed just for walking down the street to buy milk. Bob had a fixation on the real sick ones, the serial killers and child molesters, or child killers and rapists. Those who had no remorse and wouldn't accept what they had done was some sort of mental illness they were suffering from. To Bob, these were the scum of the earth, and if it was up to him, should be just taken out the back and shot, tortured first, if he could get away with it. Bob had arrested hundreds of pedophiles, rapists, murderers, and a few serial killers. He had shot a few people in his career, and a few died. He'd been shot himself in the past a few times, and some of the detectives were surprised he was still alive. All were justified shootings, and he never questioned his thoughts when he had to pull the trigger, and everyone knew it. To him, they just needed to be stopped, no matter what the cost. *That was life*, he thought. *If you fuck around with guns and with the police, you get shot.* His last shooting, and why he was now at a desk, was because of a white guy named Willy Prize. He was a scumbag junkie. They had released him early from prison because the justice system couldn't afford to keep drug addict criminals like Willy in jail forever. He was deemed a low-risk to society and released into rehab.

The first thing Willy did when he had got out of prison was to get a gun; then, he broke into a home to rob it to get his drug fix. A young girl visiting her grandfather for the weekend was home, and he raped her. As Prize left the house, the grandfather tried to stop him. He shot the grandfather who had called the police as he lay dying. By the time Sharot had got there, Willy was long gone.

The grandfather was dead, and the child was on the way to the hospital, nearly beaten to death. She was just twelve years old, and Prize had sodomized her and almost bitten off one of her nipples.

Bob became fixated on the case and worked it until a bloody conclusion transpired 120 miles away six weeks later. *During a random traffic violation stop, Willy had shot and wounded the officer to escape. The police officer managed to get a shot off, shooting Willy through the neck. Prize took off but didn't get far. The amount of blood he was losing caused him to pass out and crash his car a few miles down the road. He got himself to a house owned by an old couple. He tied them up at gunpoint and dragged them into the basement. Two uniformed officers who responded had tracked him down to the house and radioed it in. Bob had been the next on the scene just after the first two officers had arrived. He decided to kick the door in and burst through the front entrance. Bob found Prize right where he thought him to be, sitting on the couch, bleeding profusely, Prize's 357 magnum, sitting next to him. Bob had ordered Prize to push the gun off the couch and kick it away from the couch. Willy Prize did as he was told and reached over to push the gun off the couch. Bob pulled the trigger and blew half of Willy's head clean off, spattering the living room walls, couch, and floor with blood, scalp, and brain matter. This justice was completely justifiable to Bob, even though he knew it wasn't. *You won't be raping any more children now, will you, Willy Prize?* After the internal investigation was over, the LECC concluded he had not gained permission to enter the house from his direct superior. There was no ambulance called, and the use of force was excessive because of the hostages inside the house and the state of Willy Prize. It astounded Bob that they concluded that Willy Prize was the victim here because he was severely wounded. The fact he had a gun didn't seem to matter to them. What about the twelve-year-old girl? The grandfather? The police officer he shot? *Idiots!* Bob thought. Although most of the force was on his side, they commissioned him to a desk and docked his salary.

At work, sitting at his desk, he picked up the phone and called Sherry's number, but it was engaged. He looked over at his partner, Jim Levin, probably his closest trusted friend of all. "Hey Jim, you got anything juicy going on at the moment?" Jim looked up from his desk and smiled. "Only a hooker's number with your name on it." Jim grinned, and Bob grinned back. He liked Jim, no lies or games, and the first one to go through the door with him when no one else would.

Chapter Twenty-Two

Jim Levin watched his partner and probably his closest friend sitting over at his desk. *Poor guy,* Jim thought, *he doesn't belong there. He needs to get out of this shit.* Jim was as big as Bob, but not as tall, and was one of a few black men in the force and the only one with a white wife. He also had two small children aged five and six, loved them dearly, and protected them from everything that had to do with his job. He and Bob had worked hundreds of cases together and became very close friends in the academy, a friendship that continued when they earned their gold shields. Jim admired Bob for his tenacity and police work and knew he had Bob's respect, more than anyone else on the team. To Jim, Bob is a sincere guy who had his support both on and off duty. Jim had endured a long and difficult struggle, dealing with racism, in and out of the force. When there was that sort of trouble on the job, Bob would be there to back him up. Although he sincerely admired Bob, he sometimes didn't approve of Bob's methods. Jim already knew very well that Bob's hatred of sex offenders ran deeper in Bob's veins than most, and Jim always wondered if it was something more personal that affected Bob when he was younger. Jim had to cover for him several times. He would never forget some of the cases they had done together. He owed Bob his life for one in particular. They had cornered a serial rapist-killer Dennis Foster. He had a gun to Jim's head, demanding Bob hand over his gun, handle first. As Foster reached for Bob's gun, Jim elbowed him hard in the ribs. Dennis Foster keeled over. Like straight out of a western movie, Bob spun the gun backwards in his hand, using his forefinger, and shot Foster in the face, point-blank range. Jim had fallen to the floor to avoid the gunfire and was still lying there looking up at Bob. He was almost waiting for Bob to put the barrel to his lips and blow the smoke away. In the aftermath, Bob was at first scrutinized again for excessive force. When, however, Jim gave his testimony, and the press did the story on the outcome, Bob received a commendation for his bravery. It took a long time for Jim to get over that day, but he knew Bob had forgotten most of it in just one night. After that, Jim had a newfound respect for him during their investigations and let Bob get away with whatever he thought was right. Even when it was wrong to do so, he would stick up for him.

He wasn't with him on Bob's last case, Wiley Prize. Jim had gone into hospital for an operation on his back and was out of action for a few weeks. He had heard that Bob had just gone on his own, hunted Wiley Prize down, and shot him dead. That was the final straw that got him chained to his desk.

The other detectives would ask Bob for advice on whatever cases they were working on, especially involving sex crimes. They knew Bob Sharot knew more about serial killers, rapists, sex offenders, and maniacs than anyone else. Even the A.F.P. would contact him when they needed a savvy profiler for a case giving them trouble. Jim had learned so much from Bob about everything from missing girls, unsolved sex crimes, to kidnappers and murderers. There was plenty to solve, and all the state's police force didn't have the proper workforce or connections some local detectives had. So Jim was happy to stand by Bob's side the best he could. He was his partner and friend. There would be no replacing him. There was so much good getting involved with Bob, and Jim felt the privilege and stature that came with it. Even the brass feared him.

Chapter Twenty-Three

Annie managed to open her eyes. She tried to focus but still felt groggy. The first thing she saw was the steering wheel of her car. She sat up but fell back down again on the seat, too weak to hold herself up. Based on the dim light breaking through the windshield, she gathered it must be early morning. She lifted herself up in her seat; she was in the garage of her building. The windows were fogged with a slight dew. She reached for the door and pushed the handle. The door flew open, and she almost tumbled out.

She crawled out of the car and felt a rush of cool air hit her face. She was wearing the same clothes she had on two nights earlier, and they were loose and in disarray. "What happened to me?" she said out loud. Her mind was in turmoil. *Was I drunk?*

Did I pass out? What happened? She moved, and her nibbles rubbed against the fabric of her shirt, sending hot shooting pain through her chest. *Where is my bra? My underwear?* Then it hit her like a wall crashing in her face. *Kidnapped, drugged, and raped. Oh my god! Oh my god!* She got up and attempted to stagger away from the car. As she took her first few steps, she felt a stabbing pain all around her groin that almost crippled her, and her bottom was stinging. She stopped and leaned on the bonnet to balance herself. *How long have I been here?* She looked around, but there was no one in sight. Annie staggered back to her car and searched for her phone. It was off. She hit the power button to turn it back on; the battery was dead. She groaned and threw the phone in the seat. Her head was spinning, making her dizzy. She could feel herself fading and slumped back on the seat. She forced herself back out and stood to lean against the car. The world went fuzzy; she was losing her vision. She felt her body give way underneath her, and she began to slump down. Her eyes clouded over, and she collapsed to the ground, unconscious.

****

Sally made her way out of their apartment; she had a full day ahead of her. Annie had dominated her mind all night; she had hardly slept. She would not even wait until the afternoon to call the police. As soon as she got to the agency, she would phone them. She walked down the stairs and out into the garage. What she saw made her heart stop and her step freeze. Annie was lying on the ground next to her car. She ran over to her and knelt to check her friend. She lifted her head. "Annie? Annie? Hey!" Sally's worst fears were rushing through her head. *Oh my god, is she alive? Oh, Annie, what happened to you?* Sally was panicking. She pulled out her phone and called emergency services. She could barely get the words out as she explained the situation and gave them the address, begging them to come fast.

Sally placed her purse under Annie's head and began stroking her hair, tears falling from her eyes. "Don't worry, honey, the ambulance is coming; hang in there. Come on, Annie, please don't die!" The ambulance was there in less than ten minutes. Sally ran out to guide them inside the garage.

The paramedics quickly got out and checked Annie's pulse and breathing, then placed her on a gurney and loaded her into the ambulance. Sally got in her car to follow. She kept saying to herself. *You're going to be fine honey. Just fine,* through sobs. *Goddammit, what happened to her?*

Chapter Twenty-Four

Herman's mind was reeling. Last night, after he had seen Annie in The Hood's red room, he hadn't slept. He was up all night pacing, trying to figure out how she got there in the first place. So many different questions raced through his mind. *Why would she end up in The Hood's room, of all places? Why did she happen to be there at the same time I was there? What are even the chances of her ever ending up on the deep dark web and then in my particular red room?* Herman had no answers. *Thankfully I was there to save your life! If it wasn't for me, you would be dead now, lying in a ditch! I dreamed about doing things to you all these years, it can't be possible, what are the chances?*

He managed to fall asleep at four in the morning. He realized when he woke that he had to put Annie out of his mind for a while. It was time for him to find his girl. He had been searching for a week but didn't want to get caught, so he decided to change his daily routine. Cruising to the same area every day would create too much suspicion. He would start exploring a different neighborhood far from his home, then wait a few days to pass, then explore it again. This he hoped would draw less attention to himself. He was far from satisfied with his progress though. Every time he saw someone he thought could be the right one, it became too risky to take her. Somehow, he needed to exceed his expectations. If he was going to take such a risk, it needed to be better planned. She also couldn't be average; she needed to be perfect.

Chapter Twenty-Five

When Annie woke up again, she was in a soft bed in the hospital. The familiar smell of disinfectant filled her nostrils. Sally was sitting nearby and came and hugged her. "Oh my god, Annie, are you alright? What happened to you? You disappeared for two days!"

Annie wanted to speak, but her mouth was too dry. Sally handed her a glass of water. Annie felt the cool water run down her throat. She hadn't drunk anything for what seemed like days.

Sally continued, "I thought you might have had an accident or something." Annie tried to speak again, but no words came out; she just cried.

A nurse walked in, "How are you feeling, Ms Leason?" she asked, glancing at Sally. "They would like to run some tests if you are up to it?"

Annie reached over and took the glass of water and gulped the rest of it down. She looked at the nurse. "I need to call the police to report a kidnapping and rape," she said in a croaky, stern voice. The room went silent.

Sally burst into tears blurting out, "What? Raped? Oh my god! Annie, what happened?"

Annie looked at her friend. "Yes, Sally, someone took me. I don't remember much. They drugged me. I don't know who it was." She shook her head. "I only remember bits and pieces!"

The nurse looked at her uncomfortably. "Annie, you just relax there in bed. I will call a doctor to come and see you straight away; she can call the police for you. I'll get Clair Pickering; she's a very exceptional specialist. She will take good care of you."

Sally leaned down and hugged Annie again; she didn't want to let her go. Annie was grateful for Sally being there. She tried to think of something to say, but she had no words and so much pain to deal with. She was embarrassed and scared. The nurse quickly left the two of them alone, Sally held onto Annie, and the two shared the silence.

A woman came in dressed in the usual doctor's white coat and introduced herself, "Hi Annie, my name is Clair Pickering; I'm a doctor in gynecology, as well as a medical examiner. The nurse mentioned you have been through a terrible trauma; she tells me you were raped. Is that correct?" Annie slowly nodded. Clair continued, "Ok, well would it be ok with you if we got you out of bed to take a look at you? I would need to use a rape kit to examine you." Annie was glad things were starting to happen, Clair said, "let's get you out of bed, and you just need to follow me to the examination room. Are you up to walking, ok Annie? I can bring a wheelchair for you if you like?" Sally took Annie's hand. "I'm going to head back home for a while, sweetheart, and come back later if you feel up to it, ok.?" Annie squeezed her hand and forced a smile.

"Thank you, Sally, thank you so much for helping me." Tears streamed from Annie's eyes.

"Oh my honey, you'll be fine! The doctors will take good care of you. I'll bring you some goodies to munch on later on tonight, ok? Take care of yourself." She left the room and headed out of the hospital, gulping back tears.

Chapter Twenty-Six

Clair had Annie sign consent forms to release her medical examination to the police. Clair then led her to the examination room, "Ok, Annie, I'm going to need you to undress. Can we slip off those hospital jammies, and we'll keep you covered up until I need to examine a particular area." Annie did as she was told, then Clair helped her into the OP-G7 chair and put a sheet over her. She placed Annie's legs comfortably on either side of the supports, and Clair gave her a reassuring smile. "Now, Annie, I'm going to ask you just a few questions as I examine you. I want you to try to be as clear as you can and remember as much as you can. If at any time you don't want to answer, or you can't remember, you just say so, ok?" Annie nodded, and this time,

Clair gave her a genuine smile. Clair began the examination by checking Annie over externally. The first thing she noticed was the purple marks around her wrists, ankles, and neck. "Do you remember how you got those bruises, Annie"? Clair asked, concerned.

"I, I don't remember. I think they must have chained me to something."

Clair came over and leaned towards her. "Ok, let's start at the top, ok? And we'll work our way down." Annie didn't respond; she lay motionless, waiting, dreading. "I'm going to bring this down a little." Clair took the sheet and gently brought it down, exposing Annie's breasts. "Right, I just want you to relax." Clair's attention instantly turned to Annie's nipples. They were an angry shade of crimson. She took one delicately in her fingertips, and Annie winced in pain. "You're very tender there? Sore?" Annie nodded. Clair was sure they were burnt. Annie wanted to cry again, but she fought back the tears. "Annie, do you remember anything about what happened to you here?" She asked, still looking at her nipples.

Annie looked down at them. It was the first time she had seen them since being brought to the hospital. "Oh my god! What happened to them?" She cried out. Annie touched one, and the pain shot through her chest like a streak of fire. Annie sniffed and said, "I think they attached something to them and electrocuted me."

Clair went over to the medical cabinet. She returned to place soothing ointment on the end of a cotton bud and applied it gently. She then placed two light gauze pads over them and some surgical tape. "Ok, Annie, you have to stop wearing a bra for a few days until that heals up, ok?"

My god, Clair thought *this girl had been through hell.* She went back around and sat down on the stool between Annie's legs. "Ok, Annie, you're gonna feel just a little discomfort for a minute or so, ok? But I need you to relax." She looked up from the apron, watching the girl.

"Annie, did you shower before they brought you to the

hospital?" Annie shook her head. "Ok, you didn't clean yourself up with a tissue or something else?" Annie shook her head again. Clair performed a rape kit on her and placed it aside when she was done. There was something else bothering her about what she was seeing. Clair could see severe trauma around the walls of Annie's vagina, a very different type of sexual assault. She was enlarged to a degree consistent with a woman who had just given birth. However, there was very little tearing around the walls, which indicated it was enlarged slowly. *My God! S*he concluded that unless the attacker had an extraordinarily very large penis, something very large was used to penetrate her for a prolonged time. "Ok, Annie, you're going to feel a minor discomfort now. It will be over in a few minutes, I promise."

Annie turned her head to the side; she was crying again. "Ok, Annie, almost done. I just need a few more minutes to check another part, and then we're done. Ok? Just a few more minutes." Clair clicked her magnifying loupe secured around her head, down over her eyes. She checked the walls of the girl's rectum and saw that it, too, had received trauma. It was swollen and marked with tears in the tissue walls. *This was also not natural penetration.* Clair asked her as delicately as she could, "Annie, have you recently had any anal sex before this incident?"

Annie shook her head vigorously. "No! Never! I haven't been with anyone for a long time, and I certainly wouldn't do that."

Clair needed to be sure. "Ok, it's ok, sorry dear, but I do need to ask you these questions."

Annie shook her head again and shouted. "No! Jesus Christ! No! I don't do that, I told you!"

Clair talked to her in a soothing voice, trying to calm her.

"What?" Annie asked. Clair was asking her when was the last time she had sex. Annie told her not for a very long time. The few other questions she asked her were very embarrassing personal questions, and Clair could tell Annie was becoming increasingly irritated. She felt horrible for the girl, but she needed to gather all the details.

"Ok, Annie, we're almost done. I need you to turn over on your tummy just for a few minutes." Annie did as she was told, and Clair asked her to lift the apron to her hips. When Clair saw the welt marks on Annie's buttocks, she let out a soft gasp.

"What's the matter? What is it?" Clair was silent for a moment.

"Do you know who did this to you, Annie?"

Annie turned her head back to Clair, and there was anger in Annie's eyes. "I don't know; I really don't." She began crying again.

Clair was sure there was a lot more to what happened to this girl than what she was seeing, but she needed her to stay calm. "Ok, Annie, I'm just going to take a few samples of your blood for some toxicology tests, such as STD and any drugs that might still be in your system. I already took a smear test for the rape kit."

Annie fell silent, Clair drew some of Annie's blood. "Annie, ok, sweety, it's all over, you can take a shower now, and we'll get you back to your bed so you can rest." Clair slipped off her rubber gloves and disposed of them in the bin, and led Annie back to her room. A nurse helped her get back into bed.

Clair said. "Annie, listen to me. I'm going to phone the police."

Annie nodded her head and closed her eyes. Clair went to leave. Annie called out after her, "Dr. Pickering? Is everything alright down there? I mean, is it ok?" Annie was pointing to her groin. Clair smiled at her reassuringly. "Everything will be fine. You have some slight tearing, but you'll be fine. Just don't make any sudden movements, stay in bed, and get plenty of rest." Annie managed a small smile, and Clair opened the door, then Clair quickly remembered. "Oh, by the way, Annie, I have a very good friend of mine, her name is Sherry Miller, she's a social worker, and she works with a lot of girls that have experienced similar circumstances. I think you should talk to her; she's very good."

Annie hesitated, "Um, I don't know. I suppose so; I just don't really feel like talking to anyone.

Clair smiled sympathetically, "She's a special social worker, trained in cases like yours. I think it would do you a world of good to have a chat with her, just try, see how you feel, ok?"

Annie nodded slowly, "Ok, thanks, I'll try." Clair smiled again and left, closing the door behind her.

Clair was more concerned with this girl than with her other usual examinations. She was at her desk, filling out her report for the police and her private file. She concluded in her report. *Annie Leason was drugged and then systematically sexually tortured and raped, judging by her injuries.* What happened to Annie was violently unusual; the scariest part was they would most likely do it again. *This was not random. To inflict the sort of injuries done to her for hours was even more unlikely to be random unless they were already set up for it. This means, whoever this guy was, he knew what he was doing and did it in a way that left little trace evidence, or none at all.*

Clair wanted to ask Annie if she remembered anything more during the rape that might help her, but that was a matter for the police. She thought, though, she could get a better idea of what to look for but decided against it. Just getting through that examination was already hard enough on Annie, and Clair didn't want to push her. Trauma can impact people's memories, but Clair suspected Annie was drugged. If so, there will be traces that should still show up in her system days after. She hoped the tests would give her some answers. She couldn't find any traces of semen or pubic hair anywhere on her body. Annie was released clean as well as shaved. *Whatever they used to whip her with, they did not intend to break the skin.* They had also obviously attached some sort of metal or steel clips to her nipples. *Most likely electrodes,* she deducted. They must have used a steady current of electricity, which caused the discoloration and swelling. *Christ!* Clair added more to her report. The person or people who did this were meticulous, despicable, and evil. It would take at least four to six weeks before both orifices would return to normal size. She realized she would have to tell Annie about this as soon as possible; she had a right to know her full medical condition. Clair leaned back in her chair and exhaled deeply. *Oh, you poor girl, how could someone do such a thing to another person?*

She kept typing out her full report, looked at it, and read

through it again, making sure it was correct and complete. *My God,* she thought, the shock and realization hit Clair hard.

Clair Pickering had a very vulnerable, innocent young woman in her hospital. She wanted to cry for her. *I will tell her it's my duty of care.* Clair stood and left the office; she headed straight for Annie's room. When she got there, she stood outside the door for a few seconds and took a deep breath. She opened the door gently, knocking softly at the same time. Annie was sitting propped up by pillows in bed. The soft light from the lamp next to her, and the glow of the TV, were the only source of light in the room. Clair saw the bouquet on the table and an opened box of chocolates next to the bed. "Hi, Annie. Oh, I see you have had a few visitors; how are you?" Annie smiled a little but said nothing. Clair slowly walked over to her, sat on the edge of the bed, and held her hand. Annie looked at her. Clair could see her eyes were red and swollen from crying.

Annie said in a soft broken voice. "Yeah, I guess I'm ok, I'm still really hurting down there, but I'm not feeling as sick as I was before." Annie tried to smile.

Clair looked over and nodded at the chocolates. "Oh well, if you continue to eat all those, you will get sick, and then we'll have to pump your stomach." Clair was smiling. Annie managed a smile back.

"I've only had three." She said with a humble nod. "So I'm not doing too bad." Clair gripped her hand a little tighter, "Annie, have you been to the toilet yet?" she asked this in an off-the-cuff way. The question threw Annie off for a moment. "No," Annie said. "I wanted to take another shower, but I'm in too much pain to move, but I want to."

"Ok, dear, I can get one of the nurses to help you, and I will also order some stronger pain medication." Clair was smiling, but inside she was knotting up. "Annie, listen now, there is something I need to inform you about. I must tell you this because I examined you. It does concern your health, ok? I don't want you to panic, it's nothing very serious, but you need to know and be aware of it." Annie looked at her with scared eyes; her mouth trembled slightly.

"What is it? What?"

Clair sighed and gave Annie as much of a clinical report as she could, being very careful of her words not to include her speculation. When Annie didn't seem to understand, Clair broke it down and simplified her diagnosis. There was total silence in the room when she had finished, then Annie burst into tears and buried her head in the pillow. A tear appeared on Clair's cheek, and she tried to fight it. Clair brushed the tear away and spoke in a soft but determined voice. "Annie, please listen to me. You are going to be fine. It's just going to take a while for you to heal completely, but you will be fine. There is very little tearing, so there should be no chance of infection." Clair kept up the momentum. "You're going to feel quite a bit of discomfort for a while when you go to the toilet, but this will subside as time goes by. I'm going to prescribe some relaxants to help you use the bathroom and some pads." Clair paused for a second, then asked her softly. "I'll have the nurse bring you some special underwear.

You're going to get past this. I know it doesn't feel like that now, but you will." Annie was still crying. It was almost as if she had shut down and wasn't listening, Clair thought. "Annie? Did you hear what I just said?" she asked softly. Annie nodded but didn't stop crying. "I'll be admitting you for observation for a couple of more days. You'll be much better off under my direct care." Annie nodded slowly again but kept her head in the pillow. Clair slowly stood up and went to leave. "Ok, get some rest, dear. I will send the nurse in to give you the necessary medications and pads, and if you want, she can help you take another shower so that you can get a good night's sleep." Clair waited for a response, but there was none; she walked to the door and left the room quietly, closing the door behind her. She would call Sherry straight away.

Chapter Twenty-Seven

Sherry Miller was one of the finest social workers and rape counselors in the state, with a degree in psychology and a master's degree in behavioral science. She has dealt with troubled kids and young victims of sexual and domestic abuse most of her adult life. Sherry had gained a respectable reputation among her colleagues, the police, and other social services. They often sought her expert advice and counseling on certain issues involving serious child sex abuse.

Sherry stood at a modest 5'10, a divorced, fit, slender woman of 47, light brown hair with a few silver streaks on the way. Her fourteen-year-old daughter, Kathy, was from her only marriage. Sherry was grateful her divorce ended amicably. She had met him when she first started working in the city. He was an anthropologist, and his work kept him away for long periods, sometimes months, in different countries.

She knew what it was like for those kids because she'd been a victim herself earlier in her life. When Kathy was born, she finally found solace in her life, and she protected her daughter fiercely. Sherry had persevered with teaching her daughter from a very young age about the dangers and unforgiving life she could face being a young girl. She wanted her daughter to learn and understand that well. She would sometimes bring Kathy to her work and introduce her to some of the girls at the lodge who were her age. Sherry had been granted permission to bring her daughter to meet some of these girls and to share how they were starting a new life. This was a type of subliminal therapy for her daughter. It was often distressing for Kathy to experience some of the cases that Sherry handled. In the end, however, it had the desired shocked therapy effect that Sherry hoped for.

Sherry didn't like exposing her daughter to these very sad

cases, but she felt it was the only way for her daughter to understand the reality of life. She would tell her there were a lot of dangerous predators out there, and they prayed on young girls, just like her. Sherry thought as she sat at her desk. *It did have the desired effect, though;* Kathy had learned to check in with her mother whenever she was alone or with friends. Sherry had given her daughter a phone for her twelfth birthday, and along with it, various numbers of important departments, such as police, fire, and emergency rescue. One other number she had given Kathy was to a police detective friend, and now a lover of hers, Bob Sharot. The two had met at the hospital when Bob worked on a murder case. He had been interviewing a survivor who had managed to escape a killer's grasp. They met in the cafeteria, and she immediately liked him. Since her divorce, she hadn't done too well with most other relationships, mainly because of her workload and a few demons that still haunted her. The men she had met turned out to be undesirable. Their attitudes towards women were never up to her expectations. Bob was different, though, she liked his no-nonsense attitude, and they both had one very important thing in common. An extraordinary hatred for those who preyed on the young. She'd heard of his reputation already before they had met, and it never once discouraged her. He was always very respectful and kind to her, and she could see the gentleman inside that tough exterior. Sherry was always glad when he came by her clinic to say hello. Often it was not to see her but to interview a rape victim who was lucky enough to survive. It didn't bother her either way if Bob shot them to death or put them in jail, as long as they were off the streets. She knew the challenges of working in the big city, but she embraced them. She wanted to make a real difference in people's lives, and women, young children, and teens were her priority. She needed to be knee-deep among it in the city to do that.

Sherry was a country girl at heart, though, and her parents had been devout Christians. Her family was part of the new Christian faith that had swept into the newly developed houses around the countryside. She moved to the city when she had turned twenty-one after she had experienced a trauma that changed her life forever. It was the reason she chose her career.

When she was just twelve years old, a man had molested her down by the riverbank near where she grew up. That day changed her life forever. Sherry could never put it out of her mind. It still haunted her decades later. When that man had finished with her, just before leaving her there curled up whimpering, he had whispered to her in a mean gravelly voice she would never forget. "This is our secret. If you tell anyone, I will find you and kill you. And I will kill your parents too." Then he had walked away, and Sherry didn't lookup. She laid there for a long time, too scared to move. She eventually looked around, but the man had disappeared the same way he had arrived.

She hoped that the man who had molested her was now rotting somewhere six feet under. He ruined her life and her trust in men. She was now dedicated to saving others from that lifelong traumatic experience, to try to give them back what she had lost forever.

Chapter Twenty-Eight

When the police finally arrived at the hospital, it was late afternoon. Clair met them in reception and explained that Annie Leason was ,at the moment, sedated. The interview couldn't go ahead at that time, so she invited them to her office. The police understood but emphasized speaking with her as soon as possible. Clair led them into her office and sat them down. She explained to them what she had deducted from her initial examination of the girl and gave them the rape kit results, as well as her preliminary report. She told them she wanted to call in Sherry Miller, a rape counselor, and social worker, to talk with Annie. She explained that Ms. Miller might get more details from Annie about what had happened to her. The police nodded but said nothing. They had heard of the Miller woman and knew she was very good at her job. Clair would phone her friend straight after the police left and get her to come to the hospital as soon as possible. The two police officers asked her a series of standard questions about Annie's situation. They were particularly interested in her last known whereabouts before being brought to the hospital. They needed Annie's address and contact information of any friends who may provide helpful information. She told them she knew very little other than what Annie had answered during the examination. She explained some details were too private to share, only that the abuse was well beyond the norm of a sexual assault case. Clair knew some of the details about Annie's abuse were extremely sensitive. They ask her what she meant by that? She apologized and told them she hadn't received the girl's permission to divulge that type of information as yet. Clair was able to give them Sally Wui's information. She had provided her phone number when she checked Annie in as an emergency contact. They gave Clair their business cards and the detective's information who would be in charge of the case and asked that she contact them as soon as Annie was able to speak with them. Clair said she would check on her patient in the morning and see if she'd be capable of an interview. She took their cards and thanked them for coming. She walked them out of the hospital, took out her cell, and called Sherry's number.

Chapter Twenty-Nine

Sherry's phone buzzed in her coat pocket as she was walking out the door of the clinic. She searched for her mobile. When she looked at her phone, the name on the call stopped her in her tracks. Clair Pickering was a good friend of Sherry's, and they had spent many a night out on the town. They had also shared weekend vacations with Kathy and Clair's daughters. Sherry knew it must be a serious call; otherwise, Clair would just send her a text message during work hours. She paused and punched the green button. "Hello, Clair!" Sherry was looking in the distance, waiting.

"Hi sweety, how you holding up?" Clair asked. "Listen,

dear; I need you down at the hospital tomorrow morning first thing. Can you make it? I have a girl here who just came in this morning, whom you need to see. This is bad."

Sherry listened carefully. "Sure, of course, I can," she replied. "I can swing by now if you'd like? I was just heading out the door for the night." Clair thought for a moment, "Well, ok, yes, maybe that's a good idea because there are some things I would like to discuss with you about the case before you talk to her. Would that be ok?"

Sherry's concern grew. "Yes, of course. I'm on my way." Sherry walked briskly across the car park and got into her car. *This must be serious, the way Clair's voice sounded. God! When is all this going to stop? Why must we live with this evil?* She shot through traffic, arrived at the hospital soon after, and parked. Sherry prepared herself as usual and checked her face in the mirror. *Be strong;* she told herself, *be strong; they need you.*

She got out and walked to the outpatient ward, greeting one of the nurses on duty explaining to her who she was. Normally, most nurses knew who she was already, but she had never seen that one before. Then Sherry heard Clair's familiar voice calling her name. They gave each other the usual hug and walked through the corridor to Clair's office, and both sat down. Claire offered her a coffee, and Sherry took it nervously, fiddling with the cup, waiting to hear why Clair had called her there.

"Ok," Sherry said. "Spill it."

Clair proceeded to tell her everything she knew. Including the horrific welt marks on Annie's buttocks and trauma to her nipples, inflicted for some sick fuck's satisfaction. The more Sherry listened, the more shocking and horrifying the story became. Sherry sipped her coffee. "What's her condition right now? Is she sleeping? Or awake?"

Claire checked her watch. "I had her sedated a few hours ago. Then the police had shown up not long after, so she couldn't have spoken to them anyway."

Sherry stood. "I think the best thing for us to do is check on her now. If she's awake, then I think it's a good idea that I talk to her now rather than later." She looked at Clair with determination, "In my experience, the longer you leave these things, the more details the victim forgets. Their minds will try to heal themselves, tucking the trauma deeper into their subconscious."

Clair studied Sherry and knew she was right; the sooner Annie got it all out of her system, the sooner she would be better off. "Ok, Clair agreed. I'll take you to her room; we'll check on her status first to see if she is lucid enough to talk to you. I told her about you, so I think she will be comfortable speaking with you. But she's been through a lot, so I don't want to force her to if she's not up for it."

Sherry nodded, and they left Clair's office. Clair checked on Annie, then waved Sherry in. Annie was awake, staring out the window with a vacant look in her eyes. On her way out, she smiled at Sherry, mouthed the words good luck, and left. Sherry approached Annie's bed, her heart had already sunk from what Clair had told her, but looking at the young girl now, laying on the bed, it sank even lower.

She slowly approached her and smiled sympathetically. "Hi Annie, my name is Sherry Miller; I'm a social worker and a counselor for the state. I specialize in helping young people who have been through circumstances like yourself. Clair Pickering, the doctor who examined you, thought it might be a good idea if we had a chat."

"Can I sit down?"

Annie nodded, then said softly, "Yeah, but I'm not sure if I want to talk right now Ms. Miller; sorry, but it's not a good time." Annie sniffed and turned on her side away from Sherry. Annie's eyes were swollen and bloodshot from crying. She stood for a moment, then slowly made her way around the other side of the bed and crouched down to meet Annie's eyes. "Annie, listen to me," Sherry said as gently and as carefully as she could. "I know what happened to you was terrible, and I understand you not wanting to talk about it," Sherry spoke even more softly and told Annie the story of what happened to her when she was just twelve years old. "It never left me."

Annie said to her slowly and evenly. "Being raped and sodomized by a machine is a lot more serious than just being molested." Annie turned her face into the pillow and sobbed.

Sherry paused for a moment. "No, it is not the same, Annie, and the humiliation and violation are not the same. The nightmares never go away, but I can help you learn to cope so you can live a normal life."

Annie's head turned slightly to her, her eyes puffy and wet, she asked in a brittle voice. "Do you still have nightmares?"

Sherry gave her a small smile. "Every night," she said. "But when he's in my nightmares, I fight him, and I win! The more I fight, the less he comes back into my dreams. The nightmares don't fade completely, but it's facing it that will get you through. Help you find a way to survive. It's not easy, but it's possible." Sherry continued, keeping the momentum going. "I made it my life to help others with the same nightmares," she assured her.

"And I help young girls just like you face their demons and move on with their life." Sherry took her hand. "There are many girls just like you in my care, they all have those same nightmares, and I help them confront them, to deal with them."

Annie squeezed her hand. "Why me?" Annie asked. "What did I do? My life was so great. How could this happen to me?" She buried her face in the pillow.

Sherry's heart sank. "You did nothing wrong, Annie, nothing. You didn't make this monster do these things to you! If you can try to help me to help you, we can catch these people and put them in jail forever. I know it's hard, but I need your help."

Annie looked at her again. "What can I do?" she asked. "I can hardly remember anything! I know they drugged me! I remember very little of anything after that happened!"

Sherry brushed Annie's hair away from her face; she continued to speak softly with her. "Let's try to talk about it; let's start there, from the beginning. If you try to walk me through that day, you may be surprised what you can remember. Any little detail can spark a memory and help find who did this to you."

"All I remember," Annie said, "Is walking to my car, someone grabbed me from behind and stuck something in my neck, then I passed out. That's all I remember, except," she paused, and sniffed, her voice frail, "I remember it was a large room with like dull red lights, there were all sorts of things hanging on the wall, like, hmm, sex things. I've never seen anything like it. I didn't know what they were, and I remember seeing a video camera on the wall."

Sherry took this in. "Go on, Annie."

Annie looked at her with anger. "He grabbed me. I was just in my underwear. He must have stripped me while I was passed out." Her anguish grew. "He pushed me, held me down, and stuck a needle in my arm, and I passed out again. Then I woke, chained to two posts!" Her voice grew louder by the second. "He ripped off my underwear, and then he was putting things inside me!" She choked and cried again, burying her face in her hands.

Sherry comforted her, noticing the bruises on her wrists for the first time. She stood, went over to pour her a glass of water, and came back to the bed. She pulled up a chair this time and offered the water to her. "Here, Annie, drink some."

But the spell had broken. Annie pushed Sherry's hand away. "No!" she shouted. "I don't want any water! I don't want to talk about this anymore, please? It's too hard; I don't want to remember!"

Sherry realized the interview was over; she knew when to stop. "Ok, Annie," she said soothingly. "Ok, I understand, we can try another time, ok? Get some rest."

Sherry stood and watched her lying there. She had seen this image a hundred times but could never get used to it. Annie was talking and sobbing into her pillow. "Why are there people like this in this world? Why?" Sherry knew the answer, but it wouldn't help this girl at all to tell her. *It's because men cannot control their lust, their perverted urges. A famous intellectual once said, If they can't have her, they will kill her, destroy her, or disfigure her! So as not to arouse them anymore!*

"I don't know Annie, but there are, and we have to get them and punish them one at a time! Get some rest, ok? I'll be back tomorrow morning. The police will need to talk with you. They were here already this afternoon, but you were sedated when they came. The doctor thought it better to let you rest first."

Sherry went to the door. Annie called out after her, "Ms. Miller?"

Sherry stopped and turned. "Yes, darling?"

Annie looked at her with very sad eyes. "Thank you, and I'm sorry for shouting at you."

Sherry offered a polite smile. "Get some rest; I'll see you in the morning." She left the room and softly closed the door behind her. She exhaled deeply. She brushed a small tear from her cheek and walked towards Clair's office. She knocked on the door and popped her head in. "I'm going to head home Clair; we can discuss Annie's case tomorrow. I will be back to see her then."

Clair got up and came over to hug her friend again. "Thank you, Sherry."

"You were right Clair," Sherry said. "This was no ordinary rape. It was planned systematic, sadistic torture."

Sherry left the hospital and got to her car. She wanted to call Bob. *He has to know about this, but he was not Sexual Assault; he was homicide and at a desk job at that.* Sherry would wait. She would work out therapy sessions to help her remember and begin the process of healing. Things that the police might use to catch this sick-ass person. Seething with anger, she tore out of the car park, almost hitting someone on the way out. She slammed on the brakes and then sat there. She put her head to the steering wheel, small tears trickling from her eyes.

Chapter Thirty

Bob Sharot got a call from Jim Levin about fifteen minutes after he arrived at his desk. They had discovered a body wrapped in plastic in a dumpster near a public beach car park. Jim had cleared it with upstairs, and asked if Bob could come down and take a look. It was a bad one. Bob closed his phone and sighed. *It never ends. One psycho gets put away or put in the ground , only for another to pop up and take his place.*

Bob arrived not long after Jim phoned him, and they shook hands. Jim nodded at the dumpster, and they both walked towards the scene. Bob had a coffee in his hand and saw Jim already dressed for the job at hand. Bob smiled and put his coffee down to prepare himself. He wrapped his shoes in special linen to prevent marking the crime scene and a sealed lab coat over his clothes.

These days, they required their officers to wear a hairnet, but there was no way Bob would wear one, and besides, he didn't have that much hair left anyway. He looked at Jim, and they both smiled at each other's comical getup. They both looked like two blue balloons. Bob was glad to be there with his partner. He loved the job even though he dealt with some terrible cases. He was also glad he had a good man like Jim next to him, a professional who adhered to good police protocols of a crime scene. Very few detectives followed proper procedure at scenes of an active investigation.

They walked up together, being careful where they stepped and looked inside. The body lay on a pile of rubbish about halfway down. It was hard to see through the clear plastic because of the blood covering the whole body. They both leaned in to get a better look. It was a white medium-built male, naked except for his underwear. Bob tried to scan around the body but saw nothing else that shouldn't be there. He checked the time and asked Jim if forensics had done a preliminary yet.

"Yeah, they have," he answered. We can pull the body out now if we want unless you want to wait."

Bob looked the dumpster over again and then took one more look inside. "No, pull it out, but tell them to be careful. I don't want anyone touching that plastic without gloves or tearing it."

Jim walked away to pass on Bob's instructions. They stood back and watched as a small backhoe with straps attached approached the dumpster. It slowed then stopped, just at the edge of the dumpster. A man came in completely head to toe in a special crime scene jumpsuit with wrapped shoes and placed a small set of metal stairs at the base of the dumpster and climbed up. Another colleague passed him another little set of portable steps, and he placed them inside. Then he slowly and carefully climbed down into the bin, doing his best to avoid the body. He wrapped a harness around the body and gave the signal to lift it out. Two other officers in the same outfit came up with a gurney. They positioned it under the body and lowered it down onto the gurney.

Bob and Jim took off their garb and walked over to take a better look. Bob said, "Let's get it back to the pathologist for a proper forensic analysis." He ordered all the contents of the dumpster bagged and taken to forensics. He asked Jim to have the dumpster hauled away and dusted for prints. They stood back and watched the entire process, making sure there would be no contamination. Bob looked around and wondered if anyone could see the dumpster from the road. The car park was obscured from the main road.

He said to Jim, "To get to this location, you have to turn off the main road and then drive down a winding road for less than a kilometer." Jim was listening intently. Bob continued, "This beach area isn't popular for swimmers, but mainly for surfers who frequented the area."

Bob looked out and noticed a few surfers out there catching waves. He sighed. *I wished I had taken up more sports. Surfing is one of them. Maybe it would have been more calming to my demeanor.* Jim pulled him out of his thoughts. Bob saw Jim nodding in the direction of the police car that was pulling up nearby them. The station's senior detective inspector Neville Johnson got out, strode over to the two detectives, and pulled out a cigarette. He stopped to light it, then walked straight up to the two of them standing next to the spot where the dumpster had been.

"Hey, inspector!" Bob said sarcastically, "This is still a crime scene, ya know, you're not exactly dressed for the occasion." Johnson looked at Sharot with disdain. Bob knew he didn't like him as a person or as a cop. He'd told him that he thought he was a loose cannon and dangerous on more than one occasion. It was Johnson who forced him to his desk. He pushed to bring charges against Bob for that last fiasco. The commissioner, however, wasn't ready to write off Sharot just yet. Bob remembered with pleasure the look on Johnson's face when their boss told him Bob Sharot was one of the best homicide detectives they ever had. The commissioner told Neville to back off and confined Sharot to a desk. Just for a while, until the heat wore off from the politicians. To keep an eye on him. Neville told Bob he knew it wouldn't be long until Sharot was up to his old tricks again, and he'd be watching and waiting, so he could kick him off the force for good.

Neville Johnson came from a privileged family of white cops. His family had power in the community, and Neville was determined to become chief inspector one day. He wanted more power and prestige and didn't hide that he believed Bob Sharot was standing in his way. Neville knew he was a damn good cop, which ate Neville up like a cancerous tumor. He knew Sharot was first through the door and the last to leave. Sharot had the talent and the guts to get things done that he and others couldn't.

He looked at Sharot with narrowed eyes. "Shut up, Sharot; why are you even here? Aren't you supposed to be at your desk taking barking dog complaints?"

Bob ignored him. *What a jerk.*

"He's here at my request, inspector," Jim spoke up. "This is a bad one. It looks like we have a real psycho on our hands. Once we got it out of that plastic, the body's in pretty bad shape, the worst I've ever seen. Preliminary findings show the victim was bound then severely tortured. His throat had been cut from ear to ear, almost severing the head. We had everything shipped to the forensics office already."

Jim turned to Sharot.

"The killer used this spot for two reasons, inspector. One because of its location, and two for its convenience." Bob turned towards the ocean. "This is a surfers' spot, so you get very little public traffic here. It would be pretty easy to dump a body in the daylight without anyone noticing. The coroner will tell us the exact time of death, but I'm assuming early this morning. The dumpster gets cleaned once a week, so anyone who wanted to throw something in there would have easily spotted the body before this morning. The killer could have even dropped off the body on his way to work."

Neville looked out at the surfers and turned back to Sharot. "You're saying that he just turned up while all those guys were out there surfing? And dumped the body?

Bob held his breath, then exhaled. "I'm saying," emphasizing his point. "He probably dumped the body at dusk. Most surfers know that is not a great time to surf. It's feeding time for sharks. The killer likely knew that too and took advantage so he could dump the body unseen." Bob paused, then continued. "The second reason is, he wanted the body found. Whoever killed this guy got a lot of pleasure from torturing him and wanted everyone to find him quick enough to see his handy work. Christ. For all we know, the killer might be out there surfing right now, watching us do our jobs!"

Neville looked at Sharot with a blank stare, Jim chimed in. "Inspector, we've had everything dusted and taken away, including the dumpster; we'll get a couple of blues to wait around and interview the surfers. Bob and I will head to the coroners and get an update."

Neville walked up to Jim and put his face so close it almost touched Jim's nose. Jim almost gagged on Johnson's peppermint breath. Neville whispered, "Listen, Levin! You do your job but keep this psycho—" Nodding to Bob. "Out of the papers! As well as my face." Neville stood back and looked at both of them. "If I even get a sniff of either of you overstepping the line on this one, I'll have you both doing traffic before you can say parking ticket." He paused. "Is that clear?"

"Yes, sir." They both said together. Bob couldn't wait for the inspector to leave and watched as Johnson walked away. Bob wanted to shout something like 'go back to the academy and learn how to be a real cop,' but let it go. Instead, when Johnson was out of earshot, he spat, "Asshole!"

Jim agreed, "Yeah, but we gotta take this one carefully. Otherwise, it will be both our asses."

They stayed a while longer. It was five hours later since they arrived at the scene when they finally left. The two uniformed officers were almost done interviewing the surfers taking down their names and statements. Jim and Bob headed back to the office, both with the same thing on their minds. This may be the first body, with more to come, and from whatever psycho they were to deal with this time.

They had spent the rest of the evening trying to identify the victim by his fingerprints but weren't able to find a match. Early the next morning, they both headed back together to the coroner's office to get more information. They had asked the pathologist the night before to expedite the examination of their victim due to the nature of the crime. The press had already picked up on the story, and Johnson was breaking their balls about it. The two of them denied any leaks from their office and reminded Johnson that cases like that never stayed quiet for long. They walked through to the double doors into the coroner's examination room. Jim never liked this part; he never could get used to the smell of ammonia, the body parts sitting around being weighed, or in airtight plastic bags. Sealed, numbered, and stored.

Chapter Thirty-One

Herman saw her one day, on his way back home from cruising a neighborhood. He couldn't believe his eyes or his luck. He wasn't expecting to find one so much to his liking, so close to home. She was beautiful. He judged her to be around fourteen years of age, *perfect.*

She was walking alone along the side of the road. The footpath she walked along snaked into town. The day was warm, and there wasn't a cloud in the sky. To Herman, it seemed the sun rays were focused just on her. He watched the way the light bounced off her long golden hair, the way she walked with confidence. It made her seem much older than she was. The clothes she wore were loose on her body, and now and then, the breeze blew them tight against her body, against her slender, lean figure. Herman watched her as he slowly drove by. He was cautious, making sure no one was looking at him. He tried to make it look like he was searching for someone's house as he drove past her. She turned her head to look at his van; he quickly looked the other way so that she wouldn't see his face. His breathing became heavy and erratic. She suddenly intoxicated him. She was everything he wanted and more. He wondered what it would be like to have her. He wanted to take her right there and then. The urge was pounding in his chest, but he couldn't risk it. He needed to prepare for something much more clever. His head was thumping, and his body ached. He wanted to scream. He looked down at his crotch; he had pr-ejaculated in his pants without even noticing. *Oh god.*

He drove further down the road and parked, sitting in the van looking through the rear-view mirror, watching her walking towards him. *I could take her as she walked past the van; I could open the van door and pretend something was wrong with my tire.*

When she walks past, I'll grab her and throw her in. His heart was beating so hard; he thought he would pass out, the sweat starting to bead from his brow, his body quivered. She was coming up close to his van. *Now! Do it now! Jump out and ask her for directions! Do something! She's almost here! Quickly! Quickly!* He watched her disappear from the rear-view mirror, then suddenly appear next to his door. She walked past his van, not even glancing in his direction. His eyes fixated on her in awe as she walked along the path, her long golden hair swaying from side to side. Herman was almost in tears. He sat there and stared as she followed the road towards town. She reached a few hundred feet in front of him, and for some reason, Herman was expecting her to look back and smile at him. When she had gotten far enough away, he started his van and drove slowly forward, trying to keep a suitable distance from her. He followed her until she reached the start of town. Herman caught up with her and drove straight past her to park again a few hundred feet ahead. He got out and stood nearby, trying not to look suspicious. She came along on the opposite side of the road and crossed ahead. She then walked into the supermarket. Herman hurried over and followed her in. He discreetly stayed behind her, keeping his distance, watching her. If she changed direction towards him, he would pretend to look around somewhere else but still monitor her not to lose her. He was having a hard time trying to control his lust. His body was aching. Looking around, he felt everyone was watching him watch her. His legs were weak; he was scared.

Herman followed her around the supermarket and took a few things he didn't need, just to keep her in his sights the entire time. He watched her make her purchases then she made her way through the main hall, and then, she walked outside. She made it a few steps past the exit and then stopped and turned around abruptly. Herman quickly turned away, sweat dripping down his spine. Did she notice him following her? He watched her out of the corner of his vision and continue walking. He let her get a few more steps ahead, back in the direction she had come before then he ran to his van. He got in and waited until she was well ahead of him, then drove slowly behind her, stopping now and then to let her stay ahead. She walked back up the same road and along the path he had first seen her. Carefully keeping a safe distance, he waited until she turned a corner and disappeared. He drove forward and turned the corner, but she was nowhere to be seen.

"Oh my god, baby, where are you? Where did you go?" He said out loud; he drove a little further and slowed down, looking right and left at the houses. *She couldn't have gone far; she couldn't have gone this far so quickly.* He turned the van around and drove slowly back up the road towards the corner, rechecking the houses from side to side. Then he saw her; she came out of the front door of a house almost right opposite where he was and walked down a few steps and into an open garage. *She didn't see me,* he thought, relieved. *That was close.* He drove further towards the corner of the road, then turned around and came back down again. He slowly drove past the house and tried to spot her in the garage. *Be careful, Herman, don't let her see you; you know where she lives, plan your strategy.*

He noted the number of the house and the street name and then sped off home. Once there, he immediately went on his computer; he had a website specializing in finding people's names by their address. A name came up as Anderson. He searched deeper and found there were two children, Nicole and Jason. There was a phone number and business number, and he wrote all of it down. Herman sat back and breathed deep. A smile formed on his face, and he stretched his arms.

"I found you, my little angel," he said gleefully. "I found you!" Herman spent the next few days planning how he would take her. He cruised her street a few times to note the routine of the family and neighbors. He would pick his time, but first, he needed to stock up on supplies. He planned to prepare enough so he didn't have to leave his house for a while after he took her. He would keep her healthy and well-fed and stock up on any medications she might need. He got in his van and drove to town to prepare. It was time.

***

When he arrived at the supermarket, there was a family a few feet in front of him, at the bottom of the escalator. A mother and father, and their two young daughters. The two young girls had on matching shorts. He had seen these shorts on the internet. Many young girls these days were wearing them—blue denim cut-offs, with holes and rips in various places around the crotch. The cut-offs were always very short. *These little sluts, trying to deliberately show a little of their underwear, teasing guys, making them look at them, then they would curse them for doing just that.* He imagined reaching out and using his hands, grabbing at their shorts. He snapped out of it when one of the girls glanced around and noticed him looking at her.

Herman was suddenly scared that he'd been caught. Instead, she gave him an innocent smile. *Little slut!* He thought. *She's flirting with me!* He imagined drugging them, kidnapping them, and doing all he wanted to do with them. His hands around their hard little bodies, begging him not to hurt them. That power of life and death is in his hands. He could never let these feelings go, just thinking about it, though, would not get him caught. Herman was sure; just about everyone had thoughts of doing something terrible to someone at least one time in their lives. *All of this was more for men, though,* he reasoned. *I'm sure most men have thought of murdering someone, raping a girl, or just getting the sexual excitement they desire with a helpless young girl.*

Herman knew older men liked the much younger girls because they were just that. Young, inexperienced, and fresh. It was natural. But the law said it was not. Why? Herman asked himself, *Why is it against the law for an older man to be with a much younger girl?* He knew he didn't know much, but he knew a girl must be sixteen years old to have consensual sex. He didn't mind if they were sixteen, even a little older. He knew what excited him the most, *those who could be bound and helpless against their will. Those young teens would be completely submissive because they would be very scared, and that didn't bother me; why? That was against the law!*

They reached the end of the escalator. Herman came out of his dream-like fantasy a little late and tripped over the edge, almost into a family. The father turned around, and Herman smiled. The two girls giggled, but the father looked at Herman with disdain. *Fuck you! If you only knew what I was doing to your daughters in my mind! Maybe I should tell you just to see your reaction. You would hurt me, I know, and then I would kill you, of course. Tap you on your fucking shoulder. Hey, mister, I have a mental problem. I have just fantasized about kidnapping and raping your two daughters. How do you feel about that?*

As he was driving home, he thought about how things would change now that he had found Nicole. The reality pierced his heart. His basement was ready for her. A few nights had passed since he first saw her, and he was becoming desperate. He decided he would call Anderson's family number, hoping to hear Nicole's voice; when the mother answered, he hung up. The thoughts of having Nicole was bringing all his lust and urges out and were becoming too strong to control. If he didn't do something soon for relief, he would either go into convulsions, scream out loud, or cry for hours. It had happened to him that day he had first found her. He had gone into convulsions and cried himself to sleep on that evening. To help himself to remain calm, he turned on his computer and found an open red room. Then watch some young girl being tied up and raped, picturing him and Nicole. This calmed him down and relieved him. He felt better whenever he did this, and the pain would leave him.

He had watched documentaries to learn more about his mental health condition and knew it was real. It was just like the anxiety of an alcoholic or drug addict. When they can see what they need, just in front of them, but they can't have it. There was one particular documentary Herman watched about a prison for pedophiles. He watched it to understand his sickness better. They were all men; some were there for molesting or raping teen boys, others for the same crimes, but against young teen girls.

In all cases, they were there for sex crimes against children. Their victims were usually in their own families or relatives or friends of the family. Some were sports coaches. A few like

Herman were just random predatory sex offenders. He watched with fascination some of the shock and withdrawal symptoms they demonstrated when they could no longer get their sexual gratification.

Herman shook his head. *You shouldn't have gotten caught.* Herman couldn't understand how stupid most of them were to take such blatant risks. *Your own family!* He hated those who molested and raped boys. He thought about the abuse he suffered at the boys' home. As the documentary continued, he watched how they tested these pedophiles to see if children still sexually excited them even after being locked up for years—a test to see any progress in the prison's rehabilitation program. The narrator explained how the staff would attach a very thin wire around the men's penises, connected to sensors on a machine. Then they would show the prisoner semi-nude images of children in suggestive positions, some of them holding garden hoses with water spouting out near their open mouths. The machine would pick it up if the man's penis even twitched slightly. It was one sure way the therapists could then determine if that prisoner was ready to rejoin society or not. Although fascinated, Herman knew he would fail that test straight away. If he were looking at those images of young girls, it would instantly make him aroused. He thought about Nicole holding that hose; she was all he thought about.

****

He couldn't just keep stalking Nicole's house the way he was. Someone would see him there eventually, and if that happened, he would have to give her up. *What's wrong with you Herman? Why can't you just work out a plan to take her? It's because you're too weak! You have no courage! You're scared! You can't do it, can you? Can you?* "I CAN!" he shouted.

As the days passed, he watched the Anderson family more closely and with more care. Although he was taking a bigger risk, he changed his strategy each day, doing his best not to be noticed. It was working, and Herman was very good at it now. *I would make an excellent spy*. He noted that the family would drive to the beach nearly every weekend, sometimes just half the family, but always with Nicole. He would follow them to the beach and park near their usual parking place. Herman was back to wearing his special cap and sunglasses, so he could better watch them, but he did not want to draw attention to himself this time. *This was different; you can't take any risks!*

Nicole had many friends she hung out with on the beach for most of the day, and then she would meet her parents in the late afternoon to go back home. One morning as he followed them, he saw it was just Nicole and her mother. They arrived at a house, and Nicole jumped out and ran inside. The mother then drove off. Herman waited nearby. A couple of hours later, Nicole came out of her friend's house, and Herman followed them down to the beach. Herman knew Nicole's routine very well now. She would sit around laughing and giggling most of the day. Then she would get up and walk the nature path that snaked around the headland, along towards another beach. Sometimes Nicole went with her friends; sometimes she went alone. Herman always followed behind from a distance until the end of the pathway. Then they would turn around and walk back the way they came. The most intense time was when she went alone. She would reach the end of the pathway and then turn around to come back. Herman would stare at her through his dark sunglasses and cap until she was right next to him. If she looked at him, he would quickly turn his head away or look down so that she couldn't see his face.

He wanted so much to talk to her, but he knew he couldn't. *You will have your chance;* he convinced himself. Instead, when she walked past him, he would almost cry out in pain. Herman always walked further to the end, sat for a while, and thought and planned. *If I could somehow get her down here, at the end of the pathway, alone, it might just work. I have to wait until she is alone. Then if no one is around, I can drug her, then take her somewhere here and hide her until dark. Nicole had walked this path before alone. Yes. This could actually work.*

Herman walked back and stayed at the beach for hours until

sunset. Then Nicole and her friend walked back to her friend's house and went inside. Herman waited nearby again for Nicole's mother to come, but she never did. He stayed in his van watching the house. She never came back out, so he figured she must be spending the night. He was hoping he might take her tonight if she did come out. He crawled into the back of his van for the night to sleep. He already had a mattress and a blanket there from before, just in case he wanted to rape a girl in his van. *Like hundreds of others had done, but I never did.*

He spent the night hardly sleeping, excited that he finally had a plan. When he woke up early the next morning, he waited for Nicole. She finally came out a few hours later with her friend. He followed them back down to the beach, where Nicole stayed all day doing the same thing. *She really loves the beach.* She was so tanned, and her golden blond hair made her look like a young model. Later that day, her mother had finally arrived and picked her up. *So that's it. She comes here for the weekends and stays the night with her friend. Then she spends all morning on the beach until around midday, or early afternoon, then walks the nature path alone or with her friends. She needs to be alone on that nature path for me to take her. Yes! That's where it has to happen. Summer is almost here.* He drove back to his house, smiling to himself that he finally found a way out of his torment. *It would take a little more time, but I'm sure my plan will be flawless.*

Chapter Thirty-Two

The body was laid naked on the table, and the pathologist was standing over it with his hands deep in the chest cavity.

Bob spoke up. "What we got Phil?" he asked. The pathologist looked up with an insincere smile on his face. Phillip Rickson was the chief Pathologist, and the best in the country. At sixty-five years of age, with a full head of silver hair and a trim physique, he aged well. He looked at the two large detectives and shook his head. "Well," he said. "What we got here is what I would describe as a guy that went through a very painful and horrific death." Bob walked around the table and looked the body over meticulously. The pathologists continued. "Bound securely, judging by the ligature marks on both his wrists. There is tearing all around the skin of the wrists. That trauma shows, he must have put up a hell of a fight, enduring severe pain."

Jim was walking around the table, taking photos. Phil continued. "Whoever did this crushed his testicles with what must have been something mechanical. There were marks around the scrotum skin showing that. The tendons connected to the penis are almost ripped from the body. That looks to me like someone forcibly stretched it in one action. Well beyond its normal length, almost detached it." The pathologist paused, then continued. "Whoever did this put a hook-like device through the head of his penis, then forcibly stretched it, probably with either something mechanical or by someone. It was a hard tugging motion, pulling it from his body. I mean, it looks very sudden, judging by the broken tendons. The hook may have had something heavy attached to it." The pathologist moved around the body as he continued with his report. "The victim had four fingers severed with something similar to a hacksaw or a thin serrated knife. His nipples were missing when the body came in here. The skin around the area where they were supposed to be showed signs of tearing.. That tells me someone pulled them outwards, then cut them off. I found what was left of them later in his stomach. Probably forced to digest them."

Jim and Bob looked at each other. Bob looked back at the pathologist. "Go on."

The doctor continued, Jim kept taking shots, "The killer put a hook through his chin, here!" He pointed at a tear mark underneath the victim's chin. "And like a fish, suspended the victim by his weight."

Jim stood near the victim's head and took the photo. "I found traces of adrenaline, cocaine, and marijuana in his system, but these drugs besides the adrenaline could have been there before this incident. What was surprising is that I found traces of a Scopolamine type of substance. I will need to do more work on that to see exactly what the makeup of it is. My conclusion, though, is that when the victim passed out from the pain, the killer revived him with an adrenaline shot; he also kept him on some sort of intravenous. I found a needle mark on his right arm."

Jim took a photo of the needle mark. "This guy went through hell before he died, I can tell you that. My opinion? Whoever did this was meticulous and has done it before."

Bob looked at the doctor. "Why, doc? Why do you say that?" The pathologist stopped what he was doing and turned to Bob. "Because," Phil said. "Whoever did this is very well set up. He ties the victims securely puts them in a place where they can scream as much as they want, and no one can hear them. I deduced that because he would have been awake when tortured, maybe drugged up slightly, but still awake. I found no traces of anything being stuffed in his mouth to keep him quiet, besides his nipples, of course. The killer obviously has various specific tools at his disposal. These tools were specific and clear, with no traces of rust, dirt, or grime."

Phil looked back at the body. "It's hard to imagine this was just a random torture-murder. Instead, this is a very well-thought-out process. They inflicted these injuries to him over a long period."

Jim stopped taking photos and looked at the pathologist. "You mean there is someone out there that does this kind of thing often? I mean, as a pastime?"

"It's possible," Phil said. "Even if he had other ways of hiding a body. I don't believe it was random. There's just too much involved here. The cause of death was a deep laceration to the neck, almost severing the head. The weapon used a large serrated blade at least eight inches long."

Bob walked over and looked at the victim's face. He tried to imagine the terror in the victim's eyes and wondered what that guy did to deserve this. "Ok!" Bob spoke up, still looking down at the terrorized frozen face. "Do we have an ID?"

Jim looked at his sheet and said, "Yes, we finally got a hit on our fingerprint database, Brady Wightly, 29 years old. Prior arrest for striking a teacher when he was at his school. They charged him with assault, but the judge let him go; instead, they kicked him out of school. We got division checking on his family, and we'll hopefully have a positive ID from them. He's in our system now anyway."

Bob turned to the pathologist. "Ok, thanks Phil. Let me know what the toxicology report says. Is there's anything else?"

The doctor shook his head. "You know how to find me." Bob turned to his partner and asked him. "Did you get enough shots?" Jim nodded. They both waved to Phil and left the room, their minds racing. They needed to bag this one quickly. If the pathologist was right, they would soon expect another body like this one. Bob wondered what drove men to such a vicious nature. *What happens to a child who grows up to be like this? No one is born that way. What chemical reaction in the brain triggers hatred, violence, fear, and anger?*

His phone vibrated, and he saw it was Sherry. He needed a woman's presence right now, someone beautiful, feminine, smelling nice, and, most of all, alive. He didn't answer, though; instead, he decided to surprise her. *Maybe I should ask her about settling down.* He knew she went through similar tragedies daily, with young children being abused physically and sexually.

Although she didn't have to deal with dead bodies, she would sometimes tell him stories of her victims shutting down, becoming dead in their senses, in their social lives, and with their families. *It must be worse for those people because they have to live with their pain. His victims were dead, and they were out of their pain. Maybe they were the lucky ones.* He shook his head as he drove. "No. No victim is lucky!" Instead of calling or waiting, he drove to Sherry's building.

Sherry's workplace was a large structure that use to be a government tax office. Then converted a few years ago into a secure social worker complex because of the rise in crimes against women, teen girls and boys, and children. It had different living areas for the victims and was well funded. The protective shelter, nicknamed The Lodge, was to keep people out, not in. It had a gym and swimming pool, open at specific times for either girls or boys. Some therapy rooms, a kitchen, separate communal areas, and dorm rooms with bunk beds. The building was secure, with CCTV cameras and security at the front gate. Bob understood why. *There are a lot of angry disturbed people in this world. The ex-boyfriends, mothers and fathers, and predators. All were out there who either wanted to bash, kidnap, or kill them.*

Bob drove up to the gate and showed his ID. The guard waved him in, and he continued to the main entrance and found a parking space. When he arrived at the double-glazed doors, he showed his ID again to another burly security guard. Bob walked through the entrance, stopped, and waited to be buzzed through the second door. He didn't mind the protocols. Many who stayed here were recovering from various crimes, and most were serious. They needed a secure place to hide and recover. Bob walked down the corridor towards Sherry's office. *I should have phoned first. What if she isn't even here?* She was busy, and it wasn't always easy to get a hold of her during the day. He approached her door and knocked gently. She called him in, and she looked up and smiled.

"Hey, mister! What a pleasant surprise. Are you here on business or pleasure?"

Bob smiled back and walked over to her file-covered desk. He noticed photos of girls and boys with bruises, black eyes, and mugshots. He leaned over and kissed her. "I came to see you and to feel better about myself, have my day brightened." He looked down at her desk. "Every time I come here, though, it just makes me feel worse."

Sherry frowned at him, she was happy to see him, but she had enough problems with her current case, instead of taking care of his feelings. "Listen, tough guy, let's grab a coffee, it's about that time anyway, and I could use a break." They both walked out and further down the corridor. Bob turned to her. "Are you ok?" He asked, then grinned at her. "You seem more stressed than your usual self."

She smiled back, but the smile left her face just as quickly as it came. "I got a new case, a girl named Annie Leason. I'm waiting for some detectives from sexual assault to come and interview her. It's a really bad one Bob, kept for hours and tortured horrifically; I'm surprised she made it out alive."

Bob took her hand, she continued. "I know you're homicide, but I sure would appreciate it if you would come and talk with her. You have a way of getting information from people who don't want to talk."

Bob stopped and looked at her incredulously. Sherry smiled. "You know what I mean! People just naturally like you Bob, you're a very likable guy Bob Sharot!"

Although flattered, Bob did not know what she meant by that, and he didn't know what he had that people liked. They came to an open door. Sherry told him this was the kitchen facility. Bob saw a young girl washing some dishes. She glanced up and gave them a sad smile. She rinsed her hands, dried them, and silently walked out of the kitchen. Bob watched her leave.

"That's Clara," Sherry said. "Her father had been raping her since she was twelve years old. Now she is sixteen, and she has been here for almost a year. She won't go back home. She is afraid her father might kill her. His case is pending in the courts, and he is out on bail."

"What about the mother?" he asked.

"She is an alcoholic. Sherry replied. "Being charged with complicity and neglect. The state is looking after Clara until her father's court case."

Bob sighed. *What a job she has here. How does she cope and stay sane?*

Sherry made the coffee, and they sat down. "What's up? You look sad."

Bob looked at her smile; he warmed up straight away. "Oh, I'm ok. I just needed to see you. We got a pretty horrific case the other day, and it's got me rattled."

She looked at him closer. "You? Bob Sharot? Rattled? I don't believe it! What happened? Nothing rattles you!"

He smiled again. "A body that looked like he had been through a mincer, the worse imaginable torture I have ever seen, and I thought I'd seen it all. I think this case is going to get worse before it gets better."

Sherry reached over and held his hand. She gently squeezed it, and this made him feel better. He continued in an even tone. "I think this one." He paused. "It won't be a one-off." He knew he shouldn't be discussing the case with anyone outside of the investigation, but he could trust her more than anyone, and she knew the rules. So he continued. "Phil, that's the pathologist. He thinks that this guy was tied up tortured beyond imagination, details you don't need to know, over many hours, in a specific systematic way. He thinks because of this; it might happen again."

Sherry took his other hand. "I understand honey!" Consoling him. "Listen! If you need to talk about it, I'm here, ok? Just a short drive or phone call away."

He leaned in and kissed her again. "Thanks, babe," he said. "But we're on it, and we will solve it. Jim's in charge, and I'm sort of helping him as well."

Sherry smiled again. "That's good," she said. "Jim's a good man and a very good detective. How is he? I haven't seen him in a while."

Bob leaned back. "He's fine; he's doing great. He is taking a bit of a risk, though, bringing me into the case. Considering I'm supposed to be confined to a desk. Jim these days has got a lot of pull now, and with Johnson breathing down our necks, Jim just thought it better to tell Johnson straight out that I'm on the case too." He gave her a cheeky grin.

She sipped her coffee and smiled. "So how is Captain Marvel treating you, anyway? I hope he's leaving you alone?"

Bob grinned. "He's still an asshole, but he's leaving me alone on this one; I think he believes me and Jim are the only ones who can solve the case."

"Well, he's right. Maybe he's found a new course of confidence in you."

Bob snorted. "I doubt it, honey. He will always be an asshole in my book."

They talked for a while longer, and Bob promised to come and see the Leason girl. Sherry explained. "Annie might be here instead of in the hospital by the time you see her. I think she would be better off staying here with us. I will let you know." Sherry knew he had a lot of work to do, and they got up, and headed towards the exit. They promised to call each other soon. She walked him to the front door, gave him a small kiss on the cheek, and said, "Be careful out there, ok?" He gave her a wave, walked through the two doors, and went out to the car park. Bob got to his car feeling a lot better. He got in and left the building's parking lot, and blended into the city traffic.

Chapter Thirty-Three

On the third floor of the police station, all the detectives were at their desks, including Bob Sharot. Pinned on the wall behind him, was the Wightly case. He was going through the evidence they had accumulated from the murder case so far. He had the pathologist report and copies of the surfers' statements laid out on the table in front of him. He was also comparing case files from other psychopaths to see any similarities. He'd seen a lot of gruesome crimes in his day, but the nature of this one was very different. He had a feeling this one was connected to another, much older case. *Which is in the cold case files*, he thought. So below his desk was a box he had requested, marked: SERIAL MURDER FILES FROM THE PAST FIVE YEARS. He systematically organized the case files, marking the priority ones:

COMPARE FILES, to remind himself which files he needed to look at first.

Bob hadn't witnessed a murder like Wightly's' since five years ago. That meant it was either the same killer and he's back, or they were dealing with a copycat killer, and there would be more bodies popping up soon enough. He looked over and saw his partner in conversation with another detective. Bob hoped he and Jim could sit down together soon and go through these cases.

The phone erupted on Bob's desk. "Sharot!" he answered. When he realized it was Sherry, his demeanor changed. "Hi, honey. How are you?"

"I'm fine babe, but listen, I have to talk to you." Sherry quickly explained what happened at the hospital and everything Claire had told her. Now she was growing anxious. Bob was looking at the other detectives as she spoke. His sweaty hand gripped the phone tightly. He knew he had promised her he would talk to the Leason girl, but now he was knee-deep in the Wightly case. "Honey, I know I promised you, but you know I'm homicide. It's not my department. If I leave now, Johnson will have my head if he thinks I am slacking myself off this case." The other day he had mentioned to Jim about the Leason girl, and Jim hated rapists as much as he did. Bob had asked him if he could keep tabs with the sexual assault team on the real sick ones who might be suspects in the case.

Sherry pleaded with him. Bob could resist many things in his life, but Sherry wasn't one of them. He picked up his pen and wrote down the details. "Ok honey, listen, don't worry. I'll swing by the hospital in about an hour. Sound good?"

He ended the call and motioned Jim over. "You know that bad rape victim that I told you about a few days ago?" Jim nodded. "Well, I'm going over to the hospital in about an hour to meet with Sherry to get more details. Do you want to tag along?"

Jim looked at Bob's desk. "Sure, but by the looks of your desk, you might need me here instead." Bob looked down at his desk and silently agreed. Jim asked. "Did we get everything back from Phil?"

Bob, still looking down at his desk piled high, said, "Yeah, we got it all, except for the toxicology report. That's gonna take a while; maybe another week or two."

Jim looked down at his partner with a little sadness. "You know, soon you're supposed to be retired. You don't need to be working yourself to death all the time. Why don't I look over all this crap you got piled up here on your desk. I'll let you know if anything pops up out of the ordinary. You go on over to the hospital."

Bob nodded. Grateful. "Sure," he said, "Thanks, partner."

Jim grinned at his friend. "Hey, no problem. I'll tell you what, and I'll even go through these ones you got there as well, pointing to the statements from the surfers. Maybe we'll get a hit."

Bob smiled. "You're a good man Jim." He stood and felt his bones creak. With a nod towards the other detectives, he added, "You might wanna ask one of those lazy bastards over there to help you. That is if you can."

Scanning the room, Jim patted him on the back. "I'm a one-man show, Bob." Jim smiled at him and continued. "I'd only be waiting around while they drag their feet, but I'll ask two of the younger detectives to give me a hand. The others have got other cases, though, you know?"

Bob thought, *yes! They liked to cherry-pick the cases and leave the potential cold cases or the ones too hard to solve to Jim or himself.*

Bob said, "Lazy fucks."

Jim gave him another light slap on his back. "Get going Bob, I'll dive into these, and we'll compare notes when you get back."

Bob thanked him again, grabbed his coat, and headed out of the office. Jim watched him leave, then looked down at the mess of files on Bob's desk. He exhaled deeply. "Ok. Here we go."

Chapter Thirty-Four

Herman was very excited about what had recently just happened.

A few days ago, the community council had just finished

building a new nature path along the beach. They had connected

it from the end of the old path and then ran it through a

half-mile of beachfront foliage to a secluded beach called

Piper's Beach. He was sure Nicole and many others would

walk that path. Now he had many places he could hide and

grab her.

Once he took her, Herman would have to wait with her there

until dark before he could bring her back along Piper's beach

and up the old stairs to the road where his van would be parked.

No one used the old steep steps to come down to Piper's

because that meant they would have to go back up them again to leave. For Herman, though, it was perfect. He could park his van on this road without being noticed. There were very few houses there. Herman had been watching her for days and weeks. Everything was ready and planned out. He could perfectly predict her family's routine. He would wait until the weekend, then follow her to the beach, where he was sure she would take the new nature path to the end. He was now doing this every weekend, waiting for the perfect opportunity.

He had already picked the place he would hide her. He drew a diagram of his plan and then changed it until it was perfect. Herman would have to somehow lure her further along the path to Piper's beach. He needed her away from other people who would walk to Piper's end of the new path. His beach disguise helped him blend in with the other people. He scheduled two different times to go to the beach, the first mid-morning when fewer people were on the path. The early bird runners and walkers would be gone by then, and those who come after lunchtime wouldn't arrive yet. The other time was much later in the afternoon when fewer people would be on the path. These were also the same times Nicole used when she walked the path. He had taken everything he would need to stay down there until she arrived. *This is it!*

The weekend was two days away. He couldn't wait any longer. If everything went according to plan, he would have her very soon. Herman checked his basement every day, keeping it clean and prepared. The bed, shower, and toilet were ready. He had clean bed sheets for her, bathroom towels, expensive shampoo and conditioner, and pads for her period when it came. Herman didn't know much about that, but he knew it happened to women every month, something he disliked very much. He would make sure she was as comfortable as possible in the basement and feed her well. He promised himself not to mark or harm her and only condition her as The Hood did. *Yes, that's the best way of avoiding harming her.* He was learning so much from The Hood's room. He was still thinking of Annie Leason, not forgetting what happened with her. The thought of kidnapping girls from his school had never occurred to him before. After seeing Annie, though, it had crossed his mind that it would only be for sexual gratification and not harm them if he did achieve that. Herman remembered fantasizing about all those girls he went to school with. He would imagine them being raped by a stranger; it would arouse him immensely. When he had seen Annie in The Hood's room, it had very much excited him. He was just glad she didn't die in there. He wondered if The Hood would take the girls for him and bring them to his own Red Room. He could certainly afford it now. Herman's investment had tripled from when he first bought Bitcoin. *That may not be a good idea; I can't have anyone know where I live.*

For now, though, he needed to concentrate on taking Nicole.

Chapter Thirty-Five

Nicole was a quiet girl at home, but when she was out with her friends, she came out of her shell and was outgoing. She dreamed of becoming a physiotherapist, which had her parents' blessing and encouragement. Her parents were sure that she would become one of the best one day and maybe join the Olympic team. Her father was a successful real estate broker, and her mother was a science teacher at university. She had a younger brother, Jason, but like most brother-sister relationships, it was not as close as her parents would expect. Jason was always annoying her, which always drove her out of the house. Nicole didn't mind; she would spend her time staying fit by going for long brisk walks when she could.

At fourteen, her parents, friends, and teachers would comment on how exquisite and intelligent she was. They all believed that one day she would be a star. She was an excellent student and made the school's summer swimming team. Nicole was also a passionate lover of the beach. She wore very little makeup when she went outside, and unlike some girls who would look younger with a more natural look, this always made her look older than she was. She enjoyed the attention the boys gave her, and of course, she was a virgin. She had no intentions of fooling around with them. Nicole never experimented with her body. She and her mother had a very open relationship. She always shared her problems with her mother. Instead of searching the internet when her period came for the first time, she had asked her mom how to deal with it. Her mother had taught her how to behave like a lady and respect herself and her femininity. She told Nicole, "By saving yourself, you will someday meet the perfect man, and like many other young girls your age, will grow to have a beautiful family together." Nicole believed that with all her heart. She was a well-behaved but friendly girl, which brought her many friends.

Nicole loved to wear loose clothes. Even though she was aware, she had a beautiful body. The only time she let anyone see it was when she was on the beach, which kept her slightly olive skin tanned. She grew her golden hair very long, complementing her small unblemished face, straight white teeth, and blue eyes. Nicole loved to walk everywhere, day or night. It gave her time to think about her life and future. Whenever Nicole would go on one of her long walks, her mother always warned her to be careful about the dangers of being alone. They lived in a relatively safe area, and Nicole never worried. She also could be a little stubborn with her mother when she wanted to be. Her father would tell her not to walk too far alone at night. Nicole always chose a different route to walk whenever she could. She enjoyed discovering new places. Sometimes her friends would walk with her, but most days, she walked alone. Every day into town and back. On the weekends, she would hit the beach with her friends. She loved to walk the national park pathway that crossed through several beaches. A popular place also for runners and cyclists. The walk would typically take an hour one way; her mother would only let her walk it on weekends when plenty of people were about.

Nicole loved the freedom it gave her. Sometimes she would stop for a swim and rest. She always had her phone with her. If she needed to, she could call her parents; there was a signal most of the way to the end. When Nicole heard about the local community council building an extended nature path to Piper's Beach, she was one of the first to walk it. One time she and her friends had made the 350-meter journey from the top road to Piper's Beach; it had been grueling. Very few people ever took this old way. The winding steps and thick bush made it a dangerous and difficult trek.

The entrance to the old steps was at the top road and was isolated and far from the main beach. The only other way to reach Piper's was by boat. Once there, though, the beach was pristine and secluded. The scenery was breathtaking. Before the new path was built, everyone who took the main beach path would walk until they had to stop because of thick bushes and rocks blocking their way. No one ever attempted to swim around to Piper's because it was too dangerous. Since the council had cut a pathway through the thick brush, the beach was easier to access. Most people still turned around and walked back, though, because they didn't want to take the steep steps up to the top road. Then they would be stuck far away from the main beach. For Nicole, it was a new beach to explore whenever she could. She and her friends had already made the journey three times since the pathway's new construction, and once with her family.

That weekend, she planned to stay at her friend's house and spend most of the time at the beach. Her mother dropped her off early Saturday morning. Nicole told her mother she would make an entire weekend of it and swim at Piper's beach. She would then take the old steep step pathway to the top road, then walk back to the main beach. Her mother told her she was concerned that Nicole would be away from the main beach all day. She asked Nicole if she had organized her friends to go with her. "Of course, mom!" she said. "We're all walking together to Piper's. I will ask one of them to take the steps and walk the top road. Her mother kissed her on her forehead and told her to call her in a couple of hours, just to make sure she was ok. Nicole promised and jumped out of the car. She wore her bikini underneath a long loose summer skirt and a light green tank top. In her bag were her towel, sunscreen, phone, and diary. She also brought a little makeup with her and a small hand mirror. She had her favorite book on the spiritual connections between the mind and body, her prized possession. Her mother waved goodbye and drove away, an uneasy feeling washing over her.

Chapter-Thirty-Six

Jim's phone rang as he was still sitting at Bob's desk; he grabbed his mobile and answered it. Bob's voice boomed from the other end. "Hey, buddy!" Bob said. "What's up?"

Jim's mind was tapped into the files. "Oh, you know, just sitting here wiping my ass! How about you? How did the interview go?" Bob told him he got caught up, but was heading to the lodge now with Sherry to interview the girl. He wouldn't be back for another hour. Jim told him not to worry because he was still deep up to his neck in files and couldn't go anywhere even if he wanted to. Bob assured him he wouldn't be long and hung up. Jim put his phone down and sat back in the chair. A stack of files fell to the floor. "Shit!" he cursed. He bent down to pick them up, he noticed a large box and a smaller box. Jim brought the large one out and stared at it for a moment. He leaned down again and pulled the smaller box of files out. On the large box was written. SELECTED COLD CASE MURDER FILES! *What are these doing here?* He wondered. *Cold case files aren't normally used on active cases unless new evidence has been introduced.* Those files were normally stored in the cold case department. There were hundreds and hundreds of them. Unless you knew exactly what you were looking for, or if no one in the cold case office had time for you, you could spend days, even months, searching for one particular piece of evidence. Jim looked down at the smaller box and saw a sticky note that Bob had put on the box, written in red, COMPARE THESE FILES. Jim took the stack out of the smaller box and slowly sifted through them. All the files were dated back years and were unsolved; some were multiple murder cases.

"What have you got here, my dear friend?" he asked out loud. Jim shifted through more files, then stopped. He pulled a file out and opened a thick manila folder. The label read Dawson's

Murder. He vaguely remembered the case. Three family members had been murdered; the investigation ended up nowhere. The three bodies were discovered in the home; the rest of the family was overseas. Then nothing. The task force had spent over a year looking for a suspect; then, it went to the cold case office.

Jim looked at the victims and wondered about their lives, why they had been snuffed out so early. He pulled another file. This one was a serial killer who cut up prostitutes and was never caught. *It's hard to solve such cases because there is no one, no friends or family members, to miss them when someone kills street people. With no one to report them missing, the killer can get away with it for months, even years.* Jim pulled another file and continued flipping through the rest of them. There were at least twenty files in the box, and he wondered if he should just wait for Bob to get back. Maybe he would find something Jim couldn't. He picked up another file, THE EAST COAST SLASHER. Jim remembered this one. He and Bob had helped work on the case. He pulled it out and opened it. He scanned through it and came to the autopsy reports on each victim. His eyes narrowed. The autopsy photos looked eerily similar to their current victim Brady Wightly. He sifted through Bob's desk to find the Wightly photos and autopsy report, then compared the old photos with Wightly's. In the old autopsy photos, some of the victims had the same puncture marks underneath their chins. One other had his genitals crushed and mutilated. The toxicology reports showed they all had large traces of Scopolamine, also commonly known as the Devil's Breath.

One victim had large amounts of Tropane Alkaloidadrenalyn in their system, a drug very similar to Scopolamine. He'd never heard of that drug, but it had to be a generic brand sold in Australia, maybe only through prescription or possibly homemade. He made a mental note to check. He continued reading and a chill shot through him. Adrenalin. *That would have been used to keep them from passing out while being tortured. Fuck! What a maniac!* All the victims had similar ligature marks around their ankles and wrists, exactly like

Wightly's. As Phil had explained, 'Consistent with a fierce struggle, or writhing in pain.'

Jim stood, images of these victims flashed through his mind. He flipped more pages. He read the locations and dates the bodies were found. The victims were all kidnapped, tortured, and murdered. The report showed that the state crime squad in charge at the time had been sure the victims were murdered at the same location. Police had eventually been tipped off to the location of the house. The TAC had raided it but found no one except a house of horrors. There was an upstairs living area and a basement with two small rooms, each with a bed, shower, and toilet. Each bed was bolted to the wall and had a chain and a manacle connected. They had found a dead girl, naked except for her underwear, still chained to one of the beds. The coroner later determined she died from dehydration. Jim's heart sank as he imagined that poor girl dying of thirst and just a few feet away from a shower and toilet. They also discovered destroyed video cameras and some attached to the walls. Later, this large basement of the house was confirmed to be the location of all the murders committed.

The dried blood splatter found there eventually matched all the victims discovered throughout various parts of the state. Whips, bondage material, chains, and pulleys fixed to the walls and ceiling were all around. Tools used to torture and kill the victims, some still covered in blood, and plastic sheets on the floor with blood splatter on them. They also found a large two-way wall mirror and a burnt, un-salvageable laptop. Jim read that none of these things yielded any prints. The police were sure someone had tipped off the killer. It was clear someone had destroyed the evidence and left in a hurry. *If only those boys had gotten there sooner.*

They weren't able to gather any concrete evidence. The name the electricity bill had been in turned out to be false. Also, the internet account and the encrypted IP address weren't even in the country. The task force later concluded that these murders were committed through the Deep dark web. Jim was engrossed; he had heard about this many times before and the crazy things people did there. What worried him the most was these people were almost impossible to catch or track down, *unless you had maybe a sting operation set up with some very geeky people to help you.*

Jim put the file aside and thought of phoning Bob straight away, but he knew he would be busy. *Damn! What if the Wightly case is from the same nut job who was doing this shit five years ago on the Internet? As well as those fucked up people paying money to get their kicks to watch this shit?* He grabbed the file and went over to his desk, and put it on his own. Jim would carefully go through it one more time, then call Bob, whether he was busy or not.

Chapter Thirty-Seven

Bob followed Sherry into the lodge and down the corridor. He wasn't sure if he was ready for another harrowing rape case but knew it had to be done. *No point putting off the inevitable.* He thought. *I need to know who this sick fuck is, getting his kicks from kidnapping, torturing, and raping. With the Internet now, young kids are exposed to graphic violence, porn, and predators, at a young age. Their parents just don't seem to give a fuck! They let them run around take drugs because these days it's the norm; no wonder so many of them either end up as a victim, in prison, or dead! It's just so fucked up!*

They walked into Sherry's spacious office, Bob stared at the wall of young teen's photos pinned to a board that took up half the back wall surrounding the word MISSING. On each of the photos was a tag, some with a name, some without. All looked like school yearbook photos. Some were family shots, with the rest of the family cropped out. Bob had been in Sherry's office many times before, but every time he was in there, despite his best efforts, he couldn't help but be drawn back to the wall of missing young faces. Bob was sure some of them were already dead or would never be found. "I can never get used to this wall; it never gets easier to look at. The sad thing is, there are so many more of these in our missing person's bureau," he said softly. Sherry looked at the photos with him.

"Well, many of these teens are still missing, and some are quite recent, just in the last couple of months," she said.

"I have files on every one of them." She squeezed his hand. "Come on, let's meet Annie." They found Annie staring vacantly at the TV, the sound so low it could barely be heard. She was almost in a trance state. Sherry went to turn the TV off. "Wait! Please?" Annie cried out. Sherry stopped mid-stride. Annie's face contorted in terror. She turned to the TV; there was a story of a young man found mutilated and murdered a few weeks back. "I know that guy, my god, I know him! Brady Wightly. Christ! Someone murdered him?" Annie was sitting forward, her face glued to the television. She repeated almost hysterically. "That guy! That got killed! I know him! I went to school with him! Oh my god!"

Bob looked at the TV, and his first thought was, *who the fuck released the information?* He would try to find out later. He turned to Annie and asked in surprise. "You knew that man?" Forgetting for a second why he was there.

"Yeah!" she replied. "I just saw him a few weeks ago," Annie said. "He was in my class at school. I used to hang out with him and some of his friends. He was a real bastard at school."

Bob's interest piqued. He was no longer here to interview Annie about the rape; now, his murder case had entered the conversation. This may be a break in the case he'd been waiting for. He went and took a seat and pulled it close to Annie.

Sherry knelt on her other side, she spoke softly. "Annie, this is Bob Sharot. He is a senior detective and a very good friend of mine. He would like to talk with you and also take your statement."

Annie glanced at Bob, then back at Sherry. "I thought I wouldn't have to talk about this anymore?" she asked. "You said it was over."

Sherry took her hand. "It is over, honey. Bob is here to help us catch him. If you could tell Bob just a little of what you told me, it could help him solve the case."

Annie looked at them both; she turned to Sherry. "Can't you tell him everything I told you? I don't want to talk about it anymore."

"I understand that, Annie," she said. "And if you aren't comfortable talking about it, we don't have to."

Bob took over. "Annie, I agree with Sherry; we don't have to talk about it all over again, not if you're not ready. I'd like to ask a few questions about Brady Wightly, though, and the last time you saw him." Annie looked down at her hands. He continued, "Is there anything you can tell me about what happened the last time you saw him, and who else you remember seeing with him?"

"Yes, ok, well, I guess we can talk about both. I want to get it done and out of my mind. I will tell you what happened to me first, ok?"

Bob smiled and nodded. "Ok Annie, take your time. When you're ready."

Annie gave him a little smile and seemed to relax. "Well," she began, I was walking to my car in the garage, and someone came up behind me. He put an arm around my neck and injected something into me. The next thing I knew, I passed out. I woke up in a room with no windows, chained to a bed."

"Go on, Annie," he said. "What else do you remember?"

She looked at her hands again, then said, "He took me to this big room—"

Bob interjected, "The man with the hood?"

Annie's head shot up. "Yes!" She glanced at Sherry, who nodded at her as if to say, *go on*. Annie continued, "Well yeah! He was wearing some sort of handmade medieval hood."

Bob quickly asked, "Why would you think it looked homemade, Annie?"

"Because it was stitched together roughly. Like a potato sack that had been torn apart and then put back together into a hood.

It covered his entire head and went down to his shoulders."

Bob was furiously writing notes. "Go on. What else?"

Annie stared straight ahead and said, "He was wearing an apron, like a butcher's apron, but it was leather and black." She continued, "He also wore a pair of plain-looking khaki shorts and black boots with large silver buckles."

Bob looked up from his pad. "No shirt?"

Annie turned to him. "No, he wasn't wearing a shirt at all."

Bob checked the information against Sherry's information. "Ok Annie, what happened next?"

Annie started pushing her fingers against each other, building up the courage to keep going. "My clothes were already missing, except for my underwear. I must have been passed out for a long time, I guess. So I remember he brought me into a much larger room. He chained me to a couple of posts and ripped off my underwear." She paused. "He put things in me; I don't know what; they were sex toys, I think. I couldn't move." Her voice broke. "He put me over a bench and whipped me with something, and put two things with wires on my nipples then electrocuted me." She whimpered again.

Bob asked softly, "Sherry mentioned he used a machine on you? Do you remember what kind of machine?"

Annie stared at the floor. She hesitated. "Yes, he used some machine. I don't know!" she sobbed. "He used it on me for hours, and he made me watch everything he was doing to me!"

Sherry grabbed her hand and held it tightly. "You're doing great, Annie. You're doing great."

Annie continued in-between sobs. "The whole room was lit with red lights."

Bob continued writing. "Sherry told me you said there was a large mirror on the wall. Did you notice anything unusual about it?"

Annie shook her head. "I couldn't see much, only my reflection. Oh, wait!" She stopped. "I remember!" Panic began to rise in her voice. "He put me in this medieval type of restraint, you know, the ones they used to put criminals in."

Bob knew what she meant. "A pillory?" Bob asked incredulously.

Annie closed her eyes and lowered her head. "Yes, I guess that's what it was. I don't know the exact name," she said. "He would leave me alone like that, and go over to what I think was a computer screen, then he would come back and do something different to me or make the machine go faster." She cried again. Bob looked at Sherry, they were thinking the same thing.

Bob turned back to Annie with genuine sympathy. "Please Annie, go on."

Annie said, "I remember now, it's coming back." Her voice

became agitated. "While all this was happening, I saw the screen, it was a computer screen. I could see myself on the monitor. He was filming me. I could see writing moving down the screen, like a chatroom. He was walking back and forth from me to the screen. Every time he came back from that screen, he would do something different to me." She started crying again.

"I can't believe he was filming me; people were watching me!"

Bob didn't want to break the momentum, he wanted to comfort her, but they had to keep going. He quickly asked. "Annie, what happened after it was over? What do you remember after that?"

Annie wiped her tears with the back of her hand. "He held me still and injected me in my neck again, and I passed out. The next thing I knew, I woke up fully clothed in my car in the garage of my building. I got out and tried to get help but collapsed and woke up in the hospital."

Bob thought he had everything he needed for the moment; he was eager to talk about the Wightly murder. "Ok, Annie, we can move on from that for now. If there is anything you missed, tell Sherry, and she can pass it on to me." He took a breath. "For now, though, please, if you can tell me about Brady Wightly and your connection to him?"

"Well, as I said, we went to school together. He was in my class. The last time I saw him was just a few weeks ago, at our school reunion party."

Bob's full attention was focused on her; he asked, "Annie, tell me about the party? This school reunion party? Did you go alone? Were you with someone?"

Annie composed herself and spoke more confidently. "I went with my flatmate Sally Wui. We went to a bar first, then to the reunion party. After the party, we went out with some other girls and hit a few bars till almost dawn. We all left the party early because Brady Wightly was rude and abusive. He started a fight with another guy. It was annoying."

"So Brady Wightly was at that party?" he asked, his anxiety building.

"Yes!" she said. "He was there, wasted, drunk, and stoned on ice, I think."

"Tell me about this reunion Annie. Was it at someone's house? A bar? At the school?"

Annie shook her head; she was rubbing her hands together, the bruises on her wrists were still fresh. "It was a hall of some sort," she said. "Like a school hall, most of our old classmates were there, at least I think most of them. The school had organized the hall. They just sent out invitation emails to everyone."

Bob kept jotting notes down. Sherry suggested they take a break. Bob nodded. "I think we are about done anyway, just a few more questions, Annie, ok?" Annie nodded. Bob had many more questions, but he could tell Sherry was becoming protective, and it was time to wrap the interview up. "You said you think all of your friends might have been at the party? Do you remember who wasn't there? Did you know everyone who was there?"

"No," she finally replied. "There was no one I knew who didn't turn up. I'm pretty sure of that. Everyone who was there, I knew"

Bob finished writing. "Ok Annie, you say you went there with your friend Sally Wui?" Annie nodded. "Ok, well, I'm gonna need to talk with her as well. I will get a list of all the students that were there that night from the school, just in case you missed someone." He took another long breath. "My last question, well questions, for now, Annie is, what happened with the fight? How did it start? What was Brady Wightly doing? And who was he fighting with? That would be a help."

Annie closed her eyes and looked like she recalled the details. "I don't know why it started. Brady was picking on another guy. Roscoe, Roscoe Mc Fee. Brady pulled a knife on Roscoe, and another guy John Gooding stepped in and put Brady to the ground. The next thing I knew, Brady and his friends started giving us girls a hard time. So we all left."

"Ok, Annie that will do for now, but I will have some more questions for you at another time. I'll get Sherry to draw up a statement on your attacker for you to sign. Hopefully, we can catch this maniac."

Annie nodded, lowering her head. She turned to Bob. "Thank you, Mr. Sharot."

Bob looked at her with a warm smile. "Thank you. Annie, you have been very strong and very helpful. I will be in touch. In the meantime, you take care of yourself, ok?"

Annie nodded again, and Sherry told her to get some rest.

Bob and Sherry got up and left the room. Sherry gave a glancing smile at Annie as she left. They walked down the corridor, and Sherry asked him, "Do you think there might be a connection between her, the murder, and the reunion?"

Bob took her hand. "It's possible," he said. "I will need to talk to some more people who were at that reunion. Maybe the Leason girl doesn't remember everything from the night."

They stopped near the front door. Bob gave her a serious look. "Don't forget when you head back to the office to type up Annie's statement for me and get her to sign it as well?"

Sherry looked at him and frowned. "Anything else, master?"

He smiled. "Yes, please, call your friend Clair at the hospital, the one who examined Annie, and get a copy of her examination and signed consent form and the substance report. Maybe Annie had the same drug used on Brady when they were taken. Then please attach them to the statements."

She let go of his hand. "Hey, I have a lot of other work to do too, you know, mister."

Bob could tell she was teasing him, but there was frustration in her voice. "Look babe, I can hand all this to sexual assault, and you know how long those guys will take. I'm homicide after all, plus who's saying Annie will want to talk with one of those guys? They're really busy. Who knows how long it could take them. Now that Annie has given us more information, somebody has to type it all up. I'm sorry, I just don't have the time to do it."

Sherry threw up her hands. "Ok! Ok! I'll do it! Better I get it done than it not get done at all. Just remember, buster, you owe me a nice big romantic dinner, you got that?"

He took her hand, smiled, then leaned forward and kissed her softly on the mouth. She pulled back gently. "Not here, you crazy? I'll get in trouble," she whispered.

They walked through the doors and stopped to embrace quickly. She told him she would call Clair that night to ask for the reports. He left the lodge and drove back to the station.

When Bob arrived and went upstairs, Jim was waiting for him; he seemed very excited. "Hey, buddy!" Jim said. "I got something you need to see!"

Chapter Thirty-Eight

Nicole was feeling fresh and excited after she woke and dressed. Saturday morning was already in full swing. She was at a beachside restaurant enjoying breakfast at a cafe with all her close friends. They all planned to head down to the sand, take in the sun, and surf for the day. The weather was perfect for it. Later in the afternoon, they would trek the old pathway to swim at Piper's beach. Nicole told her friends of her plans to hike up the old steps to the top road and meet them back at the main beach. Then they would head into town together. So far, she was having trouble convincing anyone to join her for the long haul. She figured she would be back at the beach around five to six pm, just before dark, and for her friends, that was much too late. She decided to phone her mother and told her she would call her in about another two hours. Her mother reminded her not to walk the old beach pathway alone. Now that Piper's was more accessible, she had heard stories of girls being harassed by naked men frequenting the area. Nicole wasn't bothered, she had seen that sort of thing before at Piper's, and she always ignored those naturists. She assured her mother not to worry and explained that her friends would be with her most of the way. She said if she had any problems, she had her phone. Her mother didn't seem fully convinced, but Nicole was determined not to have her day disrupted by her mother's overreactions. She finished her breakfast, and they made their way to the main beach under the blazing sun and clear blue sky. She didn't notice the van pulling into the car park.

***

Herman almost lost control of his urge. He had waited outside near the family house from the very early morning, then followed Nicole and her mother to Nicole's friend's beach house. He had waited a few hours before she finally emerged from the house and went with her friend for breakfast. Now he was down at the beach. He was starving and had hardly slept. Knowing she wasn't going anywhere, he darted back to the van and drove a short distance to a grocery store, where he bought enough food to last the day and some of the night. *God! Wouldn't it be great if I could just drive away with her now? If only it were that simple.* He drove back and parked again, then walked down with his small rucksack and sat about 20 meters from the group. He watched her with her friends. When she went swimming, Herman went as well. He admired her perfect body, careful not to let anyone notice he was watching her. He knew all her movements. It was time to put his plan into action. He got up and went to his van, then he drove to the top road and walked through the space between the trees. There was a sign that said. 'Pipers Beach 350 meters, be careful of steep decline and loose rocks.' The same thing he had done last weekend. He made his way down the steep, winding steps to Piper's beach. Herman knew exactly where he was going. He had to finalize his plan to the last detail the weekend before. He had followed her and her friends along the nature path and then jogged past them a few hundred meters into the newly built path. He had found a particular area there, where he could sit and watch them coming without being seen.

Herman had then continued into Piper's beach. Once there, he found the perfect hiding place in the bushes that lined the whole of the secluded beach. One of many that were dotted along the edge of the sand. Those little open areas in the bushes were popular with young couples to be together privately. He explored all these places. Traces of old parties and fires remained, including empty beer cans and discarded clothing.

Herman chose a small area where he was sure no one would bother to go. It was further down into Piper's beach. To get there, you had to navigate around some rocks, then along the beach, and into some bushes. There, a trail led to his spot. Once he had chosen the place, he returned there when almost nobody was around to stash several items. He went over the list again in his head. *Towel, blanket, sunscreen, binding cord, the largest soft case bag he could find, a small rucksack with a headlamp, and a syringe.* When the day came to take her, he would bring the concoction of Devil's Breath he'd made, keeping it as cool as possible.

During the last two days, he had gone to Piper's two times to check on the items. Now he had arrived to check again and prepare. Everything was there untouched. This is where he would bring her if he got the chance. He would drug her, then keep her there until nighttime. Then take her up the old steps to the top road, put her in his van, and take her to his house. He stared at the sack; he had everything he needed. He ate some of the food he had with him and saved the rest for later.

Herman hoped the zip bag was large enough for her to fit in. He needed to carry her inside it to his van. He checked everything one more time and made his way back to the beginning of Piper's and onto the new pathway. Then he jogged back to the main beach.

Nicole was with her friends on the main beach as usual. *She is so predictable, of course. You're exactly where I knew you would be.* Now it was just a matter of waiting. He walked down onto the sand and sat nearby, watching her. *What if my opportunity never comes? It has to happen!* He tried to put that out of his mind; there was a place deep inside him that knew what he was doing was wrong. His urges were too strong to control, though, and he had come too far to stop. He had to know what it felt like. *What she felt like.*

As he watched them enjoy the sunshine, he could hear the music from their phone's portable external speaker. Just watching Nicole in the middle of the group, everyone loving her, made Herman angry and frustrated. *Why is it her? Why is it always someone else? And not me?* He saw them all stand up and pack their things. Herman cursed. He guessed they would all walk the path instead of Nicole walking it alone. He cursed again under his breath, but he didn't care. This time though, he hoped things might change. He watched them walk from their spot towards the end of the beach, where the nature path began. Herman got up, collected his things, and put them in his little backpack. He began jogging towards them and quickly passed them but kept going. He was sweating, but it wasn't from the heat.

Herman reached the end of the old path. It was much too precarious to jog the rest of the way. Most joggers turned back at this point. He was sweating and in a panic. He ran to his usual observation spot and put down his pack. He made sure he couldn't be seen and waited. They would round the bend any moment now. He wished her to him. "Come on, my baby!" he said out loud. "I'm waiting for you!" The group came into his vision. They reached the end of the old pathway and kept walking until they reached Piper's beach.

"Damn! Shit!" Herman cursed out loud. He thought they would all stay together at Piper's for a swim and then walk back together. *Every weekend, damn it! The same thing!* He left his observation area and moved further down into Piper's to hide again and watch them. They picked a spot on the beach and went in for a swim. Herman waited, panting, wishing for something different to happen. He was tired of waiting. They all stood after around an hour, and Herman watched Nicole say something to her friends and wave to them. She walked away in his direction, alone.

"What the fuck!" he said under his breath. "Shit! She's coming?" Her friends walked back, turning and laughing, yelling something out to her. She turned to them as well, laughing. She waved to them again and continued walking in his direction. He stood up and dashed further along the beach; his heart was thumping in his chest, he panicked. He had planned for this for so long, but now his mind went blank. *What do I do next? Think! God damn it! Think.*

He hid in some bushes and waited until she came closer. He looked around and saw someone was lying naked at the far end of Piper's. He couldn't tell who it was, but the person looked to be asleep. He looked back and saw that she had walked down along the shoreline. He navigated slowly in and out between the bushes. He remained hidden as best he could. She was looking out at sea. *So far, so good!* He dashed out of the bushes, ran further along and into another space inside, and ducked down. He watched her through the branches. He checked everywhere he could see. There was no one else around. He kept his eyes on her constantly. She was almost in the middle of Piper's on the shoreline. His mind was screaming. *How can I grab her? When should I grab her? What if that sleeping person sits up at the wrong time and sees me? Should I take her before she starts up the steps? No! She'll hear me, or see me coming, and scream, or run! Too risky! What if someone comes down the steps the other way?*

Herman was shaking uncontrollably and not knowing what he should do. He wanted to pee; he could hardly breathe. Watching her kicking up the sand and the water rushing over her feet made him shake all over. He tried to calm himself, but it was impossible. Instead of walking in the direction of the steps, she walked a little distance away from the water's edge and stopped.

What is she doing? She slipped off her skirt and top and walked into the water. While her back was to him, he quickly

265

jumped and ran out onto the sand. *If she turns around now, she will see me for sure! Then it's all over!*

He sprinted the short distance along the edge of the tree line and ducked into the trail that led to his secret spot. Breathing fast, he picked up the bag and fished for the syringe case. He had no idea how he was going to do it, but he had to be prepared. He took the needle out and found the little vial in the cool pack in his rucksack. Then he carefully drew the dosage. He tapped the side and made his way back to the front of the tree line. She was in the water up to her waist. She turned around to face the beach. Herman was sure she couldn't see him. He scanned the rest of the beach; they were alone, except for the sleeper at the far end. She came out of the water, dried herself off, put her towel on the sand, and sat down, facing the ocean. *Do it now! This is it! You have to do it now! Do it!* He moved out from the disguise of the trees and walked down to the sea towards her, staying directly behind her line of sight. He watched her every move. *Don't turn around! Please! Don't turn around!* He was getting closer, glancing left and right, also being too sure to keep an eye on the sleeper. He was sure she'd turn at any moment, but she didn't. He glanced around again, left, right, and behind him, checking everywhere to see if anyone was coming. He was close now. He had the syringe in his hand and was ready. He came closer, being careful not to let her see the shadow he was casting. It was like a dream for him, surreal, seeing her so close that he could almost reach out and touch her. He watched her pull out her cell phone. He looked around again one last time. *No one!* The sleeper was still lying down. *Ok! Now! Damn it! Now!*

***

She took out her phone, looked at it, *no signal* and placed it back in her bag. She started to turn, and Herman grabbed her by her shoulders and neck. She started to laugh. She must have thought it was one of her friends. Then Herman squeezed harder and covered her mouth with his hand. Her eyes bulged. He slid the needle into her neck and glanced around while her body went limp. He waited a few seconds to ensure enough of the drug entered her bloodstream. Quickly he glanced around again, hyperventilating. The sleeper hadn't moved. No one else was around. He quickly picked her up and ran with her in his arms, carrying her along the sand and straight into the bushes and his spot. He laid her down and rushed back out onto the beach, looking left and right. Seeing no one again, he rushed to collect her belongings. He turned and dashed back to where he'd left her.

You did it! Jesus Christ! You did it! He gazed at her. She was lying on the ground in her bikini. His heart was thumping so hard he felt he was going to choke. Herman stuffed her towel and clothes back into her small bag and placed them inside his rucksack. Then he laid out a blanket for her on the ground and brushed all the sand and twigs away from her body before lifting her onto the blanket and brushing her hair from her face.

The sun was still high in the sky. He had to wait. He sat down to catch his breath. Every minute or so, he would go out onto the beach and check on the sleeper and to see if anyone else had come to the beach. Then he'd go back in and sit watching her sleep. He loved her more than anything. She was an angel to him. He took a plastic container out of his rucksack and took out a sandwich with some water. He wondered if she was hungry, but it wouldn't matter. *She can't eat now anyway! What are you thinking? She will wake soon though!*

He would have to drug her again before the time came to take her off the beach. Herman knew exactly what to do now. The plan had come flooding back to him clear as anything. Once he had her secured here, his only worry would be that someone might come along the beach and walk to his spot. He would have no choice but to kill them if they got too close. *With What? I have no weapon!* He glanced around. *I can use a rock. No one will get in my way now. She is mine, and no one will stop me.* As he ate, he thought about everything he wanted to do with her. *I could make love to you right now.*

"No!" he said out loud. "Don't touch her!" Suddenly he heard voices and quickly got up and walked to the line of bushes. He peered out and saw two joggers. They turned to go up the old steep steps to the top road. *If they had shown up fifteen minutes earlier, they would have caught me.* He walked back into the trees and sat down, breathing a sigh of relief and smiling at his luck. It would be a few hours more before he could move her.

Chapter Thirty-Nine

Nicole thought she was dreaming. She was lying on a bed of grass. She could feel the wind on her skin and hear the trees rustling. Seagulls were screeching overhead. *Oh, it's so real!* A strong wind suddenly washed over her, and she shuddered. She was now cold and wanted to wake up from the dream. The dream she was having suddenly made her whole being feel sick and uneasy.

She slowly opened her heavy eyelids. The shock and realization that she wasn't dreaming came crashing into her mind. She let out a soft groan, but before she could focus on anything, she felt the pressure of someone holding her arm and then a sharp sting. She tried to move and open her eyes wider. Still, she couldn't. They immediately became heavy, and she was dreaming again. This time the dream was cloudy. It was empty. There was nothing but blackness, nothing.

***

Herman was surprised the injection wore off so quickly. Much sooner than he expected. Thankfully, he was ready with another small dose. He wasn't even sure how much to give her. She was petite and young, and he was terrified of an overdose. When he saw she was about to open her eyes, he quickly retrieved the syringe and injected her again. He had only given her half the dose on the beach. The rest had still been in the syringe, so he decided it was safe. She passed out straight away.

He looked at the sky. *It will be dark soon, and I need to prepare her.* He walked out again to see if there were any people around and went along the tree line to the beginning of the old steps. The 350-meter walk back up to the top road, most of its natural rock steps, looked foreboding. He was sure he could carry her all the way up. He headed back to his spot and sat down. As the sun's warmth faded, the late afternoon chill was coming. He looked down at her again and admired her perfect body. Then he saw she had little goosebumps all over her skin. *God! She must be cold!* She was only wearing her bikini. As much as he didn't want to, he took the blanket she was lying on and folded the excess over her. He wrapped her up like a cocoon.

"Soon, my angel! Soon!"

Chapter Forty

"Show me what you got!" Bob said to his partner, who seemed more than a little anxious. The interviews with Annie Leason had been tiring and sad indeed. Now, this girl and Wightly were dominating his thoughts. When he was climbing the stairs to his office, he wondered if he'd been a little too demanding on Sherry. But he needed those statements written up and signed. Bob decided he would ask her about them later. He shouldn't put extra work on Sherry. *That was police work!* He reminded himself, but he couldn't trust the uniformed officers with such a sensitive subject. *They could miss something. Anyway, it wasn't even their job to do it. The sexual assault boys should be on it.*

Bob was sure a very dangerous serial rapist was out there

torturing and raping young girls. He was also sure that maniac was using the internet to show the rest of the world what he was doing. What worried him the most was how he was supposed to catch a Deep Dark Web predator. They were almost impossible to apprehend, and they were always so well hidden among millions of other users, all using fake IP addresses, identities, everything. He needed to find some experts who handled that sort of thing. *Sexual assault has a couple of guys;* he reminded himself. He will need to contact them. He had to anyway. *It was their cases, for fuck's sake.* He was a homicide detective, and it wasn't even his case. *Christ, I'm doing all this fucking leg work, and everyone else is just sitting around stuffing their faces. Well, except for Jim. At least I can count on him.*

Bob wondered why he hadn't retired already. Suddenly he felt exhausted. It was like a never-ending road without a rest stop and nowhere to buy petrol. Bob felt like an old car stuck on that never-ending road. He feared he would suddenly stop and never move again.

Jim's voice made him snap out of it. "Sorry, Jim, what were you saying?"

"You ok, chief?"

Bob saw how his partner was looking at him and couldn't help but grin. "Yeah, I'm fine! So, ok, tell me what you got? What's so exciting that I'm standing here holding my dick?"

Jim grinned in a way that told Bob he had something good. "You will not believe it!" Jim said. Bob jokingly interjected quickly. "You just got tested positive at the clinic?"

Jim ignored the jab and kept smiling. "Better than that. My dear Dirty Harry, better than that!" Jim was grinning from ear to ear.

Bob pulled a chair and sat down. He breathed deeply. "Oh yeah? What's that?"

"Look at this!" Jim handed him the file that he had found in the cold case box. He threw it down on the desk in front of Bob's. Bob looked down and studied the front page. "Well! Whatta we have here?"

He flipped to the first page as Jim was talking. "Almost identical MO, on all the victims!" he said, "Drugged, tortured, some sexually abused, all murdered, video cameras found in the house when the TRG squad raided it!"

Bob looked up and said, "They never caught those sons of bitches!" He looked back at the file.

"Fucking cold case!" Jim bent down and flipped to one of the autopsy reports of one of the victims. "This one!" Jim was pointing. "Had his throat slit the same way. Wrists' ligature marks are roughly the same, but what caught my eye was the puncture marks on the body and the trauma to the guy's balls. He has been tortured in the same way our recent victim was."

Bob slowly read through the autopsy report. His mind was connecting what dots he had, and it was worrying him.

"It seems you might have something here, buddy." Bob was looking at Jim now. "I gotta tell ya, this here worries me. This is a cold case, so we're already far behind."

Jim sat down with him. "I'll bet our cold case mother fucker is back at it! He missed all the fun." Jim stopped for a moment, then decided to change the subject. "How's Sherry doing, by the way?"

Bob looked back at the thick file on his desk. "She's fine. She's got a lot of work on her plate. Say! You know that young girl who recently came into the hospital?"

Jim grunted. "Yeah! You told me two times already."

Bob turned to him and looked him in the eyes, smiling. "Well, my dear boy, it looks like the same perp who attacked our victim, Brady Wightly, also attacked this girl. Not only that, he streamed their torture on the fucking internet. Maybe this fucker was even selling tickets." He looked back down at the file and said, "Something's going on, Jim! I think we're missing something somehow."

"You think this girl is connected to the Wightly murder?"

Bob was nodding his head slowly. "I'm not sure, but we need to dig into her background a bit more. I'll have a copy of her statement soon." Bob paused. He needed a coffee. He looked at Jim, then back at the files and said, "Well, I think there are a few options we're looking at here. One, the killer of our recent boy, is one guy, and the serial rapist is another. This means it may not be our cold case asshole at all. Two, the rapist and the killer are the same guy, but still not our cold case asshole. Or three, the killer and the rapist is one guy and is also our cold case asshole." Bob looked down at the file. There was a brief silence, and he looked back at his partner. "You following me there, Jim?" Bob could see the puzzled look on his face and grinned. "My thinking is this," he said with finality. "Either this is two different perps here, and neither one of them is our cold case guy. Or there is one perp killing and raping people." Bob waited to let that sink in. Then Bob said in a pretend game show voice. "And behind door number three is... There is only one perp, and it's our cold case boy, come back from obscurity, to start up his old shit again! You get me now, jumbo?"

"Yessum masser Sharot! I'm a gotcha!"

They both grinned. Then Bob said seriously, "Ok! We need to look more into this!"

Jim nodded, then tapped his finger on the file. "Don't tell Johnson about opening a cold case file. He'll have our heads. He's also gonna be really pissed if the press gets wind of this."

Bob sighed. "Fuck him. No matter how hard we keep it bottled in, the press always finds out. They have stoolies all through this department!"

Jim nodded in agreement. "Ok, so what do you want to do now?"

Bob thought for a moment and said, "You get over to Phil's and take this file with you. See how much he can compare the wounds with the Wightly body. Maybe we can narrow things down. Tell him we need to know how these cases match and ask about the toxicology reports. See if there are any matches with this cold case."

"Ok, boss, what are you gonna do?"

Bob threw his jacket back on. "I'm gonna see if I can get

someone in tech to find us some geeks who know how to access the deep dark web. I want to keep this quiet if we can."

Jim nodded. "I'm also waiting on the results of the toxicology tests of our two victims. I want to see what that psycho pumped into them. But right now," Bob said, grinning, "I'm gonna get me a coffee."

He went to the machine and said over his shoulder. "Let me know what you have when you get back!" Jim grabbed the file and headed out of the office, he said over his shoulder, "Try putting a little rum in your coffee. Seems like you need it."

Yeah right! Thought Bob, *more like a bottle!*

Chapter Forty-One

Herman was ready. The sun had disappeared below the horizon, and only a very faint afterglow lingered. He checked on her and saw she was still well and truly out. He walked back out of his spot and could barely see beyond the trees. He would have to wait just a little while longer. There would be cars coming back from shopping and returning vacationers still on the road. *Just a bit longer.*

Herman went back, fished out his headlamp, and put on his coat and tracksuit pants. He wore a skullcap to cover his head. He checked on her again and thought about putting her clothes back on but changed his mind. He decided she was warm enough. He sat down next to her head and brushed her hair with his hand. Her hair was the finest thing he had ever felt.

Soon my love. Soon. Then I will carry you up the steps. Just a little while longer, then we will be ready.

***

One hour later Herman decided it was time. The sky was pitch black, and the crickets were howling in the wind. Herman brought out the large bag he would put her in and packed up everything except his headlamp. He kept the blanket around her and carefully shifted her body into a fetal position, placing her inside the bag. He brought the sides of the bag up around her body and maneuvered the rest of it around her head, making sure she was completely inside. He then zipped the bag closed.

Just enough room. She'll be ok. She can breathe.

Herman put on his headlamp and switched it on, adjusting the direction of the light. Then put his backpack on. He knelt and picked up the bag with Nicole inside and hoisted her over his shoulder with a grunt. He made his way out of the bushes and along the tree line to the old steps. He stopped at the first step and looked up. He let out a long deep breath, sucked in the fresh cool salt air, and started up the stairs.

****

Nicole's mother was out of her mind with worry. Her daughter hadn't phoned when she promised and wasn't answering her phone. The phone was turned off, not even ringing. She had tried calling her friends, but no one had heard from her. She might be on the top road now, walking back to the main beach. Her mother was sure Nicole would phone her, though, once she reached the top, which should have been two hours ago. Horrible scenarios were racing through her mind. Her motherly instincts were now kicking in. She phoned any friend she had a number for. No one had seen her. It was then she called her husband and told him Nicole was missing. Her husband had told her not to worry and that he was sure she probably had stayed down at the beach longer than normal. He was sure she would call soon. She explained she had already called all her friends, and Nicole would have no reason to stay at the beach so long. It was out of character. He said he would stop at the main beach and check where she usually hung out on his way home. She told him to check the top road and hurry because she couldn't wait much longer. She knew something was wrong. She waited for nearly two hours. It was dark when she heard her husband pull up in the drive. She prayed her daughter was with him. She broke down when she rushed out the front door and saw that he was alone. "I'm going to call the police!" Her husband followed her into the house. He hadn't seen her anywhere. His wife picked up her mobile and searched for the non-emergency number, and then hesitated. This was an emergency; she called the emergency number instead. She didn't care if it was too drastic. She hit the number and waited.

Chapter Forty-Two

Herman had finally reached the top of the stairs and made his way along the last stretch of the pathway. The light from his headlamp was strong, and it lit up the surroundings. He would kill the light as he got closer to the road, then navigate the rest of the way using the glow of the streetlights. She was becoming heavy. Herman hadn't stopped at all on the stairs. He needed to lay her down and rest. He pushed forward, telling himself to keep going.

Herman switched off his lamp. He was almost at the top road and laid Nicole down on the ground at his feet. He watched and waited for a car to pass, but there was none. He saw his van parked near the entrance of the pathway. A couple of other cars parked nearby, and the house opposite had its lights on. He walked out slowly, leaving Nicole behind, and went to his van. He looked around and waited. Still no one. He opened the sliding door and walked back to the pathway entrance and into the bushes. He picked her up and came back near the entrance, hiding behind a large tree. If a car came by now, he would quickly turn and put her into the bushes and hide, but no cars were coming. His mind was racing with anxiety.

This is it. You're almost home. Now it's time. Now, do it! He took a deep breath and casually walked out of the pathway, carrying Nicole in the bag over his shoulder. He made it to his van and placed her gently inside before sliding the door shut. He slipped off his backpack and threw it in the front seat, started his van, and slowly drove away.

I got her! I did it! She is mine!

He drove home carefully obeying the speed limit and pulled into his garage, closing the door behind him. Herman carried her into the house and down into the basement. He laid the bag down on the floor and took her out; he unraveled the blanket and, still in her bikini, admired her again. He picked her up and laid her on the bed he had already prepared for her. Herman placed the soft velvet-covered manacles around her wrists and ankles. The cables connected to the manacles were very strong and ran underneath the bed and were secured to the frame. Her wrist restraints were very short, so she could not reach her face with either hand. He reached under the pillow and placed a sleeping patch with elastic over her eyes, and brushed her hair away from her face. He had a table set up with water by her bedside, which he would give her when she woke. He set up his video camera in the corner and focused the lens on her. Then turned on the soft light connected to the tripod, pulled out his mobile, and took some still photos of her with his phone.

Herman went and laid a large fresh blanket on her. He checked her pulse and her restraints and nodded with satisfaction. He leaned over and kissed her on the forehead, then stood, walked back to the video camera, and hit the record button.

He walked to the doorway and turned as he placed his finger

on the light switch, whispering, "Good night, my beautiful dear princess."

He flicked the switch off, and the room went dark, except for the soft red reflection on her from the camera's recording light. He closed the padded door behind him and pushed the bolt across. He walked up the stairs and out of the basement doorway. He closed it behind him and turned the key. Herman walked into the living room and turned on his TV and computer. He took his remote and chose HDMI on his TV. There she was in the soft red light of his basement. He looked down at his computer. *Wait until they see now what I got.* He gleefully thought. *They will pay big money for her.* He smiled as he logged into his own new Red Room and typed his introduction.

Welcome one and all to the

CARDCOLLECTOR'S RED ROOM.

My room will be available soon for the right members who enjoy watching beautiful young girls restrained and violated. I allow members to bid for their sexual desires to be carried out.

See the photos below of our first sweet little pie, who will be ready for devouring soon. Leave your interest in the comments below for potential membership. Don't forget; the CardCollector always expects you to play your hand. He hit enter and uploaded the images he had taken of her. The room was officially opened for hits. He sat anxiously waiting to see what traffic he garnered, then he would decide on the membership fee.

Chapter Forty-Three

Bob looked at his desk again and sighed. He pulled the cold case file of the slasher from the pile and opened it. He had a new theory. Some pieces that were missing before were now resurfacing and falling into place. *Maybe this east coast slasher was right in front of them five years ago, but they could never connect the dots because they didn't have the expertise we have now back then.* The internet was in its infancy five years ago. *So much has changed. It's much more vast and complicated now.* He was grateful they had people in law enforcement whose understanding of the internet evolved and were experienced enough in cyber-crime to penetrate these evil domains. Trying to catch many of the major players dancing around the criminal world of the deep dark web was a massive and expensive task. *The criminals didn't create the deep dark web, though, The American Army intelligence community created it for their cyber-security defense purposes. The criminals just piggybacked their way in until they took it over.* His thoughts went back to the slasher case. *They never caught him.* Bob was an up-and-coming detective then and part of that task force. He was at the house when the TAC had raided it. *To break a door down these days, those TAC guys need permission before they can even enter from some fuck who's not even on the scene. Only if someone is being murdered inside can they enter without permission or a warrant. Those giving the permission are just sitting in some office while the real cops are in the trenches, putting their lives on the line to bring down the criminals plaguing society.* When he walked inside that house, what he saw shocked him, t*hat dead girl was chained, drugged, and raped by some animal. Everyone who was at that house that day wanted blood, and if they had found that piece of shit still in the house, they would have carried him out in a body bag. Whoever it was though, had fled in a hurry.* It gnawed at Bob for a long time that somehow someone in the force had tipped the killer off the day of the raid. As far as he knew, no one outside the department knew the plan. He lost his trust in the force that day, at least most of them. At the time, he was sure the case would never get solved. Someone high up must have been protecting the killer. *Some sick puppies in high society were getting their kicks, watching people get raped and murdered on video. There was nothing the police could do because it wasn't a crime to watch unless those people solicited such a crime to happen.* He knew what was happening back then, but it was almost impossible to prove it. Bob remembered they had even found one of those sick puppies, and they had to cut a deal with him just to catch that killer. Then it all went sour. Now Bob was wondering if they could catch another one of the voyeurs. That may be the way to get to the killer. Someone willing to give him up to save his skin. He stood to meet Jim in the task force office room. *We need to change our strategy. Maybe we need to reel in a small fish to catch the big one.* It was one thing coming up with a new strategy; it was another trying to convince others in the task force to go along with it. Everyone there had an ego, and getting past those egos was the first of his missions.

He arrived at the task force office and found Jim at his new desk. Bob wanted to fill him in right away, but he wanted to move on to his new strategy as quickly as possible before the big brass shut him down. He asked Jim to come along with him, and they found two guys in the corner of the room. Both of them had their heads buried in their computers. Bob was hoping these two guys were the ones he was looking for. One of them, Danny, stood with his hand outstretched when Bob approached. Danny had heard about this detective and respected and admired him greatly. He introduced Danny's partner. Bob waved them to sit back down. Bob pulled up a chair next to them and said, "Ok boys, we're just a few of the case detectives for the task force. We would like for you to do something very difficult and not in the normal realm of your work." He paused, giving them a sense of the challenge of the tasks ahead. Boys, we need your help in getting into the deep dark web. We need you to track our boy who's hiding in there." The two boys were silent, and Bob knew he had their fullest attention. "I know this will be very hard for you guys to witness what goes on in there, and we're not asking you to do anything you don't feel comfortable with. If you want to back out, I'll understand, but we will have to find someone else who's up to the job."

Bob knew this wasn't entirely true, but it had the desired effect. The two boys straightened their backs and told Bob that they were up to the task. Danny said they would be happy to go as far as Bob saw necessary to solve this case. Bob smiled. Jim watched Bob in awe and was not surprised at his partner's shrewdness. Bob was looking at Danny. He seemed to be the most inquisitive and smartest of the two. He knew both were specialists in their fields and knew they would know what to look for in serial sex crimes. Bob knew Danny had been in the force for almost five years and was an expert computer tech guy. Though Danny always wanted to be a cop. When they saw how good his computer skills were, they put him in the sexual assault and serious sexual offenders department. He had helped capture many pedophiles and sexual deviants who preyed upon children. Bob couldn't imagine some of the terrible things Danny must have seen on the internet. Things that would make anyone sick and break down. Things he would never want to see but sometimes had to as part of the job. They were a special small team, usually joined by the detectives in charge of a case. If some images or videos were too hard to see for them, the tech guys would move away from the screen and hand it over to the detectives, who had more of a stomach for it. After five years, Bob was sure Danny had seen it all, though. *He's conditioned.* He hoped Danny would do his job without showing too much emotion. This worried Bob sometimes, and he wondered how many people could do what Danny did. The team also comprised of psychiatrists. Doctors they could turn to if things got to be too much or too messy. They had brought in Danny as part of the serious sexual assault team, and Bob was glad he was there. Their department had briefed

Danny on the kidnap and sexual assault of the girl, and like the others in the task force, he didn't have many leads to go on. Bob was counting on Danny.

"Ok Danny," he said. "Here's what I want you to do. We need you to get into the deep dark web and find these Red Rooms. Have you heard of them?"

Danny nodded slowly. Bob continued. "I don't know how hard it is to find them, but when you do, we need you to join them."

Chapter Forty-Four

Sherry found out about Nicole when the call came in from one of her police officer friends. He explained a fourteen-year-old, Nicole Anderson, was missing and asked if she could give the parents a call. Maybe arrange a visit as well. The police had already been by the house and had taken all the details from the parents leading up to Nicole's disappearance. The girl had been missing for almost twenty-four hours, and there were no traces of her anywhere. Sherry knew the statistics. Ninety percent of missing people not found within the first forty-eight hours are usually presumed dead.

Sherry hung up and immediately started punching in their number. She wondered if she should let Bob know and figured he probably knew already. She would phone him later anyway. She spent the next hour going over other cases, then left the lodge and drove to Anderson's house. When she arrived, she was already feeling apprehensive and spent the next couple of hours there trying to convince them to have faith in law enforcement and trust they were doing their job. She had said this to hundreds of families before but knew time was running out.

After she left, she was hit with the typical empty feeling that was always left after those meetings. That feeling where she knew there was nothing more she could do or say that would bring their daughter home. She thought about Bob and suddenly missed him. She pulled out her cell and called his number. His phone buzzed, and when he answered, she could tell he had no time to talk to her right now.

"Hi Bob, I know you really can't talk long, but how are you holding up anyway?"

Bob's voice sounded strained. "Yeah, I'm ok, but we are shooting blanks on this case so far. How you doing?"

There was a slight pause, then Sherry said, "I suppose I'm ok. A girl has gone missing since yesterday, Nicole Anderson, fourteen years old. Everyone is out looking for her. I'm worried about this one, Bob."

"Shit. I hope she's found. The Uniform boys should be on that. I think there is a strong connection between the Brady Wightly murder and Annie Leason. I don't know enough as yet; we're still working on it."

Sherry was silent. Then she said, "Well, if that's true and it was this killer that raped Annie, then why did he let her live?"

"I don't know yet, honey, but I'm working on it. As of now, though, I'm going to combine the cases. I'll get sexual assault involved, and we are going to set up a state task force. Look, babe, I have to go. Call me later."

"Oh, Jesus. Ok. Take care of yourself." She sent him a kiss. Bob wanted to ask if she missed him but now wasn't the right time. He sent her a kiss back and hung up.

Bob redialed his phone and called Johnson's number. He dreaded this part. He hated having to suck up to Johnson. It sickened him, but he had to do it. *Somebody has to*! "Hello, sir." He forced himself to say. "We got a positive test on the drug used on the first victim. It also connects the recent kidnap and rape victim who was left alive."

Bob waited for that to sink into Johnson's thick skull. Then he told him what needed to be told. "Sir! The drug traces from the first victim, Brady Wightly, and the girl match those of the East Coast Slasher." Bob wanted to continue before Johnson had a chance to interrupt him. "I would like to recommend a statewide task force be set up as soon as possible. Bring the sexual assault guys up to speed, with your permission, sir, of course."

Bob wanted to vomit. He always avoided calling Johnson, sir. At first, Johnson was his usual belligerent self, doubting everything. Then he had agreed, but it would be him, not Bob, who organized the interstate police, detectives, and everyone else, to come to the station. Johnson told him he would let Bob know later that day what he and Jim would do next. Then hung up without another word.

Bob looked at the phone and closed it. He turned to Jim. "Numb-nuts said he's gonna help us put a task force together. We'll get the sexual assault guys and other big boys from interstate. Then connect them with our homicide division."

Jim threw his arms up in a mock cheer. "Don't tell me! Johnson's' going to take all the credit for our achievements? Jim didn't wait for an answer. He knew it already. "That son of a bitch! He always does!"

Bob grinned at him. "Of course!"

Chapter Forty-Five

Herman was panicking. He had Nicole, now he had to figure out his next move. His new CardCollector room became instantly popular. Ever since he had posted pictures of her in her bikini with a mask on, he began receiving hundreds of messages on his Red Room chat wall. He had two monitors with a live view of her just for him. He wanted to keep an eye on her, no matter where he was in the house.

He went down to the basement to check on her again. The breakfast he had brought down earlier was still there. He had forgotten about it. He quietly went to the bed and sat next to her. She was still sleeping, and he smiled at how comfortable he had made her. She didn't stir. He hoped she would wake soon. The last injection he had given her was a strong one, but he had to be sure she wouldn't wake up when he wasn't there. He had injected her again well before the sun was up. He read the instructions from the dark web for the dosage amounts again. He had to be very careful not to give her too much. *She's had three injections, a small one to take her. Then I gave her another while waiting to make the journey up the stairs. Then a third one early this morning in the basement.* He wouldn't need to inject her again unless she woke up before he was ready for her. If she freaked out, then he wouldn't have a choice.

He brushed her hair with his hand and watched her sleep. How beautiful she was, how soft she was. *She is perfect!* He had never been this close to perfection before. He was drunk with desire at the sight of her. Herman gently shook her shoulder to see if she would wake up, but she was deep asleep. He got up and left the breakfast there. He would return later and check on her again.

Chapter Forty-Six

Nicole was waking up. The cold feeling of being lost in a dark cave was replaced by a feeling of being warm and cozy. She opened her eyes but only saw blackness, the smell of must in the air. She felt drowsy and weak. Something was covering her eyes. She went to feel her face, to touch whatever was on her. Her hand stopped mid-movement. Her wrists were clamped. She tried using her other hand, but it was the same thing. *Why can't I move my hands?* She tried again, harder, but whatever was restricting her held her tight. Nicole felt an instant panic rush through her. She tried to pry off whatever she had over her eyes by turning her head side to side on the pillow, but it stayed on. She moved her legs and felt the same things around her ankles. She moved one of

305

her legs one way, then another. Her legs were held firm. She cried out and tried again. She could move her legs, but only just a little. Nicole tried to pull her body off the bed she was lying on, but the clamps on her wrists and ankles prevented her from sitting up. She got as far as the edge of the bed. She cried out for her mother, but there was silence. She cried out again, still nothing. She started to cry and felt the tears soak up the cloth around her eyes. Her eyes began to sting. She thrashed against the tension of the restraints, holding her arms and legs. She cried out louder, and the more she cried, the more the tears filled up in her eyes until she couldn't keep her eyes open any longer. She heard a distant noise and stayed very silent. She heard footsteps, and then a bolt slide, and a door opening. "Hello?" She whispered. Is someone there? Mommy?" The footsteps moved closer to her. She sensed the presence of someone sitting down on the edge of the bed.

"Hello, Nicole." The soft, gentle voice said.

She opened her eyes but still couldn't see. "Who are you? Why can't I move?"

There was silence for a few seconds, then the soft voice said, "Nicole, you are a special guest of mine. I had to bring you here because I need you to stay with me for a while. You don't have to worry, dear girl. You are going to be fine." Nicole tried to follow the voice and realized his face was close to hers. She could smell his cologne.

"Why am I here? Why did you bring me here? Why can't I see anything? Why is there something over my eyes? Please, my eyes are stinging." She felt a hand brush her hair, then a soft tissue wiping her cheeks, then around the edges of the mask.

The soft voice continued, "I need to keep your eyes covered, honey, because I have to be a secret. You can't see me, and that's for the best."

Nicole's panic came back. "But I don't want to be here! I want to be with my mum! Please let me go! I want my mum!"

"Shh, my love, don't worry. I will let your mum know you are fine. You will be home soon. So don't worry, my love. I will take care of you. I love you, Nicole."

Nicole writhed in her restraints. "I don't want you to take care of me! Please, Mister, let me go! I want to go home! Please, Mister, I want to go home!"

The hand came back to her forehead again. "Now, now, my love, just relax. You're going to stay with me for a while, ok? I want you to behave. No crying or screaming, ok? Can you do that for me? Are you a good girl? I promise you can go home and be with your mum, ok?"

Nicole stayed silent, and she suddenly realized she was still wearing her bikini. She became very frightened. *Why am I still in my bikini?* "Where are my clothes? Please, Mister! I need to go to the toilet; I need to go!" She was turning her head from side to side again, trying to pry the thing covering her eyes away from her face.

The man's voice remained calm. "Alright, my love. I will take you. Hold still." He took off the clamp from one of her wrists. Then took the other clamp off while quietly telling her to hold still. Then he turned her on her stomach, carefully brought her hands behind her back, and clamped her wrists together. Herman turned her on her back again, and she jolted slightly when she felt his hands on her leg. He was holding her leg still, and she felt the clamp come off her ankles and then the other one. She shivered. "Now." The soft voice said to her. "Nicole, I want you to be a good girl. I'm going to sit you up on the edge of the bed and then stand you up, ok? Are you ready? Here we go." He lifted her and turned her to the side of her bed, her legs dangling over the edge. He helped her stand and gently guided her to the bathroom. Herman led her inside and closed the door behind them. "Ok, my baby, now you need to pee? The toilet's in front of you. I will help you to it."

Nicole was shivering again. "No Mister! Please don't! I can do it! Please leave me alone! I can do it!"

She was terrified. She sensed the man very close to her ear. In a soft voice, he whispered, "No, honey I'm going to help you.

It's ok. I won't hurt you." He went down on his knees and gently pulled her bikini bottom down to her ankles.

"No! Please don't!" She cried.

"It's ok honey, you cannot pee in your swimsuit, can you?" He stayed on his knees for a few seconds, admiring her. He sat her down on the toilet with her hands behind her back. Herman stood back and watched.

"Ok honey, I will turn my back now, go on."

She sat there for a minute, unable to go. She couldn't move; she didn't know what was happening. Nicole couldn't understand anything; she sat a while longer. "Are you finished yet, dear?" His voice echoed softly in the bathroom. Always the same soft, gentle tone. "Don't look please." She pleaded.

"I'm not looking, my darling. Come on now, finish please."

He waited a little longer and asked her if she was finished.

"Yes," she said in a brittle voice. He went over and took some toilet paper and went to open Nicole's legs gently as she sat on the toilet.

"No, please don't touch me."

"I'm just going to clean you, baby. Now open your legs a little, please, ok?"

She did as she was told, and he slowly and gently wiped her clean. Nicole was crying softly. "Shh, it's ok, my love. Shh, there now. You're all clean. Come on now, stand up." He helped her up, pulled her bikini bottom back on, adjusted it for her, and then led her out of the bathroom.

"Would you like something to eat, baby? I have some food ready for you."

She didn't answer, and he led her back over to the bed and gently laid her down. Herman turned her on her stomach and clamped one of her ankles back on. He took the cuffs off her hands, then turned her over, then cuffed both her wrists to just one chain. She could now turn on her side while still being restrained. Herman put the pillow at her back to help her sit up and placed a dinner tray on the bed. He took the plastic spoon, scooped up some of the cold scrambled eggs he had made her earlier that morning, and gently pushed the spoon to her mouth. "Ok, open wide, some scrambled eggs I made before. Sorry, they're not hot."

Nicole shook her head. "No, Mister, I'm not hungry, please no."

Herman held the spoon in front of her mouth. "Yes, my love, you need to eat. You need your strength."

She opened her mouth a little, and he slipped the food into her mouth. "There you go, yes, good girl." He pushed the spoon back to her mouth again, but this time she shook her head more vigorously. Herman stopped. She shook her head again to say no more. Herman relented, took the plastic cup of water, and brought it to her lips. "Here, drink some water." Nicole was very thirsty; she hadn't drunk anything since she had gone to the beach. She drank the whole cup. Herman then laid her down on the bed. He took her free hand and cuffed it to the other chain.

"No," She pleaded. "Please don't. Please let me go." She sobbed.

"Shh, my baby. It's ok, soon. Don't worry." He cuffed her other hand, leaving one of her legs free, and stood. "Listen to me honey, I will leave one cuff off your wrist, but you have to promise me something, ok? There will be some rules. The one most important rule is—Nicole, are you listening to me?" She nodded slightly. "Ok, listen to me carefully; after I take one of your cuffs off, you cannot take your eye mask off, ok? If I see you take it off, I will have to punish you badly. It's for your safety baby, and mine. You can never take it off, do you understand?" She nodded her head. "Good, because I'll be watching. I'll always be watching."

He laid the blanket back over her body. "Now, you get some rest, and we will talk later. Ok, my baby girl?" Nicole stayed silent and heard him walk away from her. She began to cry hard now. She turned her head to the side, so the tears could run out through the slight space from her eyes and the cloth. She kept crying as she heard the man close the door and slide the bolt. She heard the footsteps get fainter and fainter. Then the faint sound of another door closing. She would cry herself to sleep, murmuring the words. "Mommy! Mommy!"

Chapter Forty-Seven

Bob was shuffling files when he looked at his phone and saw Sherry was calling. He was grateful; he needed a breather from the madness unfolding around him. "Hey, babe," he said. "Where are you now?"

"Bob, listen to me, the same man that kidnapped and tortured Annie Leason could be the same man that just kidnapped Nicole Anderson. Now I'm anxious not just for Nicole but also for the other girls out there. It's like a feeding frenzy."

She paused, Bob sighed. "Babe, listen, as far as I know, they have nothing on the Anderson girl yet. There is still no evidence she was kidnapped or any evidence that connects her to the current cases the task force is working on. But that's not to say we can't have them look into it, although we have other officers who are all working very hard to help find Nicole. But I'll have some of our boys help as well; that's the best I can do honey, ok?" he asked her patiently. "What about the parents? Anything from them?"

Sherry was silent. Then she said, "I don't think they can do much more than what they are doing already. We'll get them on TV to make a plea directly to the kidnapper, or kidnappers, as soon as possible. Maybe get the parents to put up a reward."

Bob waited. He knew there was more she wanted to say.

"Honey," she said in her smooth voice. "Can you keep me in the loop? I need to be kept up to date on this. Please? Can you do that for me?"

Bob tried his hardest to resist her, but it was impossible. She could control him when she had to, and it was working very well right now. "I will have to get the ok from Johnson and the rest, first. Ok babe? But I'll try," he said, then he added a little sugar to the unsweetened reply. "The task force is set up, so everything has to go through them, but since the serious sexual assault team are involved, I will put in a request for you to be an adviser."

"Ok, you are wonderful, thank you, but you're still going to add Nicole to the victim task force, right? There is a chance she's connected."

Bob looked up at the sky. He wasn't getting out of this as easy as he thought.

Chapter Forty-Eight

His mind was twisting in all directions. The news almost stopped his breathing. He had already seen posters of Nicole everywhere when he drove to the market to replenish his fridge. *Now two other victims being found dead will bring more pressure on police to find Nicole. I watched Wightly being murdered;* he thought with a little fear because he knew who murdered him. However, there was no question in his mind that Herman had any feelings about that boy. He didn't care about him at all; he was glad he was dead. The problem was, he knew Wightly, and he was sure the police would eventually come and ask him about Brady.

He needed to get his mind off that now and took the remote to switch to his HDMI signal and observe Nicole. He kept a constant eye on his computer and his new Red Room as well, watching in real-time a large build-up of clientele who were sending messages to him. They wanted to know when they could join, pay, and bid for things to be done to Nicole. The list had grown to over ten thousand. Herman had answered none of them. He hadn't touched her in any manner except to feed her since taking her. He helped her to the toilet when she needed it and showered her like her own mother would have done. Herman wanted to keep her sedated until he could decide what to do with her, so she slept most days. He had fallen completely in love with her and was not ready to do anything sexually to her in front of his paying customers.

Some of them, tired of waiting, had unsubscribed from his private group, others had left angry and offensive messages, some even threatening. None of them had paid yet, so it didn't bother him. Once he realized how popular she was, there was no hurry to exploit her. He was thinking of keeping her all to himself. Herman wanted her so badly, but he also wanted to wait. He was sure if she stayed longer, she would eventually grow to love him, and then whatever he wanted to do with her, she would let him.

He needed to see her in person again. Watching her sleep on the monitor was frustrating, but he couldn't be with her all the time. Herman didn't want to scare her any more than she already was. He left the living room and made his way to the basement. He opened the door and called out her name. She stirred a little but was still very weak from the small amounts of Scopolamine he gave her.

When he had researched the drug, it said to keep all dosages small and regulated, so his dosage to her was just enough to keep her weak but not completely sedated. He walked over and sat down on the edge of the bed and brushed her hair, asking her how she was feeling. "Hi, my love, can you hear me?" The sleeping patch was still over her eyes. He needed her to answer him to check how weak she was. She let out a very soft groan and moved her head slowly from side to side. She tried to speak, but she just mumbled. He took the blanket off to make sure she wasn't so sedated that she'd wet the bed. The plate of food he had left for her was half-eaten. He had left one arm free, so she could feed herself and pour herself water with an easy pour jug when she needed it. "Nicole? Can you hear me?" She turned her head and mumbled softly, "Yes."

Relieved, Herman breathed out slowly. Your food is right next to you. I unchained one of your arms, but don't take your eye mask off. Remember, I'm always watching you. He knew that wasn't true, and he only unchained her arm whenever he brought her food. He checked her often enough in case she needed to go to the bathroom. He had to take some chances with her, and she had done as she was told so far. After bringing her food one time, he left the basement, then deliberately watched her for hours on his monitor. She never once tried to remove the mask. He also took off her swimsuit, washed it, and put it away. He changed her into a nightgown so she could be more comfortable.

He placed his hand on her abdominal area and pressed down gently. "Would you like to pee, Nicole?" He pressed again a little harder. "You need to pee, baby?" Nicole mumbled something he did not understand and tried to put one of her hands where his hand was, but the chain stopped her. She used her other hand, which was free, and tried to brush his hand away. He could tell she had no strength. He was now a little worried about the dosages he was giving her and decided he would stop her doses completely until she got her strength back. He leaned down and gently kissed her on the forehead, then on her nose, then he kissed her mouth.

She weakly turned her head away and moaned slightly. "No, please don't."

Herman lifted his head up slowly. "I love you, baby; you know I love you so much." Herman put the blanket back over her and walked to the door. He was about to close the door when he turned around and said, "I'll be back in about an hour, my love. Make sure you finish the rest of your food. I'll give you a good shower and a scrub later." He said this in a loving voice, closed the door, and walked up the stairs. He had to get away. The uncontrollable lust he had for her was overwhelming. He was sure if he stayed, he would do something wrong to her, then it would be too late. There would be no stopping him then. He went upstairs and leaned against the door and breathed slowly, his heart beating fast, his chest hurting, sweat on his brow from hyperventilating.

Chapter Forty-Nine

Bob laid out his plan while sitting next to Danny, listening intently. "Danny, once you get in there, we will need you to open up accounts in these Red Rooms under various false names, keeping yourself hidden, of course. Only in the rooms, you think will help us the most. You'll be looking for rooms that offer mutilation, murder for hire, rape, and sexual torture, that sort of thing." Bob paused. "You're going to need cryptocurrency, and the task force will give you as much as you need."

Danny nodded; he had been in there many times before, usually to prevent a murder, catch pedophiles, or set up a sting operation involving the selling and buying large quantities of drugs.

He had never actually been in one of those Red Rooms, though. It excited him to try, and he found that a little disturbing. He hit his tor browser, then another. He was in deep with Bob and Jim watching over his shoulder.

This kid is very good, Bob thought. Bob turned to the other young man next to Danny. "Ok so, Ricky, right?" The young man nodded and looked intimidated. "We need you to find us a list of websites that sell synthetic dope and different illegal synthetic drugs. We're after a particular drug called Scopolamine, it's a common drug you can buy in the US, Columbia, and Brazil, but this one is a generic mixture and goes by the street name the Devil's Breath." Bob turned back to Danny. "Danny, I've been told that when you set up these fake accounts, make sure they are traceable to the corresponding Bitcoin accounts for these Red Rooms. They can be very suspicious of who joins them."

Danny nodded. Danny knew he would be up against some of the most dangerously skilled cybercriminals. Bob put his hand on Danny's shoulder. "Danny, we are looking for a particular room that has a guy who wears a hood. He'll probably be shirtless, with a black leather apron and black boots with shiny silver buckles. I know it sounds ridiculous, but it's all the info we have. Oh yeah! I forgot! The guy's hood is made of some sort of potato sack, stitched together, or something like that. Maybe hand-stitched as well." Bob thought for a moment, checking his notes from Annie's statement. "His room will have um, many whips chains, tools for torture, that sort of thing, and—" Bob paused, and Danny turned to him and waited. Bob took a breath and said, "Well, a dildo machine, if you can believe that? I don't know what particular one we are looking for. I found a couple on the internet, but I think the one we need to find isn't there. So it must be homemade or something. Anyway, the victim couldn't describe it, so maybe forget trying to get a hit on the manufacturer. OK, son?"

Bob waited for Danny to take all that in.

"Yes Sir," Danny said.

Bob smiled. He liked this one. "Let us know when you're

ready and tell us how much money you're gonna need to get it all started."

Jim watched the other boy bring up several sites on his computer that sold Devil's Breath and other illegal substances. Both detectives knew this drug was not available in Australia, but if they could somehow trace the sources, then maybe they would get lucky and track a sale to an Australian buyer. "This is gonna take a while, Sir," Danny explained. "Give me about an hour, maybe two."

Bob patted him on the shoulder and motioned Jim to come with him. They both walked over to where the rest of the detectives were seated around a large long table discussing the case.

"Good afternoon gentlemen," Bob said sternly. "I'm Senior detective Bob Sharot, and this is my partner Senior detective Jim Levin." They all stood and introduced themselves, shook hands, then sat back down. Bob brought them all up to speed on Annie's kidnap and rape. He left out the instructions he had just given

Danny for the time being. He didn't need Johnson knowing too much. He may, just out of spite, refuse the extra funds. "The possibility that the east coast slasher was responsible for Wightly's torture and murder is a certainty." *Now for my gut feeling!* "We are also certain, well, I am, that the young woman kidnapped could be the slasher's victim as well. We are still working on that connection."

One of the detectives asked the same question Sherry had asked Bob earlier. "If the slasher took the girl, why did he let her go?" It was an answer Bob still couldn't figure out, but he was sure of that too. There was silence in the room, and Bob knew he had their attention. "We are working on that now." Bob decided now was the time to bring in Sherry. "There is a woman named Sherry Miller, who is an expert in the field of sexual assault, child psychology, and rape counseling. We have been working with her and the rape victim, and with Miss Miller's help, the female victim confirmed she knew the murder victim, Brady Wightly. We are bringing her down to the station to see if she could give our sketch artist a better description. Also, if she would be willing to take a look at some shots of the slasher's previous murder victims." Bob paused, then said, "Hopefully, they may know them as well, then we will have a solid connection." Now Bob thought it would be a good time to stop, but he knew if he said nothing about what Sherry had asked him, he would hear about it from her later. "We also have a report of a fourteen-year-old girl currently missing, Nicole Anderson. Presumed kidnapped, we don't know any more than that, but we are taking that case very seriously." Again, there was silence. Then Bob asked if there were any questions.

The detective at the end of the table caught his attention; he asked Bob, "What's the connection with the fourteen-year-old and these murders?" It was a good question, and Bob cursed Sherry a little for talking him into mentioning it. "Well, none at this time, but we don't want to rule out the possibility that there may be a connection. If that's all gentlemen, I'll let you all get back to work."

Bob thought that he had just made a dick of himself at the end there. *Thanks, Sherry.* What he didn't know was they had already heard about these two detectives, especially Bob Sharot, and none of them had any doubts about their abilities and professionalism. These two were famous.

Chapter Fifty

Nicole was in and out of consciousness. She didn't know what time it was or how long she had been in this strange room. She had heard the man come into the room many times. Every time he came in, her fear returned. She was sure one of those times he'd do something to her, but he never did. Whenever he took her to the toilet, she could never go because she could feel him watching her. He promised her he didn't, but she had no choice in the end. She had to go.

After pleading with him, he finally relented and let her go by herself and clean herself. He wouldn't, however, let her shower alone. He insisted on washing her. She said no many times, but he ignored her. She hated the showers. Nicole felt him touch her in her private places, she would tell him to stop and jerk away, but he told her it was the only way to make sure she was clean. She felt his hard thing brush up against her. Nicole knew, at fourteen, she knew. She also knew he was doing it to himself in the shower next to her. He would go silent for a little while; she could feel different splashes of water on her besides the shower, then he would groan a little and continue washing her. She never said anything, but he did it every time they were in there.

He still kept the mask on her, and she was grateful she couldn't see him even though she did try to imagine his face. His voice seemed soothing, but it didn't make her feel more relaxed around him. She would think of her mother during shower times. She was thinking about when she was a child. When her mother used to bathe her, these thoughts got her through it. To overcome the panic and fear of some stranger seeing her naked and touching her, cleaning her. It also stopped her from screaming. She never screamed. He had told her never to scream, or he would punish her. She didn't know what that punishment would be, but she was too afraid to test him. Instead, she thought about her family and friends and tried to pretend she was safe and somewhere else. Nicole cried a lot but tried to stay strong, knowing her mother would want her to. *Why is he doing this?* She asked herself. *What does he want with me?* She lay on the bed and opened her eyes under the mask. She turned on her side and searched carefully for the cup of water with her free arm. She drank slowly and placed the cup back in its usual spot to find it again. She felt for the half-eaten plate of food. It was the same as before, and cold. She laid back down and stared into the mask over her eyes. Images were flashing in front of her, laughing with her friends, her family worried sick about her. She pictured them hugging her. She imagined the sun on her face, and for a moment, she felt like she was free. She closed her eyes again; there was nothing she could do but try to sleep. A tortured sleep was all that came.

Chapter Fifty-One

As the days blended into weeks, Herman grew increasingly determined that nothing would happen to Nicole in his basement. He had built and prepared for so many things and still had not yet tested any of them. He felt more doubtful that he even wanted to use them on her. *How can I hurt something so pure and gentle and soft? Why would I want to destroy that? She will not love me that way.* He tried watching The Hood's Red Room, but it was closed. *Where is he? Out getting another victim, I know?* He constantly checked other Red Rooms, afraid of what he might find. *What am I looking for? I don't know; maybe someone else knows me in one of those rooms. Are they going to die because of me? No! Stop it! You're being paranoid!*

He had to think clearly, find a reason the people he knew at school were being snatched and tortured in front of him. Being with Nicole was his only release, being close to her and smelling her. Every time he would watch a Red Room, and there was a young girl, Nicole was all he could think of. He would lose his urge to go down to the basement and do something with her *because she was too perfect.* He should have chosen a young girl that was less desirable. Someone he wouldn't care about using for his Red Room. Now it was too late. *I could always get another girl. Maybe I could do things to her while Nicole watched. Or she could at least be in the same room so she could hear. No, that would just make her more afraid of me, and I need her to love me.* Every time he sat next to Nicole, he would go upstairs and watch a Red Room after. *She would never last in my Red Room. She's too fragile,* he thought. *Any blemish on her, any drop of blood, or bruise would cause me too much pain.* He was making sure she was eating well and keeping hydrated. He cleaned her sheets every two days, and the air in the basement circulated the best he could. *She was changing*; he noticed. She started talking to him more and more, asking him his name, how old he was, what about his friends? His family? Herman had to lie. He told her his name was Robert, from his time in the clinic. He had also told her the story about his sister Beth, using her real name. How he just wanted to take care of Nicole the way he was never able to take care of his sister. Although even when he and Beth were together, he never had any thoughts about sexually hurting Beth. That was not how he thought of Nicole initially, however, because now that has all changed. *She is just like Beth,* he thought. *I see Beth in her in so many ways.* It was soothing that Nicole cared about him, and he loved her even more for it. *Is Nicole loving me now? She can see how well I take care of her, and she will love me more.* He left his computer and went downstairs, and when he entered the room, he smiled when he saw Nicole was finishing the meal he had made for her.

She stopped eating. "Robert?"

He smiled. "Yes, my love, it's me." He walked over to her.

She sat up and felt for her cup of water, and Herman guided

her hand. "Thank you," she said.

He smiled at her, still cradling her hand. "How are you?" he asked.

She smiled just a little." Oh, I'm so full, and you? Did you eat as well?" she asked in a soft voice, without fear.

He softly stroked her hair. "Yes, my baby, I did. How does your head feel now that I stopped your medication? Do you still feel dizzy?"

Nicole laid back down. "I'm much better." She rubbed her forehead. "You're a splendid cook Robert."

He began to cry.

"What's wrong Robert? Are you ok? Was it something I said?"

He squeezed her hand in his. "No baby, but I'm feeling so sad. I really don't know what to do."

Nicole squeezed his hand back a little tighter. "Don't be sad Robert. I know you won't hurt me, will you? I know you are a kind person, so it's ok, don't cry."

He laid his head on her stomach and cried. She put her hand on his head and brushed his hair. "It's ok Robert, it's ok, I know you are good, I know you don't mean to keep me here. Maybe you should let me go soon; I think it's time now, don't you think? We can still write to each other."

He was still sobbing; he buried his head in her lap, his voice muffled. "I don't know, I don't know."

They both stayed still for a while as she stroked his hair. He lifted his head and looked at her. "I have to go out for a while, baby. I will be back later, ok? Get some rest." He got up and walked to the door.

She called out to him, "Robert please don't be too long."

His eyes softened. "I won't be my baby, don't worry." He left and went back upstairs to his computer.

"Ok. Where are you? You fucking hood?"

Chapter Fifty-Two

Nicole had been planning for days now, and she was sure her plan would work. Instead of staying silent with him, being afraid, she would try to talk to him engage him. She had heard about this through social media. *She once read that forming a friendship with your captor can save your life*. Now that she was sure he wouldn't harm her, if she could be nice to him, he might let her go.

When she first talked with him, there was silence. He seemed very nervous around her. The nicer she was, the more meek and afraid he became and would even cry. She almost felt a little sorry for him. Nicole could tell he was hurting inside, but she didn't want to know why and didn't care. So she thought of anything to talk about, anything at all. Her dreams, what she wanted to be when she grew up, things to take his mind away from what she thought he wanted from her. Nicole was never sure if he was lying or not about his name or his family, but it didn't matter. He was trusting her more and more. She planned to earn his total trust. She needed him to see that letting her go was the only way they could be together forever. *It seems to be working.* She began asking him if she could take her mask off when she entered the bathroom, let her go in alone, and shower alone. He would ignore the question or say something like, *we will see,* but it was never a no. His level of care became almost that of her mother, and she knew she was getting through to him. *My mum, oh I miss her so much! I need her now, help me, mummy.*

Nicole wanted him to let her go to be back with her family, with her mother. She began to cry, unable to stop the tears. Finally, she pulled herself together. She would fight this; she had to control herself and stay strong if she wanted to win, *even if I had to fight to get out of here!*

Chapter Fifty-Three

A few days later, Nicole was sitting up pretending to be happy eating a sandwich he had just made her. "What's the weather like outside today, Robert?"

He was sitting on the edge of the bed, watching her. "I don't know, baby," Herman said, feeling comfortable for the first time in a while. "I haven't been outside for the past few days, but I noticed through the window that it was sunny."

Nicole stopped chewing. "Oh, I wish I could feel the sunshine on my face. I would love to go swimming. Can you take me swimming, Robert?"

He smiled at her. "I'm not a very good swimmer, honey, I might drown. Eat your sandwich."

Nicole took another bite and said with her mouth full, "I can teach you. I'm one of the best in my class." She chewed quicker. "Let me take you Robert, and we can go somewhere, just you and I; no one has to see us."

He looked at her, unsure what to say next. He placed his hand gently on her and began moving his palm up and down her leg. "Um, Robert." She searched for the plate to place the uneaten sandwich on, Herman guided her. "I'm getting my pains again, and you remember those pads you brought me? The ones you bought for me a couple of weeks ago? They are not good; they hurt me."

His hand stopped. "What? You have pain now?" He didn't want to know about her feminine problems. When he was young, his sister had shared nothing like that with him. He had never wanted to look at Beth's used underwear when she threw them in the basket. It was only when he had molested a few girls that he had seen it, and it turned him off. A few days after he had taken Nicole, her monthly episode had come, and she asked him to buy her pads. He didn't know what to buy her, so he had to guess. He had driven miles to an out-of-town pharmacy, worried that walking in and asking for these things would be too suspicious near his home. Especially since his local pharmacy knew his face, he had given her the package and let her do whatever she had to do alone in the bathroom. He had asked her how long that sort of thing lasted, and she had told him. Then he just stopped talking to her. He wouldn't even come close to her for at least two days, only to bring her food. He had given her a nightgown to wear, but she asked him to buy her some underwear to be more comfortable during her episode. He had agreed and bought her a few pairs from a store far from his house. He refused her a bra. He forbade her from wearing underwear at any other time. Herman would check her now and then, and when she soiled her underwear, he would make her wash them. He didn't care whether she could see or not.

He was looking at her now and felt a small amount of rage build up inside him. He took his hand off her leg. "I thought it only comes once a month?"

"It does," she said carefully. "But it can come early if I'm stressed." She looked in his direction and deliberately bit her lower lip softly.

"Are you stressed, baby?" he asked, confused. "Why? Don't I treat you well?"

She searched for his hand. "Yes, you do Robert, but I'm stressed because I don't see the sunshine at all. I can't feel the ocean breeze on my skin. If I can't have those things, sometimes I get very stressed, then I bleed all the time."

Herman suddenly felt helpless, his rage increasing inside him. *What am I supposed to do now? She expects me to take her to the beach?*

"Baby, listen to me," he said, trying to keep his voice soft and level. "I can't take you outside. I just can't. What do you expect me to do?"

Nicole could sense he was becoming angry. "Robert, it's ok, I understand. Maybe we can go somewhere together where no one is around, a part of the coast. Just me and you. Then I could swim for a while, and you can watch me."

He thought about this. *Maybe I could inject her, then take her to a secluded beach area in my van. Let her swim in the ocean and then bring her back. But then I would have to take off her mask. Could it be possible? Maybe I could wear my mask while she swims so she can't recognize me. Yes, I could do that. I just can't stand her being in pain.*

"I will think about it, ok baby? Maybe I can find a way."

Nicole smiled at him. "Yes Robert, thank you. I think it would be great. We could have such a good time. Don't you trust me? You know I'm well behaved."

Herman stood, feeling defeated. He walked to the door and turned to look at her for a moment. "I do trust you, baby, yes you are very well behaved, and I love you very much for that. Let's see what happens. I'll be back later to see you." He left and locked the door. Nicole felt defeated, she began to cry softly, she knew he would be watching her, but she didn't care. Her tears were real; she was crying

346

for her freedom.

Chapter Fifty-Four

Herman returned to his living room and sat down, watching her on the monitor. Nicole was crying. *Shit, why is she crying now? She was fine a minute ago! What have I done now? What does she expect? Haven't I been good to her?*

He changed the channel back to regular TV. He needed to know the latest updates on her search. *Where were they looking for her,* he wondered? The TV anchor explained the current statewide search underway, and police were searching all areas of interest, including bushland and coastal areas. *I knew it, coastal areas! Nicole knows this, I'm sure, and she's trying to trick me into letting her swim in the ocean, so I'll be caught. Why would she do that to me?*

He stood and started pacing the room. *What's she trying to do? Why am I being so nice to her? Why aren't I doing what I want with her? That's why I brought her here, isn't it? And now she's taking advantage of me.*

"No!" he shouted. "She is not like that! She is good! She just wants to stay healthy; it's you who are ruining her!" He fell to his knees and cried out, putting his hands to his face. Suddenly, there was a loud knock on his door. He looked above his hands. Panic tore through him instantly. He stood and tiptoed to the door and waited silently. The knock came again, but this time harder. *Who would knock on my door? Who knows, I live here? Maybe it's The Hood? Shit! Who the fuck is this.?* "Um, hello? Who is it?" he asked, forcing his voice to sound normal.

There was a moment of silence; then he heard a firm voice on the other side of the door. "Hello? Mr. Kapper? Herman Kapper? My name is officer Jenkins, and I'm with the police. Could we talk to you for a moment, please?"

Herman's body became weak, and fear rushed through him like a virus; his breathing became erratic. He forced himself to relax and responded calmly, "Just a minute."

What do I do? I don't have a gun! How did they find me? How did they know I was here? Someone told them someone found out who I was.

He thought quickly and took off all his clothes except his underwear. He ran his hands roughly through his hair and unlocked the door. He opened the door just enough so they could see he wasn't dressed. He barely opened his eyes to give them the impression he'd just woken up. "Yes? Hello," he said, slurring his words.

****

Police officer Jenkins was tired. He and his partner had been knocking on doors all day, and they were finally on their last one. He was a little surprised that someone would be sleeping in the middle of the afternoon but figured the guy must work nights. "Sorry to bother you, Mr. Kapper. Did we wake you?"

Herman leaned against the door. "Um, I usually take an

afternoon nap, I have a medical condition, and my meds are pretty strong."

The police gave Herman a quick smile. "Oh, I see, well yes, I can understand that. Anyways, we are currently investigating all the students who attended the All Saints Anglican high school reunion party some weeks ago. Were you at that party, Mr. Kapper?"

"Oh yeah," he said. "I went to that, but I left pretty early. I wasn't feeling so good, so I left early and went home."

The police officer checked his notes. "Ok sir, it's just that we don't have any record of anyone seeing you there that night. May I ask what time?"

"Um, I think it was early, yes, around 5.30 pm. I went there early because I had a few things to do around town beforehand and then headed to the party. When I got there, I guess I was still too early. There was no one there, not even the teachers, so I waited for a while. I thought I had the wrong address. Then I felt very sick, so I just left and came back home."

The other police officer looked at this man, trying to judge his honesty. "You didn't see anyone else there that was hanging around? Anyone suspicious, maybe?"

Herman slowly shook his head. "No, not that I can remember. Oh shit, it's about that guy, right? Um, what was his name? Yeah, Brady, shit. That's right, murdered. Oh my god, yeah, I went to school with him." Herman paused for a moment. "Yeah, Jesus, that guy, he was always a good guy, and everyone loved him. How could anybody do that to him? Do you know when his funeral will be? I would like to pay my respects. Do you have his family's phone number?" Herman's voice rose. "I should ring them and tell them how sorry I am. So terrible. I hope you catch those bastards."Officer Jenkins was tired of it all. His legs were aching, and they hadn't eaten yet. "Sir, we cannot give out that information. I'm sure if the family wants you to be a part of that, they will reach out."

"Oh yes, of course, look, maybe I should help." He sounded

slightly hysterical. "I can be good at helping. My doctor says I shouldn't sleep so much, anyway, maybe I can help you."

The police officer threw up his hand. "That won't be necessary, sir. Thank you for your help. We will contact you if we need any further information from you." They turned and walked to their car.

Herman came out and followed them. "Yes, sure," he said, more excited. "I would love to be a cop. I wanted to be a cop all my life. My father was an undercover cop. He put away some bad ones. Do you think I can ride along with you guys sometime?"

The two police officers couldn't wait to get away from him fast enough. They didn't answer him. Just before they got into the car, Jenkins said to him. "You should get inside now, sir. Get some rest. Hope you're feeling better."

Herman stopped on his front lawn, smiling and waving at them like a schoolboy would, as they were reversing out of his driveway. He turned around, slipped back into his house, and closed the door.

The police drove off, and Jenkins turned to his partner and shook his head. "What a nutcase. That guy looks like he couldn't even tie his shoelaces. It looks like he's a dead end as well. Let's eat."

Chapter Fifty-Five

Herman rushed back down to the basement, over to Nicole, and sat beside her. His breathing slowed. She was completely unaware of what had just happened. "Robert? You ok?"

He smiled down at her. "Yes my baby. I just went out for a quick run to get my strength. Are you hungry? Thirsty? Can I get you anything?"

Nicole put her arm out to feel where his hand was. Instead, she touched the bare skin of his leg. She moved her hand nervously up towards what she thought would be his hand, but it was still bare skin. She shivered.

"Where are your clothes, Robert?" Her voice was brittle.

"I'm not naked, baby, see?" He took her hand and pushed

\

her fingers gently against the side of his underwear. "You see? Not naked."

"Oh, ok, that's good. Why are you only wearing your underwear?"

"I went for a run and was about to take a shower," he explained. "I just came to see if you needed anything; besides, you can't see me naked anyway. You've got your mask on." He laughed a little, and he watched her reaction.

She forced another smile. "Yes, of course, that's true, ok you take a shower. I don't need anything right now except for those pads. You promised me Robert, you remember?"

The smile left Herman's face. "Yes, I remember," he said evenly. There was a moment of complete silence. He stood up and pulled his underwear down to his ankles. She froze and didn't say anything.

"What pads do you need now?" he asked in a commanding voice.

"Um, just buy the next size up for me, Robert. That should be fine, and then my pain will go away quicker."

He walked over to her and leaned down. She trembled in silence. "I hope so, my baby, cause I can't have you dirty at all, ok? You know I hate that when you're dirty." The words were menacing. He touched her chest and stroked it. "Robert? Please? No."

He kept rubbing her chest just above her breasts, the nightgown adding no protection. "It's ok baby; you know how good I am to you. If you are perfect and clean, everything will be fine ok? You know that, don't you? Hmm? How perfect you are?" He slid his fingers further down, brushing over her nipple. She flinched.

"Please, Robert, don't, please, if you truly love me, you won't. I want us both to be perfect. We both have to be ready."

He stopped and pulled his hand slowly away. "Yes, my love, of course. You are right. It has to be perfect." He leaned over and kissed her forehead softly. "I will be back later, ok, rest now." He stood and saw how aroused he was. Herman fought his urge and quickly left, naked, from the basement. He went straight upstairs and logged onto his computer. He found a Red Room he was looking for and switched on the TV monitor to watch her. He then turned back to the screen and watched the rape of a young girl. She was bound with rope, and he didn't care whether it was real or not; it looked real enough. He looked at Nicole on his monitor, then back at the computer screen. He did this while satisfying himself, crying out her name over and over again.

Chapter Fifty-Six

After Herman switched to the news, his eyes became glued to the screen and his mouth opened in complete disbelief. The story had just broken. The case of the east coast slasher was now believed to be responsible for the recent mutilation and killing of Brady Wightly and the brutal killings of six people five years ago. They reopened the prior cold case. A nationwide manhunt was on. Police still hadn't determined if Nicole Anderson, the missing fourteen-year-old girl, had fallen into the hands of the slasher or if she was located somewhere else. The news anchor suggested the killer possibly kidnapped Nicole Anderson, and they all feared for the worst. Police said the killer was also suspected of the recent kidnapping and torturing of a young woman. They hadn't been able to identify the slasher and said their investigation was intensifying.

. Herman became immediately furious. He flew into a rage, standing up and pacing his living room. *This fucking hood, he's ruining everything! The cops will be much more intent on finding Nicole because of this fucking guy!*

He wanted to find The Hood and confront him. But had no proof of who he was or if he even knew Herman. The anchorman asked a police spokesperson if the victims' release were connected. Herman stopped mid-pace and stared at the TV; the spokesperson replied that so far, the police were not releasing any more details, but they were not confirming or denying any connection with what had happened to the girl.

"Fuck!" Herman screamed. This was terrible for him. If they caught him with Nicole, they would blame him for Annie's kidnapping, the one he paid thousands of dollars to save. He could never prove that. They would also blame him for other murders the Hood committed, and The Hood would get away with everything. Maybe he would have to disappear, take Nicole with him, somewhere they could be safe together.

Herman's hands began to sweat as he flicked his monitor to one of his Rooms. The bids on the girl in the Red Room he was watching were things he knew he could never put Nicole through. He was beyond caring about anyone else except his love for her.

Knowing she was comfortable in his basement gave him a secure feeling he hadn't felt since his sister Beth was alive. However, he still hadn't decided what to do with Nicole, which weighed heavily on him. *Maybe I could let her go eventually, but I don't know when that would be.* He wanted to keep her forever and grow old with her, but he knew that could never happen. He would have to either eventually let her go or kill her. If it came to killing her, he would choose a painless death. *A deep long, forever sleep, and I would hold you, my love and die with you.*

Do I really want to put her into the seedy world of child pornography? And other deep dark web activities? His mind was racing with decisions. *She can make me so much money. Yes, but then she's soiled? Destroyed? I can't ruin her. She must remain pure.* All those fantasies he had about her, all the things he wanted to do to her. He was touching himself every night in frustration. *Now she is here at my mercy. She is mine to do whatever I want with.* But he was afraid of her. She controlled his every thought. When he felt excited and wanted to take her, he would touch himself, sometimes in the shower, when she couldn't tell or watch her on the monitor instead. *She makes me too afraid to go near her and try something like that.* Herman remembered the first time he was washing her in the shower, and she had brushed up against him and flinched when she realized his dick had touched her skin. She had moved away from him, and he had silently cried. The water from the shower hid his tears, even though she couldn't see them. He forced his crying to be quiet, exploding in his mind, saying sorry repeatedly. When he couldn't control his fantasies about what he wanted to do to her, he would touch himself, then cry and sob—telling her on the monitor how sorry he was. Now he risked losing it all. They would catch him because of the fucking Hood, and he would never have the chance for Nicole's true love. *That cannot happen,* he asserted. *He must die! The Hood must die! It is the only way.* He was sure The Hood was setting him up. *How to find him?* That was the key. *How to find him?*

Herman switched off the TV and stared at the blank screen. He was feeling a fear that made it suddenly hard to breathe. There may be more of his old school friends being tortured and raped in front of him. Herman was certain The Hood would have information about his clients. *What if the police caught him and got a hold of him? Then they could find their way here and take Nicole.* He was trusting her much more now. *I was wrong about her trying to trick me. She just wanted to be home, that's normal, I can forgive her for that, and she is such a good girl. She never screams and barely cries.* They had become much closer, but it also made his emotions even more vulnerable for Herman. He was submissive to her now. She had convinced him to let her leave the mask off when he wasn't in the basement. "What does it matter?" She had asked him. "You're not here for me to see you, and when you come, you just tell me, and I'll put it back on for you."

At first, he reacted with fear. *She will see everything in my red room and despise me for them. The whips and chains, and my special sex chair. She will completely freak out.* He told her he thought it wasn't a good idea because he had very disturbing things in the basement that she shouldn't see. It was for her own good that she should leave it on, but she was insistent. "My eyes hurt when it's on, and it's ok about your basement. I know that whatever you have here, you're not going to use to hurt me. I guess as long as it's not dead bodies or anything."

He had smiled at that, and she was right; he wouldn't use any of those things on her, so he had agreed. The day she took her mask off for the first time, he had quickly closed the basement door and rushed upstairs to put the video feed on his large TV screen to study her every move. He had waited for the shocked look on her face that he was sure would come. He had watched her move nervously around the room, brushing her hand against some of his whips and chains that were hanging in various places.

This aroused him watching her touching these things. Nicole had gone over to his special chair and walked around it, studying it. She was clearly in shock. She then went into the bathroom, sat on the toilet, and cried. He was heartbroken, but it's what he expected. He had gone down and told her to put her mask back on; he was coming in. She did as she was told, and he had stayed with her for hours, convincing her he would never use those things on her. Eventually, she had believed him, and things became much better. She still had to wear her mask, though, when he was around. He had asked her to take close-up photos of her eyes with a cheap Polaroid he had, so he could stare at her eyes when he was away from her. She did this for him without question. Things had become so good, but they also had changed. Now he had to beg her to let him shower with her, but she would have to keep her mask on. *Why do I beg her?* She had let him shower with her sometimes, and she would also let him wash her, but she would not let him touch her everywhere. She asked him to please not touch her in the places she didn't like. He did whatever she wanted, and when she washed her private parts herself, he would touch himself right next to her in the shower. He wasn't sure if she knew, but sometimes he was sure she did. She never said anything, though.

She knows, he convinced himself. Herman knew he could just ignore her requests and do whatever he wanted with her. That, however, would destroy her purity, and she would be uncontrollable and hate him. He could never deal with that. She had such powerful control over him, and he was weak every time he was around her. He checked her monitor now and noticed she wasn't in bed. *She must be in the bathroom.* He switched the camera to the bathroom feed and saw her in the shower. He went through the kitchen and down to the basement, went to the bathroom door and knocked.

"Nicole, baby?" there was a brief silence. "Yes Robert, I'm here." Herman rested his head against the door.

"Can I come in?"

"Robert I'm in the shower. Can you wait a minute? I'm almost finished."

He closed his eyes and cried lightly. He turned and leaned against the door and banged the back of his head very hard against it three times.

"Robert? What's wrong? Are you alright? Wait, I'm coming, wait for me please."

He put his palms to his face and slid down the door to the floor. He cried uncontrollably.

"Robert?" He heard her soft voice on the other side of the door. "I'm here now, Robert. Do you want me to open the door?" He could let her open the door if he wanted to, but she would see his face. It would be all over then, she would have to stay with him forever. Then he could never let her go. The urge to open the door was unbearable for him, he asked her with a sobbing voice, "Do you have your mask on?"

"Yes, Robert, I do."He felt the door move against his back. "Robert, you're in the way, please move so I can come out." He shifted his body and the door opened, she crouched and felt for him, and found his arm. She sat down on the floor next to him and found his head and stroked his hair. He leaned over and buried his head in her stomach and cried.

"It's ok Robert, it's ok, I'm here now."

Chapter Fifty-Seven

Bob was leaning over Danny's shoulder and had no idea what he was looking at. It amazed him how experienced this guy was and how valuable guys like him were to law enforcement in catching cyber criminals.

These particular people weren't cybercriminals. Bob thought. *They were animals! These were actual people kidnapping, raping, torturing, and killing other people and children for money.* Bob watched Danny work, he thought about the phone call he had received from Jim; they were still trying to track down the mysterious informant from the east coast slasher case, but to go further, they needed permission from the AFP's head office commissioner.

Bob had told Jim to tell those fuckers they had better cooperate, or he would expose their reluctance to the media. This prompted a harsh phone call from Neville Johnson, telling Bob if he even went near a newspaper or camera crew, he would be busted down to dog catching at the local pound. Bob's threat did seem to work though, not long after, the AFP had phoned Jim back and told him they would send all the information they were allowed to disclose to Bob's office. It was probably just a way for them to save their asses, but he didn't care. He had also received a call from Sherry, updating him about the missing Anderson girl. There was a delay in getting Annie to the station, and as soon as she could, they would be down there. Bob had explained that he was tied up for a while anyway, so hopefully, they could go through some photos with the girl by the time they were both free. He had also told her they still had no progress on Nicole's disappearance, and they couldn't say if Nicole was connected to

Annie's kidnapping.

The task force was working day and night. He promised to keep her informed and in the loop on the case as much as possible. Whether he had permission to or not, in his mind, Sherry's help was a critical part of the investigation. Danny was talking to him, and Bob leaned down over his shoulder. "Ok." Danny said, "Here we go! These are the Red Rooms and all their sites that we can choose from."

Bob leaned in closer. Danny continued. "Each of these rooms costs around $10,000 to $50,000 to join, depending on the rooms and what you are looking for. The money needs to be paid in Bitcoin. There are many to choose from, and from what you told me to look for, I haven't come across anything with an image of a hood yet. I typed in murder and torture. There are quite a few, some may be fakes. I can try to narrow it down."Bob looked at the screen, and there was a list of dark screens with red borderlines around the edges and strange symbols in the top corner of each site. Inside these borders was a piece of information or a conditional agreement in bold red writing.

"Click on this one Danny, let's see what it says." Danny clicked on a site that showed images of women screaming in agony. He slowly read the introduction.

Welcome you. If you came here, it means that you, like us, are connoisseurs of these wonderful genres as Snuff Death, Gore Cry Necro, penalty punishment. Torture.

Be warned! Onlookers and fans have no place here. We won't tolerate them. To have access to our private collection, you must have Bitcoin. Not everyone can afford it, but only true connoisseurs and foodies. Those who want to join us will have access to the collection of private material! Be notified about the online torture broadcasts of executions and much more. As mentioned above, not everyone can because it is expensive to get to us, but if you are not confused, read below how to do it. 1) Fee for access is 00.188 BTC, which should be sent to 1GUsj5kyres8bnkgYDJdgTK7Hsk

2) Send us a message in which you specify only the address from which you paid for access

(igh4FD842ivdyjmgfchjhc54dhntttor.com)

3.) If you did everything correctly, we will send you further

actions to take.

We once again remind you only need to send with no

additional characters. The subject is available and specifies

what you want. We do not answer any other letters. We are

looking forward to being true connoisseurs! Everyone else can

leave.

Bob stared at the screen for a few more seconds, still resting his hand on Danny's shoulder. "What does all that mean Danny? How much is 00.188?"

Danny was still looking at the screen. "Sir, BTC is a Bitcoin cryptocurrency, and it works out to be about $13,000 Australian. Bob whistled softly. *This would get expensive,* but that wasn't a problem since his task force had unlimited funds.

Danny continued. "Sir, that $13,000 is just for only one room. There are hundreds of red rooms; each room has a joining fee from around that amount and upwards."

Bob was still looking at the screen as Danny searched more rooms. "Sir, some of these rooms are for spectators only, which means they cannot take part in the actual murder or torture of the victim. I mean, they can't tell whoever is doing the murder what to do." He paused. "Other rooms can. Whoever is the highest bidder gets to call the shots on how the person dies or how she's raped and tortured."

"Danny, I want you to join a few of these rooms, pay whatever needs paying. I want you to look for the rooms where this sick fucking guy is hiding. Narrow it down to the site where his sick customers can participate specifically in the torture, rape, and murder of people. Can we do that Danny?"

Danny looked at the screen. "Um, it will be very difficult, Sir. They use cryptic IP addresses that send the user's address worldwide. It bounces from country to country. They could be physically here in Australia, but their IP address might be in, say, Korea. It's almost impossible to know, but I will do my best, sir."

Bob felt somewhat reassured but not hopeful. *God,* he thought, *What happened to good old standard police work?* Danny interrupted his thoughts. "Sir, um sir, I'm going to need to watch some of these rooms because some of them don't specify what happens to the victim until people bid. I'm not sure if I can handle all of that."

Bob looked at the young guy and could tell he was already afraid. "Alright, son, you get in these rooms and get your partner next to you to help. When these sick fucking shows start, you let me know, and you can both move away from the screens. Then Jim and I will take over, but we will need you close to guide us on anything we might need to type, ok son?"

Danny nodded. He turned back to the screen. "Sir, I would like to bring in another guy who is even more clued up on this than I am. He would be a big help, I think."

Bob thought for a moment. "Ok son, get him in, but I want to see him first and talk with him before he goes ahead and does anything. Is that clear?"

Danny nodded. "Yes sir!" Danny picked up the phone, called his cybercrime buddy, said a few words to him, then told him to get his ass down here and hung up. He began typing again. "Ok!" Danny said out loud. "Here we go!"

***

It took a couple of days for his accounts to be verified by whoever was running the rooms, and now he was a lifetime member of many of them. They had created six fake accounts so far and spent over $180,000 in cryptocurrency. They were searching not just for a hooded man but for anyone else that wore masks or some sort of headwear. Danny was becoming increasingly disturbed by what he was watching. The perpetrators in the rooms were all hooded. Danny needed more information and was told it was coming. He had typed in the name, The Hood, and came across one currently closed room. He was monitoring it. The searches between himself and his partner had yielded three murders so far, all execution-style. The one Danny was watching now had a banner explaining they would bring a woman in. She didn't know what would happen to her, only that she was going to die. Danny watched as two masked clown figures dragged her into a broken-down unpainted room and tied her up. They tortured her with knives and burned her with hot metals until they finally slit her throat. Danny wasn't sure how much more he could watch. He tried to keep it hidden, but he felt he would collapse at any moment in despair, crying out for the victims. His partner had to watch children being sexually abused and said he wanted to quit.

Danny was grateful he didn't have to watch too much of that. They weren't looking for pedophiles right now. Since their conditioning took them both to child sex sites, they never had to watch those videos for very long to catch the people behind them. They only had to trace their IP addresses. Most of the pedophilia they found were thankfully just photos, but they still had to look through the photos in case they were a missing person.

There were some videos, however, that weighed heavily on their minds. That poor woman being tortured and murdered didn't seem to bother him as much as the brutal sexual rape and murder of a child. He admired the detectives who had strong enough stomachs to watch it all and still keep their shit together. Now they had to watch these snuff films because they needed to identify this Hood's next victim, so maybe they could find out who he was. It was too much to endure right now. He turned around and looked for the detective. *What was his name again? Sharot, yes, that's right, where is he?* But he couldn't find him.

"You ok there, son?" Jim Levin said. "You need some help?"

Danny turned back to the screen. "Um, I think so Sir, ahh."

Jim got up from his desk and walked over. "What's up son? Do you need a break? Why don't you get some air? I can take over for a while."

Danny was grateful. "Thank you, Sir, yes, I think that's a good idea."

Danny got up and walked out of the room without saying a

word to anyone.

"Ah, Danny!" Jim called out to him, not understanding the next step at all. "Are we ready for this?"

Danny turned around. "Oh yes sir, sorry, um, just hit enter, and that's it."

Danny gave him a reassuring smile and Jim turned to the screen. Bob had told him to monitor the boy, and if there was any sign, he might lose it, he was to relieve him and give him a break for a while. Jim looked for the enter button and hit it. The screen changed in front of him, and a man was beaten with a large stick. The victim was hogtied and half-naked. Two men were standing over him with hoods on, both had long canes in their hands and were taking turns beating the man all over his body except his head.

"Jesus," Jim said softly out loud. He couldn't believe people paid thousands of dollars to watch this shit. He wondered what it would be like to just burst into that room, rip the large

379

cane stick out of their hands, and start beating *them* with it. Then throw them in cuffs. *Now that would be a show.*

Bob was at the station with Sherry and Annie, they were waiting for Annie to give a more detailed description of The Hood. He took his phone out to call Jim's number. "Hey, buddy, how are we doing on the dark web there?"

Jim was looking at the screen. A girl was hanging upside down, being whipped. "Um, I'm on it, partner. I'm watching some fucked up shit at the moment. I had to relieve one of your tech boys. I think he's outside throwing up."

"I need you to get those other D's off their asses and put them in front of those screens, it's about time they got in the deep end."

Jim was smiling. "Ok boss, but I don't think they're gonna like it, but I'm on it."

***

Bob closed his phone, he thought about the report the AFP had sent him and Jim. *Shit! I'm sure there were a few cops in that task force who were connected to the slasher case; bringing it up would definitely be sensitive and embarrassing for them, fuck 'em.*

"I'm gonna need the best sketch artist you have here. Where is he or she?"

The desk Sargent thought for a moment. "He, I think is at home." Bob walked over to him. "Get him down here now, tell him it's urgent. If he gives you any flack, tell him to look for another job sketching tourists." The Sargent picked up the phone and called.

This was going to be a long night, he thought.

****

Annie gave the artist the most detailed and closest description she could. When the artist had finished and studied it, he felt reluctant to show it to Bob Sharot. Bob looked at the sketch. "You're fucking kidding me? What the fuck is this? Robin hood?"

The sketch artist swallowed hard. "That's the details she gave me boss, even right down to the colors and stitches in the hood."

Bob looked at it again. "Well, a lot of good that's gonna

fucking do. Imagine I send that out statewide?" Bob was angry and frustrated that this was going nowhere. "Ok, have the sketch sent over to the task force office and give it to the tech boys on the computers. Tell 'em that's what we're looking for in those Red Rooms.

Bob was shaking his head; *this just gets worse and worse.*

Chapter Fifty-Eight

Nicole's disappearance was added to the task force investigation and pursued vigorously. It had been two-and-a-half weeks since she disappeared. Bob was increasingly frustrated about why they, or anyone else, still knew nothing about finding her. They interviewed all her friends, tracked down all known sex offenders in the area, and brought them in for questioning. After the second day, the media had already picked up the story and ran daily stories about her disappearance. The community had gotten involved and placed posters of Nicole's smiling face all over the state. They completely saturated social media with her photos, and sympathy poured in on all the chat platforms. Her friends had told police about her last movements, and they had searched the beach area where she was last seen. This included all the bushland by foot and helicopter. Hundreds of locals had joined the police, walking the same pathway she had been up the old steps, to the top road. They had found nothing in the surrounding bushland of the secluded beach. Some bits and pieces of rubbish they found, they bagged and sent off for fingerprints. The parents had put up a reward from a go-fund-me page posted on the internet. So far, it had raised almost $100,000. They were also on TV nearly every day pleading for their daughter to come home and, if someone had her, to please let her go. He still hadn't found a solid connection between his case and the Andersons'. The twenty police officers put in charge to check on each person's whereabouts leading up to the day of that reunion party and then on the night, had finished. Now in his hands were the date and time of Brady Wightly's. Most students had solid alibis at the time of the victim's death; some didn't. Most of those who didn't were finally located and confirmed to have solid alibis. *So that just leaves a few,* Bob thought. *That shouldn't be too hard to sort out.*

For Bob, all the students they located so far could still be in danger. He had to assume the worst. They couldn't protect them all, but they advised them all to take careful precautions at night and not to venture anywhere alone if possible. Solving Nicole's kidnapping, the murder of Wightly, and the Leason rape case would be difficult. He had the toxicology test results back from the pathologist and the substance test from the Leason girl. The same drug was used on both of them, which confirmed what Bob already suspected. He was hoping he could solve them in one go. The thing that nagged at him still was whether this could all be the work of one person. The question was constantly swimming around his head, never sure if he'd pin down an answer. *Why would one person who may or may not have known these victims, and who knew each other, torture and kill one of them, torture and rape the other, and then let her go?* He knew it had to be someone in one of those Red Rooms. Maybe someone was making specific requests, paying these people and making special bids for what they wanted to be done. Or, it could be the Red Room owner themselves. *So many questions and no answers.*

Bob hoped that Danny and the other techs were getting somewhere because he needed a miracle right now. Little did he realize, but it was about to come.

Chapter Fifty-Nine

Bob arrived back at the task force office and found Danny buried deep in his computer. "Hey Danny, how's it going? Did you get something yet?"

Danny looked up at his boss. "Sir, I think I got something, there is a room called The Hood. It's been offline for a while but recently came back on. This guy does everything, murder, rapes, beatings, and of course torture." He tapped a couple of keys on his board. "Here is his profile image."

Bob looked at the screen. It was an image of a Red Room. A lot like the others, except this image, showed some sort of basement with whips and chains and sex toys. In the image's foreground, there was what Bob thought looked to be a potato sack, torn apart and sewn back together in the shape of an executioner's hood. Bob pulled out the sketch from Annie Leason's description and studied it. "I'll be damned, that's it! That's our man! Danny, can you get a trace on the scumbag's IP address?"

He was squeezing Danny's shoulder now; Danny was shaking his head slowly. "I'm not sure Sir, I've already tried the whole site, including his IP address is encrypted. I have paid to get in, it cost us a lot of money, around $30,000. There is no guarantee, but it does look to be our guy. I can keep trying to hack into his server, but I will need time."

Bob patted his shoulder, "Get on it, kid, get on it."

"Yes sir," Danny said without looking back up.

Chapter Sixty

Nicole's scheme to placate him was working. When she first tested her idea, she was afraid she was too submissive. She thought if she gave him too much too quickly, he might just lose control and hurt her in ways she couldn't imagine. When he finally allowed her to remove her face mask, she had seen all the things he had supposedly prepared for her, and it shocked her. So much so she wanted to vomit.

Instead, she went to the bathroom and cried; she knew he was watching, but her tears were real. If he tried to use all those things on her, she would rather commit suicide than go through all that torment each day. He promised her he wouldn't, and she truly believed him. He was resting like a child, seemingly asleep on her lap. It had been at least an hour since she'd been afraid to open the door to him.

He could have come in at any time, and she knew that, but she was sure she had his will in control now. She lowered her head down and whispered his name. There was no response. She said it again, still nothing. *Is he sleeping?* She couldn't help but take the risk, it was dangerous, she could ruin everything, but she had to know, her only chance to know. So slowly and gently, she lifted her hand to her face and pulled the mask from her eyes. She looked down and finally saw the man that had kidnapped her and held her for so long. She saw his medium-length thick dark hair, his firm jaw, and tanned skin.

I know you; I have often seen you at the beach; I caught you looking at me so many times. Oh, it's you.

When she saw him at the beach, she had thought he was handsome. Even though he was much too old for her, she had enjoyed his attention. Now she hated it, she hated him, and she hated this place. She desperately wanted to leave and go back to her family. She was always sick with worry for her mother, who she knew had to be broken. Tears slowly fell from the corners of her eyes, and as she pulled the mask back over her eyes. She needed to be strong. She needed to keep doing what she was doing if she was going to make it out; It was working. She had complete control over him. When she told him not to touch her in her private places, he didn't. He obeyed her like a child. Whenever she wanted anything, he would get it for her. In exchange, she allowed him to wash her, to bathe her, even though she couldn't see him in the shower. She knew he was next to her, looking at her. She also knew what he was doing to himself while they were in the shower. She could hear his short rapid panting. She did her best to ignore it; she let him because if it meant that he would not touch her in bad ways, then it was ok. She was grateful for wearing the mask when that happened because she didn't have to watch him.

Chapter Sixty-One

Bob was at a desk in the task force office when Danny called him over. "What's up Danny? Tell me you got good news."

Danny kept his eyes on the screen. "I think so, Sir, The Hood's room has just announced that he will have a show starting soon. It doesn't say exactly when, but just says to stand by for another mutilating experience."

Bob was anxious. *Who the hell was this going to be? And how do we stop it?* "Ok Danny, how are we going to get a trace on this prick?"

Danny was silent for a moment. "At the moment, Sir, I'm still trying to trace his IP, but it's extremely difficult. The address is so well encrypted it's going to take a while, and I can't guarantee if I can crack it. Sir, may I suggest we contact the FBI in the states and ask them for advice. Maybe they have a new system they could share with us. They have done it before with major pedophiles and drug rings. It probably wouldn't hurt to try." Bob knew the kid was right, but the last thing he wanted was for his department to look incompetent to another department. "Ok, kid, make contact with them and their cyber department. See if you can get any hits from them. Maybe we can save someone's life here before it's too late."

"Yes sir, I will get on it now."

Bob walked away feeling slightly deflated. They had no new leads and nothing on the missing fourteen-year-old. He was convinced she was either being held captive or they were too late, and she was dead. Jim came up to him. "How are you doing, buddy?" Putting his hand on Bob's shoulder. Bob sighed.

"Ahh, you know, not so fucking great.

Chapter Sixty-Two

Mrs. Parkman hadn't been able to sleep since her husband had died. She would sometimes slip out of bed and sit by her window late at night and dream of the wonderful things she used to share with him. The moon shone straight through into her bedroom, guiding her easily. She loved this time of the night. It was peaceful, and the cool air helped calm her.

She had seen the man walking down the middle of the street and thought he must be drunk. Then a van pulled up beside him, and a large man got out and attacked the other man.

Oh my god, what's he doing? The big man did something to the drunken man, and he fell onto the road.

Mrs. Parkman stood to get a better look and saw the big man turn around and look in her direction. She hid behind her curtain, hoping he didn't see her. She heard the van door close and had peered around the curtain again. The man on the ground was gone.

Oh dear, that man in the van just took him. The van drove off; she tried to read the number plate, but she was too far away. Instead, she went over to her phone and called the police.

Chapter Sixty-Three

Danny had been monitoring The Hood's room when he had shouted to Bob and Jim to come over to his computer. The three of them watched The Hood brutally kill a man and couldn't believe what they were seeing. As soon as they saw the hooded man push a hook-like device through the man's chin, they knew this was their perpetrator. They were completely helpless to save him.

Danny did his best to trace the IP address but was unsuccessful. During the screening, they had gotten a call from another detective that had received some info from the local police. A woman who rang quite a few hours ago reported she was sure she saw a man being dragged into a van and driven off. Bob couldn't believe his ears. Some flatfoot had seriously fucked up and treated the call as just another elderly woman complaining about some drunk making a racket outside her home.

Although Bob didn't know the complete story, he was sure it was related to what they had just watched. Bob and Jim had flown down the stairs and were now driving to the address. Jim asked on their radio for two more cars to join them to do some footwork around the area. They needed to interview the other residents.

Chapter Sixty-Four

The elderly woman invited Bob and Jim in. Bob immediately began grilling her on everything she saw. He went to the window where she claimed to be sitting when she saw the man being taken away in the van. He judged the distance to see if she could have seen more than what she had told the local police.

" Ma'am, you say it was a white van with no windows, but there was a sliding side door. Is that right? Do you think you can remember the license plate? Anything at all?" It was a wild question, and Bob knew it. Even he would have trouble reading a license plate number during the day from where he was standing. Let alone late at night.

The woman just shook her head. "I just saw a drunken man walking down the middle of the road; then a large white van pulls up beside him. A large man got out. I couldn't see his face; it was too dark. He went up to the drunk and did something to him; then the drunk man fell to the ground. The large man opened his side door and put the drunk man inside his van. He closed the door and looked around, and turned in my direction. I was scared he might see me, so I hid behind the curtains. When I heard the van start, I looked down again and watched the van drive off. That's all I saw."

Bob and Jim thanked the woman and left, feeling no closer than they were when they arrived. Then Bob had an idea. He called the task force and told them to set up a secret coded message to all the police radios throughout the city. Their killer may have a police radio. Instead of looking for a white van with a sliding side door, he called it a grey Ford sedan. He asked all eyes to stop and interview anyone driving the description of that van.

"If they have to talk about it on the radio, make sure they

use the code grey Ford sedan instead. Tell them to make something up to give them reasonable suspicion to search the van if they have to. There could be a body in it, and I want everyone to keep a lid on this from the public. We don't want this perp to get wind that we're looking for any vehicle at all. Then at least it might keep him from locking the van up in his garage or dumping and burning it." He knew this was going to be a nightmare. They had little time before the body would be disposed of. The pathologists rated the time of death of Brady Wightly and the East Coast Slasher's victims as within twenty-four hours before being dumped. *Jesus, there must be thousands of large white vans with a sliding door out there, but we have to start somewhere.*

Bob's phone rang as soon as he closed the call. It was Danny, telling him he might have a break in the case of The Hood without getting a trace on the IP address. He can't be certain, but he needed Bob back at the task force office as soon as possible. Bob told him he was on his way. He then phoned Phil, the pathologist, told him to expect another murder victim soon, and informed him of the murder they just had to watch on the deep dark web.

Bob was thinking about what the witness had said. He was sure The Hood injected the drunken man the same way as the others. Jim turned to Bob. "We still got nothing on the Nicole Anderson kidnapping. I guess the one good thing is that she hasn't turned up in this psychopath's Red Room."

Bob nodded. "Yeah, I guess so. I still don't know about that one, Jim. I mean, a girl gets kidnapped, tortured, and raped, then set free. A guy gets tortured, mutilated, and murdered, now a second who also may be connected to the other two, and we still don't know what the connection to the girl is besides knowing each other in school. Then in the middle of all this, a young fourteen-year-old girl gets kidnapped and disappears. It doesn't make sense. We must be missing something."

"Maybe whoever took Nicole thought it would be the right time to take her because everyone would think it was the same maniac doing all the other crazy shit."

Bob shook his head. "No, I don't think so because that would bring even more heat on whoever took Nicole. No, I think Nicole was taken by someone who wanted to take her, whether there was a major police investigation on an unrelated kidnapping or not. I think whoever took Nicole must be obsessed with her and took her despite the risk."

They drove the rest of the way in silence, both thinking hard on their next moves. Bob was thinking about Danny, and what he might have for him. He was also wondering when that body was going to turn up.

****

They got back to the task force office around eight pm, and Bob headed straight to Danny's console. "Hey Danny, talk to me."

Danny was furiously typing. Bob looked at his screen. A dozen different things were going on, Bob understood none of it. "Well, Sir, after The Hood's Red Room show closed down, I sent a ping to the IP address, knowing it would just bounce me around to a dozen different VPN addresses. So I sent it multiple times in a matter of seconds. Instead of waiting the usual one time as most people do, I sent these ping tracers. I created an algorithm that could analyze the header when I sent them. Then it gave me a general server location before it bounced me somewhere else. I isolated the server's last location and then pinged it again to get a more accurate response."

Bob had no idea what the boy was talking about, but it fascinated him nonetheless. "Danny, in English, please, if you can?"

A small smile formed on Danny's mouth. "Well, Sir, it's like the game hide and seek. When someone is hiding from you, and you're counting to twenty before you open your eyes. Basically, in this case, you peek before you reach twenty. Unfortunately, you only see the direction they went to hide in this case.

Bob was frowning. "Ok Danny, so how much of an area are we talking about where he might be hiding?"

Danny looked up at him. "Well, sir, in the hide and seek scenario about the size of, say, a twenty-block radius."

Bob exhaled. "Jesus, that could be hundreds of homes. Ok give me the total area you think it is, and I'll go from there. If I'm not here, give it to Jim or the other task force boys. Good work Danny, keep at it."

Danny turned back to his screen. "Yes Sir, it shouldn't take me too long. Give me about twenty minutes."

Bob squeezed the boy's shoulder and went over to the rest of the task force team to update them on Danny's progress. He also made sure his instruction on the van search was clear and that it was to be kept extremely quiet. Just then, Jim walked over to him. "Bob, I just got off the phone with the pathologists. Phil has confirmed it's the same guy."

It relieved Bob. Now they had only one asshole to look for. However, there was still no word on the Anderson kidnapping. Bob hoped they could kill all their birds together with the one stone. He only prayed that the young girl was still alive.

Chapter Sixty-Five

The Hood woke around midnight. He quickly got up and took a large slug of whiskey. The strong harsh bite of the alcohol burned his sleeping throat and widened his eyes instantly.

He had heard about the witness on his police scanner, but it was too late to do anything about it now. *There would be police everywhere. Don't worry, they can't find your name or address, just relax, there is no way they could have seen who I am.* He put on his overalls and went out to where the body was still wrapped and ready. He went back through his chambers and turned on the police radio, and went out to his garage to open the van door to get the body in. As he came back in, he listened to the police scanner.

They were looking for a grey Ford sedan possibly involved in kidnapping a male victim. The Hood smiled, *well they won't be finding me driving a shit box like that.* The Hood went back to the basement, picked up the body, and put it over his shoulder. He carried it through to the garage and put it in his van, slamming the door shut. The Hood knew where he was going to dump it. He had a beach spot picked out. He hit the button for the electric garage door. As he waited, he checked his loaded pistol just in case. He slipped it between the seats in the console and drove out slowly. The night seemed much darker than usual. He tried to see where the moon was and noticed clouds obscured it. *Good, the darker, the better. As soon as I get rid of this trash, I will shut everything down for a while. Maybe come back online in another few years. This is all getting too risky.* The Hood knew he wouldn't find another customer like the one he had just finished with, not for a long time. He made over $400,000, and with the rest of his Bitcoin, he was now well and truly a millionaire. *I'm done. I don't have to work again for a long time.* The Hood drove through the empty roads, keeping under the speed limit at all times. His van was in excellent condition. There would be no reason for anyone to stop him.

****

Senior constable Roden and constable Fisher were driving out of a small road where they had just spent the last hour solving a domestic dispute. They pulled up at the intersection's stop sign when they saw a white van drive past. At first, the two were silent, then they glanced at each other, reading each other's thoughts instantly. They pulled out and trailed the van from a distance. Fisher got on the radio and relayed the information immediately to the task force team's office.

Bob and Jim and two other detectives on the skeleton crew were still there. They were going over the map that Danny had drawn to plan how they were going to canvas the entire area. It had taken Danny a lot longer than expected, but they now had a fairly strong location to do a house-to-house canvas and check vehicles matching the witnesses' description. They all stopped when the radio message came through, and they listened in silence.

Bob was the first to speak up. "Tell 'em to stay back and follow only; try not to get spotted. Get a backup team with them now, and notify the TAC boys to stand by on alert. How many cars do we have in that area?" *White vans fitting that description being out this late at night? Maybe this could be it.* "Jim, you come with me."

The two police officers trailing the van couldn't quite make out the license plate because they were too far back. They were told to stay back, but Roden was becoming too anxious. If he could nail this bastard, he would be quickly on his way to detective. He slowly increased his speed. Fisher looked over at him. She was worried, but she trusted her partner. Fisher had seen him in action before, and she was sure he could handle this. She also was thinking about the accolades she could get if the two of them could bust this guy. *If it's him.* "I'm gonna pull him over," Roden said.

Fisher suddenly felt the adrenaline surge through her. She checked her utilities and pulled her flashlight from her belt. "I'll let dispatch know," she said.

Roden flashed his lights. The van drove on, keeping the same speed, so he gave the siren a few short bursts. Fisher picked up the handset to call dispatch and tell them what they were doing. Roden watched the van pull over to the side of the road. "Wait," Roden said. "Maybe it's not him. If it was, he'd be running; you wait here, run a check on the license plate for me, ok?" Fisher wasn't sure, it was against protocol to let her partner go out there on his own, but he outranked her. *Maybe he's right; maybe it's not the guy they're looking for.*

She picked up the handset and called in the rego number as she watched her partner pull his flashlight out and walk to the van's driver's window.

***

The Hood had seen the police car at the intersection. He had no reason to worry if they pulled him over. They weren't looking for his van. He had watched them pull out and drive up behind him, so he took his gun out of the console and laid it on his lap. When they flashed their lights at him, he had let his driver's window down to prepare himself. When he stopped, he quickly leaned over and had opened the passenger door just enough so it would open with a nudge. He had moved across to the middle of the seat and waited.

***

The way they were parked, the van obscured Roden from her vision, and she immediately grew anxious. She couldn't just sit there and wait any longer. Fisher got out and turned her flashlight on as she walked around the opposite side of the van.

***

The Hood watched the first cop walk up to his window. As he got closer, he got into position. As soon as he saw the cop's head come into his vision, he fired two times, hitting him in the face and chest. He knew that once he shot him, the other one coming up on the other side would come around to the driver's side.

***

Fisher heard the two shots ring out. She doubled back around to the driver's side, at the same time fumbling for her gun in its holster. She saw her partner collapse on the ground, a bullet wound to his chest and head as she came around. She managed to pull her gun out and point it at the driver's window, trying to see the person in the side mirror. Although she saw no one in the reflection, she decided what she was going to do in seconds. She took the stance and shouted. "Drop your weapon, put your hands out of the window now!" But there was nothing. The Hood quietly exited the passenger door. Fisher heard a noise behind her and spun around, but before she could react, she heard the shot and felt the pressure of the bullet hit her face, she heard another shot, and again, the pressure of the bullet entered her side. She fell to the ground, she could feel the warm blood covering her face, she tried to move but couldn't. She watched as the dark figure walked up to her, she wanted to plead for her life, but her face was numb. She could feel the cold air on her face and could tell some of it was missing. He stood over her and pointed the gun down at her. In slow motion, the gun fired, and the last thoughts that tore through her mind in milliseconds were her whole life, her husband, family, and her mother.

Chapter Sixty-Six

The Hood quickly got back in his van. He could hear the dispatch over the police radio asking for the two constables. He threw the gun on the passenger seat, started his van, and quickly drove off. *Damn, why did they pull me over? Well, they got it now. They would not take me. Damn, I'm good! They weren't expecting that.* He drove fast to the beach area and quickly dumped the body near the edge of the dunes. He got back in his van and drove back to his house at the legal speed limit. He took a different route; it would be longer but safer. The van's registration was in a fake name with a fake address, all he had to do was get back to the house and be safe.

The Hood pulled into his driveway and straight into his garage. He locked the door and pulled out his police scanner. He listened carefully. There was nothing about the two cops he just shot or about the hunt for the man who shot them. *Something's wrong,* he thought. *Why aren't they talking about it? Maybe they think I'm listening.*

The Hood was getting worried. He hadn't expected to be pulled over, and now he was feeling like they were closing in on him. He still felt quite safe in his house though no one knew his address. His neighbors didn't know him, nobody did, but it didn't matter. The Hood decided it was time to go. He had his other car, a four-door family sedan, and plenty of money. If he wanted to, he could always start up again somewhere else. He needed to get the hell out, fast. He got to work. He grabbed what he could, then threw acid on the rest. He had all his hard external hard drives and laptop. His heart raced; they'd be there soon, he was sure of it. He ran back to the car and flicked the switch to open the garage door. He placed his gun under the seat and waited for the door to open.

Goodbye, sweet house, you have served me well, time to get the fuck out and have some fun.

Chapter Sixty-Seven

The two constables had not responded. Bob, Jim, and some other task force detectives were already on their way. When they arrived at the scene, there were three other units already there, the tactical boys were still on their way. They quickly got out and surveyed the damage. There was little they could do. "Jesus Christ, why the fuck did they stop the van? Why the fuck didn't they listen? Doesn't anybody follow fucking orders anymore?"

Jim went over to the others and spoke to them quietly. Two female officers were crying. Jim came back with a solemn look on his face. "Looks like Roden, the senior police constable. He pulled the van over. He's shot first, then his partner obviously got shot trying to rescue him. He killed her almost point-blank,

416

execution-style. We got the license plate; we're running it now."

Bob wanted to scream, but it wouldn't have been appropriate. His mind was racing, he had to think. He suddenly thought of Danny's map. "Ok, I know what we gotta do. Hey everyone, listen up." Bob was raising his voice which got everyone's attention immediately. "Ok, this is what we gotta do. There is no reason to think that this asshole wouldn't still dump his body. For all we know, he has dumped it and is on his way back to his place. We need to cover, no, seal off all the areas around Hastings road, Miller Road, Queens Street, and Rivers Drive. It's a pretty big area, but that's the area we got from our cyber team. Chances are, we can squeeze that area tighter and tighter, and maybe if we are lucky, get a sighting on our psycho. We know he has an IP address in that area, so come on, let's go!" He turned to the other police constables. "Get this area sealed off completely, and the pathologist will be on his way. He turned to Jim. Call the TAC, tell them they can join in search of that area."

Jim came back over to Bob. "Bob we just got a trace

address on the registration of the van; it's nowhere near the area you want us to search."

Bob took his partner's arm. "Listen, my friend; I will guarantee you that address you got is fake! This guy has been one step ahead of us this entire time. He is smart and very fucking clever, I'm going on Danny's hit, now we gotta move."

Jim wasn't about to argue. When Bob had his mindset on something, there was no way of changing it. "Ok partner, I'm with you, let's do this."

They both got in the car, and as they were driving off, they saw a news camera crew pulling up. "God damn it, how the fuck did they find out about this so quick?" Bob shouted at the windscreen, and Jim shook his head slowly.

"Police scanners, my dear boy, everyone's got one." Bob suddenly realized what Jim had just said made perfect sense to him, he got back on the radio and ordered all chatter involving the case to cease and use their mobile phones instead. "The killer likely has a police scanner, so everyone needs to be very careful what they say from now on."

Chapter Sixty-Eight

Nicole was playing a dangerous game. She was letting him get close to her and giving him more and more attention. The risk was he might lose control and hurt her. She knew he could at any moment, and this terrified her. The dangerous risk was in his mind, he could rape her, and she would let him, but so far, she was feeling safer than she had ever felt since he first took her. Now she had to find a way to convince him to release her. The darkest thoughts of all were that he would love her too much and never let her go, or even worse, kill her.

"Robert?" She said soothingly. "Come on, it's time to wake up. I'm cold, I need to be warm. Robert, hey."

He groaned, adjusting his head. She stayed still, waiting for him to get up first. He shifted slightly. "Robert, please come on, wake up, I want to get back to bed. I'm cold, this floor is dirty."

She felt him stir. He groaned again and moved his head further down to her pelvis. He gently tried to push his head between her legs, kissing all around her pelvic area. "No Robert, please don't, please remember?"

He shifted again, softly moaning like a little boy who couldn't get his way. She tried to hold his head still, but he kept forcing it down. "Robert, please don't. I hurt there. Please stop, no don't." She tried to move away, but suddenly he was awake now, and gently tried forcing her legs apart. "Robert, please! Please don't do this! I thought you loved me, you promised me you wouldn't hurt me, please."

He stopped what he was doing for a moment. "Baby," she heard, and she could tell he was looking up at her. "I won't hurt you. I promised you that. I'll never hurt you. I just need to know, baby, I just need to know. I have always wanted to know. That's all, nothing more."

Nicole cried. "No Robert, please I don't like that please don't. It will hurt me. Let's eat something. I'm hungry." She was hoping to distract him, but it wasn't working.

"Just a little," he said, his voice muffled from the bathrobe. "That's all, ok baby? Then I will stop, you know I love you." He pulled the bathrobe apart. She tried to push him away, but he was too strong.

She was crying. "Please Robert. No, no, please stop." Deep down in her secret place that no one ever knew, she always wondered what it felt like when a boy did that to a girl. She had thought that if she ever found the boy of her dreams, she would let him do that to her. But not like this It wasn't supposed to be like this. She sat there, up against the bathroom door, crying, her legs held apart by his hands, she was trying to push his head away, but couldn't. *What did I do wrong? Did I go too far in denying him even to touch me? I let him wash me, isn't that enough? Maybe it wasn't. He is obsessed with me. What will happen after he finishes? What's he going to do then? Rape me?*

All this planning, my idea to get out of here untouched, will be gone, shattered. She forced her mind to think of something else, she was at the beach, the ocean water in her hair, and the sun upon her face, she was treading water. The waves crashing over her head, she was out in deep water but strong enough to stay afloat. She was safe.

Chapter Sixty-Nine

She felt defeated. It shouldn't have happened. Although he had

not penetrated her, she still felt dirty and violated. When he had

finally finished, she was ready to kick and scream if he tried to

put himself in her, but he didn't. He had not allowed her to take

another shower after what he had done to her. Nicole had tried to

convince him to let her clean herself, but he had refused because

he wanted some part of him to remain on her. He had also refused

to let her wear underwear. He got up and led her back to the bed.

Now she was lying alone, her mask was off, and her cheeks were

marked with tear stains.

She was staring at the ceiling. Although not chained to the

bed anymore, she still felt chained to the room. She reached down under the blanket. Her inner thighs were still wet from his saliva, she felt sick. She tried to wipe herself with the sheet. Now she had to wait for him to come back down. He had promised to make her a wonderful candlelight dinner. She decided she would be more aggressive with him. *Being submissive was a mistake.* She needed to show him anger and dominance; it was the only way to gain control of him. *If I keep being so submissive, he will rape me.* She had to be smarter. She would tell him that if he wanted her to love him, he needed to take her for one swim at the beach. It was the only idea she had, but she hadn't yet thought about how she would escape him once there. She would figure that out when the time came. Maybe she could swim away from him. He had told her he wasn't a good swimmer, but she was, and she knew he wouldn't bind her wrists in the water, so she might just have a chance. It was a risk, an enormous risk. *I could drown, but it would be better than living as his sex slave.* She was sure her plan could work. Now she just needed the right time. She would commit to it during dinner.

***

Herman had prepared a beautiful dinner that he had learned from videos and recipes on the internet. He laid everything out on a large tray and lit two candles, two glasses, and a bottle of white wine for the first time. Herman never drank alcohol, but he wanted this time to be special. He had kept some expensive wine when he first moved into the house; the wine was for when he had guests, guests who never came. He had thought about his life the last few days and his purpose for being. The Hood was now gone; he was free to start his special Red Room with Nicole by his side. *Maybe I can convince her to join me, and we could run our Red Room together. I could teach her everything I have learned.* There was torment in his heart, so much to worry about. If the games they were playing with him on the dark web were still out there, even with The Hood gone, then he would never know what might happen next. *If someone knew when I was online watching The Hood and knew who was in my class at school, then maybe he knows where I live. Maybe he knows about*

426

Nicole. His head hurt from all the worry. He couldn't lose Nicole. She was his only source of happiness; he was sure now she loved him. *She let me do that to her; she cried, but she let me.* He had to make a choice; It had been long enough, and he needed to decide what his future would be. He decided tonight would be the most special night of his life.

He breathed in deeply, the scent of her still on his face. Tonight, he would ask her to marry him. Then he would enter her, and they would be together forever. Nicole could then stay with him without a mask and tied up. He wouldn't force her to marry him. If she refused, he would accept it, but that would be the end. It was a world he hated so much. She was his whole life now his only reason for living. There was no one else except his sister Beth. She had been his whole life. *Now Nicole had taken her place.* He knew that now; she was the closest thing he'd ever have to Beth. If he was going to die, he would lay next to Nicole and take her with him. They would sleep together forever.

Herman picked up the syringe he had prepared and placed it on the tray. He carried the tray down to the basement. He called out that he was coming in. He waited for a moment. "Is your mask on, my love?"

"Yes Robert, it's ok."

He came in and went over to the bed. "Can you sit up, please, baby? I have a beautiful dinner for you." He held the tray as he watched her make room on the bed for him, and he placed the tray gently on the bed.

"Oh, it smells good Robert, what is it?"

He smiled at her. "It's something special I made off the internet honey, it's called chicken cordon bleu. I never heard of it, but it looked delicious. I even have candles lit for us, although I'm sorry you can't see them. A bottle of wine too. I think it's a very nice wine."

"Robert, that's wonderful, I'm a little young to drink wine, but you can drink it."

He opened the bottle and poured two glasses. "Oh no, it's ok. There is no one here but you and me, so it's ok. I want you to be mature and enjoy some time with me, ok?"

She nodded. He guided the glass into her hand and brought it to her lips.

"Cheers, my baby, to us forever."

"Cheers Robert, thank you." She took a sip and cringed slightly. He prepared her plate and put a bib around her neck, then cut up some food for her. He gently put it up to her mouth. "I know it's easier for you to eat alone, my love, because you don't need the mask. I wanted tonight to be very special for us because I have a very special surprise."

She chewed slowly on her food, a slight streak of worry quickly crossed her face. "Really? What is it?"

"Shh, eat first, my love, then I will tell you. I want you to enjoy my cooking. I want you to enjoy everything forever with me, my love."

"That's funny," she said, "because I have a special surprise for you too Robert." She chewed some more and waited.

"Well, you can tell me what it is my love. I hope it's good

news." He slipped some food into his mouth and studied her. "Come on," he said with a mouth full of food, "what is it?"

She swallowed. "Let's finish eating first, Robert, then we can talk." They ate in silence for a while, and when they both had enough, Herman put the tray on the floor then turned to her. "Ok, so tell me your surprise, baby, I can't wait any longer." He was watching her, her long golden hair falling down each side of her perfect face, the glow of the candlelight dancing on her perfect skin, the small mask covering her eyes. He loved her more than ever right then.

"You first Robert, I know you have prepared so much for me tonight, tell me."

"Baby, what I have to say is going to change our lives, so I need to hear what you have to say first, please? I insist."

"Well Robert, this is difficult for me to say, but we have been together a long time now, and you have treated me so well. You kept your promises not to hurt me, and I am happy about that. So I want to tell you that, um, I, I love you Robert. I truly do, but I need you to fulfill one thing for me. Just one thing if you can, to complete my love for you."

He looked at her as though she had just saved him, literally just saved his life. "Wh—what? Do you love me? Oh Nicole, oh my baby, I can't believe it." He began crying. She searched for his hand and found it.

"Yes Robert, but my love can only be true if you grant me my one wish."

He dried his eyes. "Yes my love, anything, of course, what is it?

"First, tell me what my special surprise is, Robert. I want to hear that first, ok?"

He sniffed, looked down at the syringe laying on the tray, and pushed it further away from the bed. "Well," he said softly. "Baby, I love you so much it hurts, and I can't wait any longer, so, Nicole Anderson, will you marry me?"

Nicole was shocked, *does he actually think I would marry*

him? He is crazy, Oh God!

"Wow, Robert, that's so sweet of you. Well, um, yes Robert, ok, I will marry you if you grant me my one wish. I will pledge my love to you forever."

He put his hand on her thigh, she could sense him very close to her, and before she could react, he kissed her lips. She forced herself not to react badly, she let him kiss her. Then she gently pulled back and found his hand, softly stopping it from moving further up her leg. "Robert, please let me ask you to grant my wish before we are together properly."

"Yes, my dear love?" he asked. "What is it? Anything."

She took a deep breath, her heart beating fast with fear, then in her softest smoothest voice, the one she used on him when she wanted something, she said. "Well, remember we talked about me going for a swim in the ocean?" Nicole didn't wait for an answer. "I want you to take me to the beach for one last swim before we marry, and then after, I will give myself to you. Then we are together forever." The silence was deafening in the room.

"Ok, baby," he whispered. "We can find a way to do that. I will grant your wish. Now it's time for you to open your eyes to me." He reached up and slowly took her mask off.

Chapter Seventy

Nicole kept her eyes closed for a second, dreading if she should open them or not. If she did, she would see his face, and he may never let her go. She decided to risk it all and slowly opened her eyes to look straight into his. The first thing she saw was the reflection from the candlelight flickering inside his deep green eyes. She saw sadness in them. She studied his face. *Such a handsome boy,* she thought. *A beautiful man, but such a monster, a crazy monster, a sick man in his head.*

She swallowed hard. "Robert, why?" He said nothing. She mesmerized him. Herman had seen her eyes in the photos she had given him, but now they were inches from his, and he felt completely lost in her gaze.

He shook his head. "Oh my dear Nicole, you must know everything now that we are no longer hiding from each other. My name is not Robert." He paused for a moment, then finally said. "It is Herman, Herman Kapper, and you are the most beautiful girl I have ever seen. I want you to see the person who loves you more than anyone ever could. Now we are together forever, just as you said."

She hid the fear, always suspecting the name he told her was fake. Now she was forcing herself, willing herself to remain in control. *I knew it, I took the risk and lost. Now that I have seen him, I know his name. He will never let me go.* He closed his eyes as he leaned towards her, slowly kissing her. Nicole would have to let him. She watched his face come to hers, and he kissed her. She kept watching him as he slowly pulled back, opening his eyes. As he did, she quickly closed hers to let him think her kiss was sincere. Then she also opened her eyes and gave him a small smile. He went to move in again, this time with his body. Closing his eyes again, she gently put her hands up to his chest and stopped him.

He stopped and opened his eyes. "Robert, I mean, Herman please, can we, I mean, we must wait until my wish is granted, only then can I be fulfilled in my heart and be completely happy. You can wait just one more day, can't you? Then we have forever to do whatever you want."

He leaned back from her, his soft eyes still not showing anger. *Good,* she thought, *yes, please stay like that.*

"Alright my love," he said. "Yes, I can wait another day for that because, after that day, we will make love. It will be worth waiting for, but I'm so excited for you now my baby, please let me touch you just a little until then?"

He leaned towards her again; she had to think fast. If she let him touch her, he might lose control like, and this time he won't stop at just one thing. He will go all the way. She knew what she had to do, and slowly stopped him again. "Herman, please unchain me."

He looked down at the manacle around her wrist and then back into her pleading eyes. He took the key from around his neck, unlocked the clamp, and let it fall.

She smiled at him. "Herman, look at me, she reached down and put her hand between his legs. He looked down at what she was doing. "Herman, keep looking at me," she asked him softly. She could tell he was shaking. Nicole put her finger to her lips for him to be quiet. He kept his eyes on her, and she forced her eyes deep into his, both of them locked in a stare. *You need to do what you have to do, do it to survive, no one will ever have to know, not even my mother, but…*

She reached down without taking her eyes off his. She unzipped his pants. He let out a soft moan. "Shh," she whispered. "Look at me." He stared at her in wonderment and amazement. She was sure he was going to cry. She had never done this with her hand before with a boy, but she knew what to do. Her girlfriends had told her. They had all laughed about it. *Boys love it,* they had said. *It's what they expected if you don't let them have sex with you.* She let her mind travel back to the ocean and the chance of freedom. She was treading water again, the sun beating down on her face. She was alone and free. Suddenly her attention turned back to her captor, a warm liquid was all over her hand. She wanted to vomit. He let out another louder groan. Nicole pulled her hand away, hoping she had done it right, still watching his face. She quickly wiped her hand on the bedspread, trying not to look at what she had done, or show disgust.

She whispered to him. "Herman, now you know I am true for you. Now you will take me to the beach tomorrow before we marry and make love. She pulled his head a little closer and kissed the top of it. He was silent, looking like he was in shock. "Now I want you to go upstairs and take a shower and clean yourself up, ok? Then get some rest. Tomorrow is going to be the most special day of our lives. The first day of our new beginning."

He stood without saying a word and fixed himself like a little boy. He sheepishly left her, closing the door behind him. She heard the upstairs door close and lock. She quickly got up and ran to the bathroom to wash her hands thoroughly. She drank some tap water and spat it back out. She looked at herself in the mirror and hated what she saw. *I'm not free yet.* She wanted to cry again, but she refused to let it happen, then she suddenly realized something, *he had never locked the basement door, but the other door was locked! Oh god! He left my mask off.* She knew he could be watching from the cameras all over the basement. He could watch her in the bathroom, but there was nothing she could do about that. She went back and sat on the edge of the bed, looking down at the tray of leftovers. Next to the plate was a large syringe full of a clear liquid.

What the hell is that? Was he going to use that on me? Her eyes carefully darted around the room, remembering where the video cameras were, she didn't dare touch it yet. *He must have left it here by mistake. Or maybe on purpose to test me? If not, will he remember to come back for it? It will be bad if I take it now and he comes back for it, he'll never trust me again. He may even kill me. I could always say I was going to kill myself. He would believe that.*

The revelation hit her hard, and she let out a gasp. *He was going to kill both of us if I refused to marry him!* She lay there staring at the ceiling, trying to figure out what she needed to do. Things had now radically changed. Time was running out. She needed to come up with a plan to save herself. *Maybe I could end it all here with this,* as she looked down at the needle. *No, I won't let him win. I'll fight until the very end.* She began to plan.

Chapter Seventy-One

The next morning, Nicole was ready. She had only one chance. Last night she had waited for hours until she was sure he was asleep. Nicole was never sure what time he went to bed, and she never knew if or when he was watching her. She took a chance. When she thought the time was right, she grabbed the syringe off the tray and hid it under her blanket—praying the whole time that he wasn't watching her. When she had taken it, she sat still, waiting for him to come down and attack her. He never did. Now she was awake and ready to strike the moment he leaned over the bed. She practiced the move in her head repeatedly and was sure she could do it. *Put it in his neck, just jam it in there and push the plunger down.* Then she would run for her life, as fast and far as she could. *He will be bringing me breakfast soon, he always does. Please help me get through this!*

She had given up on her beach idea. He'd never take her there anyway. Besides, there were too many risks and ways it could have gone wrong. The syringe gave her hope. She had to get it right, though, because if she failed, he would know she'd been lying to him all along, just playing with him. She knew this would send him into a wild rage. A rage there would be no coming back from. He would kill her.

Chapter Seventy-Two

Herman woke from a dream that he wanted to last forever. He walked with Nicole along the beach, holding hands and laughing together. People stared at them with envy. She was lying on a bed of flowers, and he was on top of her. His love for her was unfathomable. He couldn't believe what had happened last night, and his mind was still spinning. After he had done exactly what he was told to do, go upstairs, take a shower, clean himself up and go straight to bed. His dreams were vivid and exciting, and he had woken up the same way, springing out of bed as if still in a dream. He slipped on his pajamas and went to the kitchen to prepare her breakfast. Suddenly he was anxious, the reality of the day sinking in. *Why did I promise to take her to the beach? Even if we go somewhere secluded, someone could spot us. Her photo is all over the place. People will recognize her. What if the police pull me over for a random check? Is she in the back of my van? No, we cannot go, and I will tell her strongly. I must be strong with her. She has too much control over me. I have told her so much about my past, even about Beth. That boy I killed in the boy's home, and the others I wanted to kill. She knows everything now, even my name and what I look like. She can't ever leave this house.*

He finished making her breakfast and looked for the serving tray. *Where is that damn thing?* He grabbed another one, placed her breakfast on it, and headed down the stairs, reminding himself to be strong. He was about to announce that he was coming when he remembered she no longer needed a mask. *Oh yes, that's right, her beautiful eyes.* He walked in, holding the tray, forgetting he hadn't locked the door.

"Hello my love, good morning, Nicole. How do you feel today, my beautiful love?" Nicole was lying on her side. She opened her eyes just enough to peek through her lashes. He walked over and noticed the other tray was on the small table next to the bed. He crouched to place the tray he was holding on the floor and stopped. He slowly lifted his head and looked at the tray on the table. *Where is my syringe? Where did it g...* Suddenly Nicole flared up, screaming. Her arm quickly came out from underneath the blanket, and she hurled herself at him while he was still in a half-crouch. Nicole screamed again and rammed the needle into his neck. He flinched out of the way, and the needle plunged into his shoulder at the base of his neck. Nicole desperately tried to plunge all the liquid into him, but he fought her off. She recoiled back on the bed up against the wall and pulled her legs in, crying and screaming. Herman tried to stand, the needle still poking out of his shoulder. He stared at her in disbelief as he reached for it; he grabbed it and pulled it out. Nicole was crying and hyperventilating. His mouth flopped open and shut, attempting to create words. Then he fell, collapsing on the floor.

Nicole jumped off the bed, ran to the open door, and up the stairs. She went through the kitchen and desperately looked around at the unfamiliar room, searching for the exit. When she found it, she ran towards it and began unlocking it, crying and fumbling with the locks. She got it unlocked and threw the door open, and rushed out straight into the arms of a large man standing in the doorway. She screamed as he caught her. "Hey, what's this?" he said. She felt a wave of relief. She was safe. She was free.

"Please Mister, help me! He kidnapped me, a man, he is still there, he's inside, please help me!"

The man gripped her. "A man? Calm down. Where is he? Are you alright? Take it easy, let's have a look. Come on, it's alright. I've gotcha."

Nicole was still frantic. She struggled against the man's tight grip. "No please, I don't want to go back in there. Please, Mister, just get me out of here, call the police! Please, you have to call my mother Mister!"

The man held her tightly and leaned down so they were face to face. "Now listen, young lady, just calm down and tell me where this man is?"

Nicole tried to calm down, but it was impossible. In between breaths, she told him what had happened and how the man was down in his basement on the floor, unconscious from the syringe she stabbed him with.

He held onto her. "Is that right? Well, we better take a look now, shouldn't we." She stiffened, sensing something was wrong. He wasn't letting her go. Instead, he held her too tight and slowly forced her back inside the house.

"No! Let me go! I don't want to go back to that house! Call the police! Let me go!" She tried to pull away from him, but he was too strong. He forced her back inside the house and slammed the door shut.

"What are you doing?" she screamed in shock. "Let me go!" She tried to wiggle free from his grasp, but he held her easily.

That's when she noticed the syringe, and her heart stopped. She screamed as he held her, and he plunged the needle into the side of her neck. As she collapsed, the last words she heard were, "Now then, my little lollipop, let's go down to the basement and see Herman."

Chapter Seventy-Three

Bob's phone rang, it was Danny. "Hey Danny, how are you doing there?" Bob liked that kid, and he reminded himself to recommend a promotion for him.

"Hello Sir, how are you doing?"

"So, tell me Danny, what's happening?"

"Sir, the main reason I'm calling is we got a hit on the Anderson girl."

Bob sat straight up. "Ok son, go on."

Danny could hardly control his emotions. "Well, sir, you were right, I found her in a Red Room."

As soon as Bob heard that his heart sank. *Oh no, please*

don't tell me some sick bastard's done something to her.

Danny continued, "From what I could see, she seems unharmed at the moment. She looked unconscious and was chained to a bed."

"Was she clothed?"

"Yes Sir, she was. She had on a bathing suit, a bikini Sir. There are only a few photos of her, and they all seemed to have been taken at the same time."

Bob was thinking, looking straight ahead. He'd have to tell her parents about it. He would call Sherry and ask her to go with Jim to tell them. "Ok son, what else?"

"The Red Room is called The CardCollector, and as far as I can see, nothing is happening in the room. There's something else Sir, and it's just a feeling, really."

"What is it, Danny? If you have a gut feeling, I wanna hear it."

Danny swallowed. "Sir, the room is in an opening soon

mode. The background photos of the girl's room look like a replica of The Hood's Red Room. As if the CardCollector room is copied down to the last nail. Maybe this guy was an avid customer of The Hood. Whoever controls the CardCollector site must have access to The Hood's room. However, there's not even a subscription page or info about how to join. Just a shit load of watchers."

Bob frowned. "Watchers? What ya mean? Like waiting for something to happen to her?"

"Yes Sir," I guess they're all waiting to join the room. As I said, the photos seemed to have been up for a while. He has thousands of watchers so far. I don't know why he hasn't opened the room yet."

Maybe he's reconsidered, Bob thought. "Ok son, you did very well as usual. From now on, you don't take your eyes off that room, ok? And if you can get a trace on it, you call me the moment there is any change."

"Yes sir, I will, "

Bob was still staring at the wall, his mind spinning with anxiety. "Yeah, ok son, is there anything else?"

"I got in touch with the FBI's cybercrime division. They told me there are some ways to trace the encrypted address, but they can't share the information due to national security reasons."

Bob sighed. *Fuckers!* "Ok, Danny thanks, well you tried, let's talk soon."Bob hung up and immediately called Jim. He started to fill Jim in, but he was already up to speed. He and Johnson were trying to figure out the best way to tell her parents. Bob suggested he take Sherry with him. She would know how to handle it better than any of them. Jim was grateful and told him he would clear it with Johnson first, but he'd take Sherry anyway if he objected.

"Tell that fucking guy—oh, never mind. Ok, I'll call Sherry now; I'll get her to call your cell in a little while."

He hung up and called Sherry's number, cursing Johnson.

"Hello babe, listen, I got some bad news. Well, it's good news and bad news. We found her on the internet. She's in one of those fucking Red Rooms that Hood guy was using."

There was a brief silence on the other end. "Oh my god, Bob, you gotta get her out of there. Please don't let anything happen to her."

"Listen, babe, I need you to do me a favor." Bob gave only as many details as she needed and asked if she would assist them in talking to Nicole's parents. Sherry told him not to worry, she'd handle it, and she would call Jim shortly. They exchanged a few pleasantries, but neither was in the mood for a long conversation. Bob put the phone down on his lap and tried to think.

Chapter Seventy-Four

Herman was coming around. He slowly opened his eyes with a groan but couldn't see anything. There was something over his head. He shifted his body but couldn't move. His arms and legs were strapped to the chair he was sitting in. He struggled back and forth, but he was bound too tightly. "Well, Herman, welcome back. You have been out for a long time. Good to see you're awake, just in time." Herman turned his head from side to side to gauge where the voice was coming from. It was close.

The voice continued. "I wanted you to be here, in your basement, Herman. I must admit, you've got quite the setup here.

I'm impressed. I didn't realize from your video feed how much work you put into this room. This is a real great god damn Red Room; well done. Although it looks a lot like The Hood's room, don't you think? A little too much like it, if you ask me."

"Who are you? What the fuck is this? Where is Nicole?"

"Oh, your little lollipop? Yes, she sure is lovely. A fine choice. One of the loveliest young girls I have ever seen. She's gonna be a genuine pleasure."

Herman struggled violently in the chair, shouting. "Don't you fucking hurt her. You hear me? She's mine! She's my wife, goddamn it!"

The voice let out a laugh. "Your wife? Come on, Herman, you don't really think a fourteen-year-old girl that you stalked and kidnapped is going to be a happy little housewife, do you?" He chortled. "No, I don't think so. No Herman, she will be in the best show the deep dark web has ever seen. By the time I get through with her, not even her own family is going to want her back."

Herman was breathing heavily. "We love each other." But Herman knew that wasn't true. *She betrayed me. She lied to me and tried to kill me. But I still love you, Nicole.* "Please don't hurt her." Then he screamed and struggled. "Please don't fucking hurt her!"

The man was still talking. "But you can have her back after I'm done with her. Don't worry; I won't kill her. You can have what's left of her."

Herman sensed the man coming very close to him, and suddenly the covering over his head was ripped off. The bright red lights of Herman's basement blinded him for a second. When he could focus, he saw the man standing there. He had a similar mask that Herman had used on Nicole, only this one was bigger and covered his whole face except for holes for his eyes, nose, and mouth. His hair was tied back in a bun. He was dressed in a suit, with no tie, shiny shoes, and was holding a baton. Herman thought he looked familiar but couldn't place him. The man walked over to Herman and pushed the baton against his leg. A flash of pain streaked through his whole leg and into his body.

The smell and sound of electricity filled the air. Herman screamed, and his body convulsed. "Cattle prod. You got one of these Herman? I'm sure you don't, very effective. I have used these on a few girls."

When Herman composed himself, he glanced over to see the man pushing Herman's Red Room chair his way with Nicole strapped to it. She was unconscious, naked except for her underwear, and her legs were tied wide apart.

"Jesus Christ, Nicole, Oh my god, Nicole," Herman screamed in anguish. "Don't you hurt her? If you hurt her, I'll kill you. You hear me; I'll kill you!"

The man walked over to him and waved the cattle prod in front of Herman's face. "Ever imagine what one of these could do to a lollipop's pussy Herman, hmm? A lot of damage."

Herman felt helpless. "Please, who are you? Please don't hurt her; I'll do anything you want, you need money? You can take it all."

The man laughed, pacing the room. "Oh, I will Herman, I will take a lot of money from you. You see, I'm going to live stream your little sweetheart and take all your subscription money Herman, and you're going to watch."

Herman exploded with anger. "No, you don't go near her! I'll kill you!"

"Listen, Herman, relax; when I start streaming, you can enjoy it; I may even let you join in. There will be no sound, not until I start with her, but right now, your subscriptions are pouring in. Let me check here." The man pulled a desk over in front of Herman, and he changed the level of the laptop so Herman could see. In front of him was a video still shot of Nicole strapped to his chair, a large flashing pink banner scrolled across the screen.

Welcome to the CardCollector's Red Room. We will have a young teen lollipop destroyed for your viewing pleasure. You can bid during the live stream show for whatever you want to be done to her. The show starts in two hours, and lifetime subscriptions are now open. Please deposit 0.79 Bitcoin and follow the prompts. Once we receive confirmation of payment,

your subscription will activate.

The man pulled the screen away and paced again around the room. "So you see Herman, I'm just doing what you wanted to do, but you never had the balls to. You never dared to step over to the other side.

It feels wonderful. An incredible sense of euphoric freedom. That's why you don't belong on the deep dark web Herman; you're gutless. You belong with all those other little lambs out there. Waiting for people like me to come along and gobble you up."

Herman started moving violently in his chair, kicking and screaming. *I'll get out of this chair and kill him.*

"Now Herman, I can't have you going nuts while I'm busting this girl's cherry, can I? I think I'm gonna have to put you out for a while." He walked over to the table and took the syringe. He waved it in the air. "You remember this, don't you? This is how you took your little lollipop, isn't it? Who do you think fed you that information?" He took a small bow.

Herman looked at the man in disbelief. "Swift?"

The man stopped and turned. "Very good Herman, yes that is my username, and you can call me that if you like. But you've known me by another name as well."

"Who are you?" Herman whimpered.

The man stood, clasped his hands behind his back, and started pacing in front of Herman. "That is the million-dollar question, isn't it? I have been watching you since you left that clinic." He stopped and leaned his face down inches from Herman's. Slowly he removed his mask. Herman squinted; he wished to rub his eyes but couldn't move his hands. The face in front of him looked familiar. His mind struggled to grasp who that smiling man was.

The man feigned offense. "Herman, after all, we've been through. Do you not remember me?"

And then the images flickered behind his eyes, the pool, being molested, the hope he felt when he told him Annie liked him.

"Ah, you remember. Nice to see you again, old friend." He took a syringe and plunged it into Herman's neck.

Herman collapsed in the chair. John untied him, dragged him over, and laid him on the bed. He injected him one more time to make sure he would be out for at least twenty-four hours. He went back over to his computer. The money was still transferring into his account. He went over to Nicole and checked her heart rate; it was steady, she would be out for a while longer. He had given her a large dose. He went back and looked at his computer; the transactions were almost done. *Good,* he thought with a smile, *not long now and almost a million dollars richer.*

Chapter Seventy-Five

"Sir, sir," Danny looked around, desperately searching for Jim. He saw him coming out of the restroom and immediately caught his eye. Jim came over quickly and leaned down by Danny's shoulder. "Sir, look," Jim looked at the screen as his heart sank. He read the pink banner flashing across the screen.

"Jesus Christ, my god," he said, his voice breaking. "Can you trace it, Danny? Please tell me you can trace it?"

Danny swallowed hard. "I'm trying Sir, I am, but this encryption is beyond me, and I don't know what I can do."

Jim stood. "Keep trying son." Jim pulled out his phone and hit Bob's number. He answered on the second ring.

"Boss, we got a problem," Jim explained what he had just seen and that he was worried they were going to be too late.

"There is only one hour left, Bob; who knows what they will do to her then."

Bob was just as anxious. "Ok, tell Danny to subscribe."

"Are you sure? Shouldn't we be out—"

"Did you hear me, Jim? Tell him to join that fucking room; we need to track and record everything that's happening to her."

Jim felt like he could throw up; if he could find the people behind it, he would tear them apart with his own hands and gladly go to jail for it. Bob told Jim he would call him back and hung up.

He thought about the federal police contact he had and immediately called Derick's number and waited. "Derick, it's started, we need your help. We only have an hour before the Red Room starts, and the Anderson girl is going to be at the mercy of this freak. Can you help us? Maybe hack into this guy's computer and trace his location? Anything would help." Bob knew he

463

sounded desperate, but he didn't care; he *was* desperate. "Bob, I wish I could, but we don't know who is controlling that room, and there might not be any way to hack into it, but I will try. It's The CardCollector's room, right?" he asked. "Yeah, that's right," Bob replied frantically.

Derick was already on his computer furiously typing. "Ok, well, let's see what I can do, but I will tell you, without subscribing, it will be even harder."

Bob interjected. "I already have one of my boys joining as we speak. Can you get here and take over somehow?"

Bob knew what he was asking was impossible. The man was in another state and would never make it in time. "I would like to Bob, but I'm sure you know I won't make it in time. Those shows usually only last about twenty minutes or so; then it's all over. Give me the number of your tech guy, and maybe I can talk him through some things. I can't promise anything, but I'll try."

Bob hung up and sent a text with Danny's number. He

called Danny to tell him to expect a call from Derick. Instructing him to do everything that Derick suggested. Danny was hardly listening; he was furiously typing and trying to trace the VNP. Bob leaned back in his chair, and for the first time in his life, he was suddenly scared of failing. He looked over and saw Johnson marching towards him. "Oh shit," he said under his breath. Now what?"

"Well, Sharot, if it isn't the hero from the wild west. How you doing there, gunslinger? Shoot anybody on the way to the office?"

Bob would not take the jerk's bait. "Hey chief, no, not yet, but I can put a couple in you if you'd like." He stood and smiled as he breezed past him. "You're still on thin ice Sharot, don't forget that. Just because you nailed a few psychos doesn't give you the right to be a maniac asshole."

Bob stopped mid-stride. He would not let this ride anymore. He turned around and walked back slowly. Johnson stood his ground, but his face looked less confident. A few other officers and detectives had noticed and weren't trying to hide that they were watching the two men.

Bob walked right up to Johnson and put his face inches from his. "Listen to me, 'cause I'm only gonna say this once, I know you don't like me, and that's ok because I don't like you," Bob said in a low menacing growl. "But the only maniac asshole around here is you. Whenever you feel like behaving like a real cop, instead of sucking up to the brass whenever they want their cock sucked, you just let me know. I'll take you on some real cases. The puppies can't run with the hounds Johnson. So until then, you just keep running around here like a good little puppy, chief."

Johnson couldn't hide his shock and humiliation. His mouth opened and closed, but he was obviously lost for words.

Bob turned around and walked off, finally getting off his chest what had been bottled up for such a long time

Neville looked around and saw the looks on the faces of the others. His face flushed bright red. "You're finished Sharot, you hear me? You got no right talking to me like that. I'm your superior, you're done Sharot! Done!"

Bob kept walking, ignoring him. Johnson turned to the others. "Get back to work, or I'll have you all writing parking tickets at the zoo."

Chapter Seventy-Six

John looked at the software he created to trace and detect being traced. *They're trying to track me.* He saw they were narrowing in on his output signal. *Wow! Whoever is doing this is good.* He knew it had to be the police, which meant he didn't have enough time for the lollipop. *Damn, should I take her with me? Too risky.* He would have to leave her here. *That's ok; plan B was a better one.*

The girl was still very much passed out; he looked over at Herman, completely out and sprawled on the bed, naked except for his underwear. He checked the screen one last time and was satisfied with all the payments he had received so far. He typed in the sequence timer for the show, then closed his laptop and checked the room one more time. He had worn thinly-lined gloves, so he wasn't worried about fingerprints. Everything was as it should be—*time to go now. The cops will get a solid trace soon. It was nice seeing you again, Herman. We'll be seeing each other again someday.*

Smiling at him, he went over to Nicole and stroked her hair. *You too, sweet lollipop; a shame we don't have time to play. Maybe we will cross paths again one day.* He grabbed his laptop, left the basement, and went out of the house, careful to wipe any fibers he might have left. He got to his car; he already had the number and sent the message. He drove off slowly, smiling; *well, that was exciting, now to disappear for a while and watch the real fun begin.*

Chapter Seventy-Seven

Bob was frantically searching through the pile of files on his desk. He was looking for anything that could connect The Hood and Nicole. He had all the information from The Hood's car as well. Danny had dissected most of it for him, and now he was trying to figure out how these people were connected, The Hood, CardCollector, and Nicole. He still had no idea who the CardCollector was, but he was closer. Thanks to Danny, he found out that the CardCollector was a regular customer of The Hood.

"Jesus," he said under his breath. "This must be one sick fuck." Bob's phone alerted him he had a text message. He picked it up, read the message, then slowly stood—shock combined with excitement. The two emotions rushed through his body, and he almost screamed.

He ran out of the room and flew down the stairs. He had the phone to his ear and was calling Jim. When Jim answered, Bob was already out the door. He said he was on his way to pick him up and told him to wait for him outside on the corner; Bob drove through the streets like he was the only one there, he tore around the corner and saw Jim standing outside waiting, shifting his weight between each foot in anticipation. He pulled up, and Jim jumped in the car. Bob immediately sped off the second the door closed. "What do you have, Bob?"

Bob took out his phone and handed it to him. "Read the message," he said. At the same time, he was keeping his eyes on the road.

Jim took the phone from him and read the message. "Jesus Christ, is this for real?"

Bob was staring straight ahead. "I reckon it has to be, there is no sender information, but I would bet a million bucks that it's the same son of a bitch who's been playing us all along."

Jim read the message again. "Are we gonna call for backup? We should, you know, Johnson will have our badges this time if we don't."

Bob kept his eyes forward; he was weaving in and out of traffic, heading out of the city. "Yeah, whatever, call them but don't use the radio. Call the task force first, then Tactical, and tell them to stay off their radios. I don't want another fuck up like last time. I'm guessing by the time they get to where we're going; they'll be too fucking late as usual anyway."

Jim pulled out his phone and called the task force; they put Danny on the phone. "Hey, Danny, what's up?' Jim listened to Danny and Bob look over a couple of times to judge his partner's facial expressions and determine what was being said on the other end of the phone. He hung up, and Jim explained that Danny could narrow down the address to less than a block radius, and the task force was on their way there now. The red room show would start in 20 minutes.

Bob shook his head. "Shit, that doesn't leave us much time."

He put his foot down and turned on his siren. Although they were in an unmarked car, they had all the trimmings of a police cruiser. They sped on through an intersection and several sets of red lights. They reached the turnoff in fifteen minutes. Bob practically took the corner on two wheels as he spun the car around and down the road. They were coming to a cul-de-sac, and Bob scanned the numbers of the house.

"There it is, goddamn it." Jim pulled out his pistol and cocked it. They screeched to a halt on the house's front lawn and ran to the front door.

Bob slammed his large fist on the door and shouted. "Police, open up!"

"We gonna wait for permission to break down the door?" Jim whispered.

Bob looked at his partner, then back at the door. He lifted his large leg, ignoring the pain from his old injury. "Fuck no!" He kicked the door as hard as he could, splintering it down the center.

THE END

EPILOGUE

The two detectives burst through the door and found Nicole and Herman Kapper still unconscious in the basement after clearing the house. Both were taken to the hospital, where Nicole fully recovered from her ordeal. Herman Kapper was placed under guard during his stay at the hospital until his recovery. He was then subsequently taken to the police station and charged with aggravated kidnapping, illegal confinement of a minor, child molestation, possession of child pornography, as well as sexual solicitation of a minor for financial gain.

Nicole was placed in the lodge for girls under the care of director Sherry Miller. She was eventually reunited with her family, keeping the trauma she had been through very private and quiet. It was difficult for her to overcome, but with the help and support of Sherry Miller's rescue lodge for young girls and boys, and her family, she would lead a somewhat normal life.

In court, Herman Kapper professed his love for the young teen and insisted he had no intentions of harming her. He claimed his old school friend John Gooding, alias Swift, was the real CardCollector and set him up. Kapper's lawyer claimed the CardCollector / Swift used Herman Kapper and Nicole as bait to gain large sums of money, organized the torture and rape of his friend, Annie Leason, and the murder of Brady Wightly. Kapper's lawyer also claimed that Mr. Kapper had every intention of releasing Nicole. He was due to be sentenced to 30 years in prison, but the defense argued diminished responsibility due to the severe sexual abuse he had endured as a child and teen.. The defense also brought up the case of Herman Kapper being abused in an institution home for boys while under the government's care. The sentence was reduced to fifteen years to be served in the

Aradale Asylum clinic psychiatric clinic for the criminally insane. Herman and Robert were eventually reunited once again.

Given the circumstances of his sentencing, some say he could be eligible for parole if diagnosed to be mentally fit in less than ten years. People are already protesting this and demanding a longer, more conclusive sentence. The sentence is currently being appealed.

Annie Leason was shocked to find out the boy she knew and liked in school could do that to her. She began spending more time with her other female classmates, who helped console her from her terrible experience. They began taking turns staying at each other's apartments, looking out for each other, and talking about their future.

Sherry continued to run The Lodge and was guaranteed another five years of government funding. She and Bob Sharot eventually got married. Bob retired from the department a hero but never strayed too far from what he loved. He kept in touch with his old colleagues. Every once in a while, he'll put his skills to use and assist Sherry with a case, but most days, he's enjoying the quieter life.

Neville Johnson got kicked off the force for corruption. He was caught with a young girl in a hotel room. Although the girl was of age, it didn't sit too well with his wife. He eventually became a private investigator.

Jim Levin received another promotion and took Neville Johnson's posting. Danny was promoted to head the cybercrime division. Derick Peterson left the Federal Police and also became a private investigator. He deals with missing teenagers and cybercrime.

John Gooding, the man they called Swift, seemed to have disappeared off the face of the planet. Nobody figured out if his real identity was John Gooding. And rumors had it; he had plastic surgery and a whole new identity. He is still wanted by the police, the AFP, and many other agencies. There is currently a $500,000 reward for information leading to his identity and arrest. They can still spot where his presence has been on the deep dark web. Even with some of the best techs in the country, The Swift remains elusive. Many try to track his footprints and where he will go next, but it's impossible. As technology grows exponentially and out of control, the Swifts will always be out there. They are hiding among us, in all of us.

PERSONAL NOTE FROM THE AUTHOR

This book recognizes and respects the real, timeless, and often soul-destroying law enforcement battle of good versus evil. It is dedicated to special cybersex-crime divisions dealing with and preventing child sexual abuse and sexual assault. The admiration for these elite officers should always be unwavering. This is an unending battle against those who engage, profit, or exploit these crimes. Either for their gratification, financial gain, or the self-gratification of others. The following crimes are; Child Sex Abuse, Domestic Sexual Violence, Sexual Assault, Kidnapping for Sexual Gratification. Online Child Stalking. Child Exploitation. Illicit sale, Production and Distribution of Child Pornography. The Solicitation of Torture, Rape, and Murder.   Most of these crimes exist on the deep dark web, regardless of the victim's age, sex, or race.

These officers are put on the front line and subjected to watch and record the horrors committed by those integrated into the deep dark web to solve these crimes. Often they are traumatized and need to be referred to a psychiatrist

Those who commit these crimes are all around the world. There are two very important points the reader should take away from this book. Disturbing as they are.

One: The people who are very willing to pay large amounts of money to watch, enjoy and share these horrible crimes take place on the deep dark web, and the ones who take part in providing this service.

Two: These people live secret lives among us. They can be your next-door neighbor, friend, family member, relative, member of the church, boss, or even member of your government.

Without the first, the second would not exist. There must be accountability for those who deliberately pay money for these crimes to flourish.

Cryptocurrency and encryption IP addresses make these criminals almost impossible to catch. So we all must be vigilant, help our law enforcement, and do our best to keep our children safe from the clutches of the deep dark web.

ABOUT THE AUTHOR

Graham Cain (GC LAM) was born in Australia and continues to follow his dream of becoming a crime fiction writer. The Card Collector is his first novel. He plans to write a prequel to follow up from The Card collector. Graham currently lives in South East Asia.

www.ingramcontent.com/pod-product-compliance
Lightning Source LLC
Chambersburg PA
CBHW020241120726
47904CB00001B/45